T0147098

Whole Latte Murder

The All-Day Breakfast Café Series by Lena Gregory

Scone Cold Killer
Murder Made to Order
A Cold Brew Killing
A Waffle Lot of Murder
Whole Latte Murder

Whole Latte Murder

All-Day Breakfast Café

Lena Gregory

LYRICAL UNDERGROUND
Kensington Publishing Corp.
www.kensingtonbooks.com

LYRICAL UNDERGROUND BOOKS are published by

Kensington Publishing Corp.
119 West 40th Street
New York, NY 10018

All Kensington titles, imprints, and distributed lines are available at special quantity discounts for bulk purchases for sales promotion, premiums, fund-raising, educational, or institutional use.

Special book excerpts or customized printings can also be created to fit specific needs. For details, write or phone the office of the Kensington Sales Manager: Kensington Publishing Corp., 119 West 40th Street, New York, NY 10018. Attn. Sales Department. Phone: 1-800-221-2647.

Lyrical Underground and Lyrical Underground logo Reg. US Pat. & TM Off.

First Electronic Edition: April 2021
ISBN-13: 978-1-5161-1046-9 (ebook)
ISBN-10: 1-5161-1046-3 (ebook)

First Print Edition: April 2021
ISBN-13: 978-1-5161-1049-0
ISBN-10: 1-5161-1049-8

Printed in the United States of America

All-Day Breakfast Café
Cast of Characters

Gia Morelli – Owner, All-Day Breakfast Café.

Thor – Gia's Bernese Mountain Dog.

Klondike – Gia's black and white kitten.

Savannah Mills – Gia's best friend, real estate agent.

Pepper – Savannah's gray and white tabby kitten.

Captain Hunter Quinn (Hunt) – Gia's sort of boyfriend, Savannah's cousin, Captain, Boggy Creek Police Department.

Leo Dumont – Savannah's fiancé, Hunt's partner.

Harley Anderson – Gia's friend, homeless man.

Earl Dennison – Older man, Gia's first ever customer at the All-Day Breakfast Café.

Cole Barrister – Retired, full-time cook at All-Day Breakfast Café.

Trevor Barnes – Owner Storm Scoopers, ice cream parlor on Main Street.

Brandy – Trevor's German Shepherd.

Zeus and Ares – Trevor's guard dogs, Akitas.

Willow Broussard – All-Day Breakfast Café's full-time waitress.

Skyla Broussard – Willow's mother.

Zoe – Owner of the Doggie Daycare Center.

Donna Mae Parker – Harley's ex-girlfriend, flower shop owner.

Joey Mills – Savannah's youngest brother.

Michael Mills – Savannah's brother, works in construction.

James, Luke, and Ben Mills – Savannah's other brothers.

Cybil Devane – Mysterious older woman who often walks in the woods.

Chapter One

"I can't believe people actually torture themselves like this. On purpose." Savannah Mills tapped one long salmon-colored nail against the top offender in a heaping stack of bridal magazines piled on the All-Day Breakfast Café's counter. Light reflected off the rhinestone heart on the tip of her nail. "I think it would be easier to elope."

"Oh, stop." Gia Morelli slid one of the magazines out from the middle of the pile. "You're not eloping."

"Well, what am I supposed to do? I don't want to have to start cutting people off the invitation list, but we can't afford what it would cost to invite everyone to one of these venues." Savannah rested her elbow on the counter, propped her chin on her hand, and sulked. "I don't understand why planning a wedding is so difficult. It shouldn't be. Right?"

Gia didn't know what to tell her. When she'd gotten married, the entire affair had been arranged by the company her ex had hired to create an event that would boost his status in the financial community. She just showed up the day of, stood where they told her, and smiled at his guests. She should have realized then where that marriage was headed.

"Hey? Earth to Gia." Savannah waved a hand in front of her face. "Did you hear a word I said?"

"Um…"

"Ugh." She threw her hands up and flopped against the back of the stool. "What kind of maid of honor zones out while the bride is on a rant?"

"I'm sorry. I'm trying to think of something that will work without it costing a fortune." But Savannah was right. The cost of a wedding venue was excessive, and she and Leo didn't have that kind of money. Gia had been saving to try to help them out, but it was slow going. And Savannah refused help from her father, saying he had a hard enough time just keeping up with the bills.

Easing the death grip she held on the magazine, Gia opened it to a random page and set it on the counter. If she hadn't known how badly Savannah had always wanted a big wedding, with her extended family and an abundance of friends there to celebrate with her, Gia would have whole heartedly encouraged the elopement idea.

An image caught her eye. A laughing bride and groom, still clad in their formal wedding attire, playfully splashing in the surf. "Have you considered a destination wedding? You don't have to go somewhere far away; I'm sure Florida is full of beautiful locations. Maybe the Keys?"

Savannah's gaze bored through her.

"What? It was just a suggestion."

Cole, a good friend who often manned the grill despite the fact he claimed to be retired, tapped the page she had opened. "They do look awfully happy."

Gia shot him a grateful look, then braced herself to earn Savannah's wrath.

"But that puts the cost of attending on my guests, and I already know some of them won't be able to afford to attend."

She couldn't argue that. The cost of traveling, hotel rooms, food, plus missing time from work would make it difficult, if not impossible, for some people to attend—Gia included, since it would mean closing the café for a few days, at least. "I know you want a big wedding, but is it really worth the stress you're putting yourself under?"

"Maybe you're right." Seemingly defeated, Savannah folded her arms on the counter and rested her head on them. "Maybe I should just give up trying to plan the perfect wedding."

Guilt nudged Gia. "Oh, stop. Come on. This can't be all that difficult. What are the most important things to you?"

Savannah shrugged and continued sulking, an unusual look for someone who was usually filled with energy and almost always saw the positive in any situation.

Cole handed Gia a notepad and pen.

"Thanks." She tapped the pen against the counter. "Come on, Savannah. Help me out here. What do you want most out of your wedding?"

She sat up with a sigh. "Mostly, I just want somewhere all of my family and friends can gather to celebrate with us without it costing an arm and a leg."

A seemingly legitimate request, and yet… Gia set the pad and pen aside and flipped through page after page of advertised venues, not that they hadn't gone through them all already.

"I have an idea." Earl, the elderly gentleman who'd been her first customer and had since become a good friend, took a sip of his coffee, then set it aside and grabbed a magazine off the pile. "Instead of looking for venues that won't cost a fortune, why not see about having the reception on the beach or in a park?"

Savannah sat up straighter. "You think that would work?"

Oh, thank you, Earl!

"I don't see why not." He flipped through page after page without stopping. "You'd have to set up a tent of some sort, in case the weather was bad, but other than that, I think it would be beautiful."

Savannah shook her head. She still looked semi-interested, but skepticism was creeping back in. "What about food?"

Cole grabbed the pad Gia had discarded. "What kind of food do you want? We could cater it, I'm sure."

Savannah frowned. "I don't want you guys to have to cater it. I want you to have fun."

Willow, the All-Day Breakfast Café's only full-time waitress, though that might change later if the woman Gia was scheduled to interview turned out to be any good, stopped to chime in. "What if we all pitched in to make the food ahead of time, then I could get a few of my friends to serve the day of?"

"I don't know." Savannah chewed on her lower lip. "Where would we keep the food? It's not like there are refrigerators in a park. And even if we did a buffet, the food would still have to be heated up. How would we keep it warm?"

An idea started to form. Gia glanced at the clock over the cutout to the kitchen. Their late morning lull would be ending soon, and she wouldn't be able to do anything about her brainstorm until later on when Trevor opened Storm Scoopers, the ice cream parlor down the road, and she could talk to him. "If I can work out the logistics, would you be happy with an outdoor wedding, somewhere pretty that wouldn't cost too much, even if we had to have it catered?"

"Are you kidding me? I'd be thrilled." She tossed the magazine she'd been looking through back onto the pile. "I really only care that everyone can come and have a good time."

"Great, then leave it to me." Gia added her own magazine and Earl's back onto the stack, then shoved the whole pile on a shelf beneath the counter.

Savannah's already big blue eyes widened. "Seriously?"

"Yup, I have something in mind I think might make you really happy." At least, she hoped it would. Savannah was her best friend in the world. She'd been there for Gia more times than she could count. The least she could do was help her plan a wedding that would make her day as special as she was.

She took her phone out of her pocket and shot Trevor a quick text asking him to stop in on his way to work. "Now. Are we still on for this afternoon?"

"Yup. Two o'clock. I'll pick you up here so we can start gown shopping." Savannah grabbed a muffin from one of the cake dishes on the counter. "Hopefully, a gown will be easier to find than a venue."

"Well, it can't be much harder. At least, chances are, it'll cost less." Gia set a plate on the counter in front of Savannah, along with a can of Diet Pepsi. "Do you want a real breakfast?"

"Nah." Savannah waved her off. "Thanks, anyway, but my client is meeting me here any minute. We can have lunch afterward if you want, before we go shopping."

"That works." Gia offered Willow and Cole something to eat. Earl had already finished his breakfast, so she offered to top off his coffee. When they all declined, she set a plate on the counter for herself and put a banana chocolate chip muffin on it.

May as well eat a little something before she had to interview the potential waitress, a chore she dreaded. Hmm…maybe Cole wanted to interview the waitress while Gia manned the grill.

"Oh, wow, I gotta run." Earl stood and grabbed his fisherman's cap from the stool next to him. "I'll catch up with you guys later. I promised my daughter I'd pick up my grandson from soccer practice this morning."

"I'll see you later." Gia sat next to Savannah and broke off a piece of her muffin. She paused with it halfway to her mouth. A fruit cup would probably be a better choice, given that she was trying on maid of honor gowns that afternoon too.

Savannah glanced at her watch. "I hope Buster gets here soon. If not, it's going to cut into our shopping time."

Earl stopped partway to the door and turned back toward her. "Buster?"

With her mouth full of muffin, Savannah nodded. "Mm-hm."

Reversing direction, Earl yanked his cap off and headed back to the counter. "Buster Clarke?"

"Yeah, why?" Savannah wiped her mouth and spun her stool in his direction. "Do you know him?"

Earl propped one foot on the bottom bar of a stool and leaned an elbow on the counter next to Gia. "Yeah, I've heard of him. Guy's bad news."

Savannah frowned. "What do you mean?"

"He's a two-bit hood and a loan shark. I know a guy who got in a little over his head with that man and wound up in the hospital with two broken legs."

Savannah gasped.

Cole leaned on the counter on the other side of Savannah, caging her and Gia between them. "How'd you get mixed up with him?"

Savannah shoved her plate aside with her muffin only half eaten. "He came into the office and sought me out. He's looking at an expensive house, the old Oakley Manor House."

"That's the one out by the fairgrounds, isn't it?" Cole asked.

"Yes. It's a seven thousand square foot house on five acres of property. It was a bed and breakfast at one time, but it sold a while back, and the owner never opened it again. He never kept up with it either, and it fell into disrepair, but now it's in the process of being restored as a private home. It'll go for over a million dollars once finished."

Earl scowled. "Guess crime is profitable, if Buster can afford a house like that."

Savannah ignored him. "If I can sell it before construction is complete, I get a bonus. A nice bonus that would not only help us pay for our wedding, but would also put me ahead of Ward Bennett for sales."

Earl looked at Cole, then shifted his gaze back to Savannah. "Let Ward Bennett sell him the house."

Savannah bristled. "Look, I've already invested a lot of time in this, and Ward will get a share of the commission as it is, since the Oakley Manor House is his listing. Trust me, I'll be careful, but there's no way I'm giving up this sale to that weasel Ward."

Earl scratched his head and put his cap back on.

From what Gia knew of Earl—which was a lot considering he came in for breakfast every morning and spent at least half an hour chatting with her, some days hanging out all morning long—he wasn't easily ruffled. If he feared for Savannah's safety, it was with good reason. "Maybe you should consider giving up the sale. I have an idea that will make the whole wedding cost a ton less, and it's better to be safe—"

"Enough." Savannah stood, lifted her tote sized, teal purse off the stool back, and slung it over her shoulder. "I'm not giving up this sale. And stop talking about him; he's meeting me here any minute, and I don't want him to walk in and overhear."

Earl glanced over his shoulder toward the door and pitched his voice low. "Why is he meeting you here?"

"So we can drive out to the house together."

He lowered his gaze and shook his head. "Would you consider doing me a favor?"

Done with the topic, Savannah fished her sunglasses out of her bag and propped them on top of her head. "What's that?"

"Take your own car, and let him take his."

She started to argue, but Earl held up a hand. "Look, Savannah, you and Gia are like daughters to me, and I'm only giving you the same advice I'd give any of my own girls. If you insist on doing business with that man, at least take precautions. Tell him it's getting late, and you have to meet up with someone right after the showing, so you've decided to take your own car."

Savannah caught her bottom lip between her teeth.

"It's not even like that's not true." Gia didn't know Buster Clarke, but for Earl to be so worked up over it, the man must be bad news. And Savannah heading out to a deserted house in an area even more remote than Gia's community with a man she didn't know but whose reputation preceded him, did not sit well. The thought of calling her boyfriend, Savannah's cousin, Captain Hunter Quinn, shot through her mind at warp speed.

Savannah pointed a finger at Gia. "Don't even think about it."

"What?" The innocent look she aimed for was probably ruined by the *'you caught me'* expression she was most certainly wearing. Sometimes, having Savannah's thoughts run so similar to her own had its down side.

"Listen, guys." She kissed Earl's cheek and patted Cole's hand. "Thank you for worrying about me. I really do appreciate it, but this is my job. I don't have a choice but to do it, even if it's not always comfortable."

"Are you sure, Savannah?" Cole leaned closer to her. "I'm covering grill, and I'm sure Gia wouldn't mind rescheduling her interview so she could go with you."

A pang of hope shot through Gia.

"Aww...sweetie, thank you." She kissed his cheek as well. "You guys are the best, but I'm okay. Buster hasn't done anything inappropriate either of the times I've met with him so far, and once was at the office after everyone else had left. He's been nothing but professional, no matter what he does in his personal life."

Gia stepped forward, a sinking feeling in her gut that she shouldn't let Savannah go alone. "Savannah…"

Savannah's gaze shifted past Gia's shoulder and out the front window. "Shh. He's here. You guys behave now. Please."

The front door opened, and a middle-aged man strutted in, his mostly black but peppered with gray hair slicked back with more grease than Gia scraped off the grill after cooking five pounds of bacon. His perfectly tailored suit hugged the solid build of someone who spent a good chunk of his day in the gym. He reached a hand out to Savannah. "Savannah, dear. So good to see you. I'm sorry I'm late."

"Um..." She glanced at Earl, Cole, and Gia grouped together beside the counter. "No problem, Buster, but would you mind if we take separate cars out to the Oakley Manor House? I have a meeting right afterward, and I'll need to head straight there once we're done."

He shifted his gaze to the trio beside the bar, looked them up and down, and then dismissed them to look at Savannah. "Of course, dear. That's fine."

"Thank you."

Buster turned and headed for the door without acknowledging any of them.

Savannah shot them a wink, then followed.

Earl whirled on Gia. "I'm not comfortable with this. Sloan was hurt really bad by that guy."

"Did he press charges?"

"Nah, Buster's slick. He had a couple of his goons take care of Sloan when he couldn't repay the loan he'd taken, then threatened to come back for his wife and kids if he went to the police."

Bile burned its way up Gia's throat. "What ended up happening?"

"Sloan learned a hard lesson about the dangers of gambling. He paid back every dime, including the astronomical interest, and was grateful to be done with the whole thing. Once he finished rehabilitation, he went back to work, though he still walks with a limp."

Gia's gut cramped. "You said Buster had Sloan's legs broken because he couldn't pay him back. Where'd he come up with the money to satisfy the loan?"

Red blotches crept up Earl's cheeks. "A friend loaned it to him."

"Did he pay it back?"

Earl shook his head. "Sloan's a truck driver with a pack of kids and a wife who doesn't believe in working. He has a hard enough time keeping food on the table without having to pay back that kind of money. That's how he ended up in trouble in the first place, just tryin' to make ends meet."

Gia hugged him. "You're a good man, Earl, and a good friend."

He blushed even deeper, then turned to stare out the front window in the direction Savannah had gone. "Then why do I feel like I failed Savannah?"

"She'll be all right, Earl. She does have to earn a living, and showing houses is part of that. Besides, growing up with five brothers and a pack of male cousins made her tougher than she looks." She hooked an arm through his and nudged his side. "And, I happen to know she carries a can of mace somewhere in that massive purse, and she's not afraid to use it."

Gia glanced at the clock. Three hours before Savannah was supposed to meet her back there to go shopping. She had a feeling it was going to be a long three hours.

Chapter Two

Gia wiped her sweaty palms on her apron, then tossed it into the hamper. This was ridiculous. She was the interviewer not the interviewee; what did she have to be nervous about? It's not like she had to hire the woman. If she didn't seem like she'd work out, she wouldn't hire her. But that was the problem. Gia's track record for choosing which employees would work out was less than stellar.

Although, Willow and Cole had worked out perfectly.

Besides, she could always fire someone if they didn't do the right thing. Of course, firing trumped interviewing on her most dreaded business owner responsibilities list. She sighed and took a detour into her office.

Coward.

A quick glance at the clock on her phone told her she wouldn't have to return to work before heading out with Savannah, so she took a moment to freshen up. She ran a brush through her long dark curls, taming them as best she could between the humidity and two and a half hours spent standing over the hot grill with Cole. She used a wet wipe to clean the dark circles from beneath her eyes, courtesy of the eyeliner and mascara that had run while she'd stood over the steam all morning, then reapplied a fresh coat of each.

And with that, she promptly ran out of stalling options. Ugh…She'd already left the woman standing out front waiting for the better part of ten minutes. It was time to—in Savannah's words—pull up her big girl pants and get this done.

With a new burst of confidence, she strode through the doors to the dining room and stopped short. Sweat trickled down her back. Only one customer sat alone, a woman at the counter sipping a cup of coffee.

She appeared to be in her late twenties, early thirties, mid-length brown hair pulled back into a neat pony tail. Her capris and tunic style shirt were neatly pressed. She watched Willow like a hawk as she finished up with the few customers still remaining in the shop after the lunch rush. Nothing about her screamed don't hire me, and yet...

Gia approached slowly. "Excuse me, are you Marie Winston?"

"Yes, I am." She smiled, stood, and held out a hand. "Gia Morelli, I presume?"

"Yes." Forcing a smile of her own, Gia shook her hand. "It's a pleasure to meet you. I'm sorry to have kept you waiting."

"Oh, no problem. Willow was kind enough to give me a cup of coffee." She gestured toward the cup on the counter. "To be honest, I'm not sure the caffeine was such a great idea. I'm already nervous, and it just made me more jittery."

She seemed friendly enough. And honest about her feelings. Which was good. She supposed. "Sit, please. There's no reason to be nervous."

Marie sat, and Gia moved to stand behind the counter opposite her. Then she paused. Maybe she should have taken a stool and sat. That might better convey the cozy, homey feeling she encouraged in the café.

She resisted the urge to roll her eyes, barely. This whole interview process was lost on her. She should have let Savannah or Cole do the interviews. Or even Willow. "So, do you have any waitressing experience?"

The woman twisted an engagement ring with a small round diamond around her finger. "Well, not really. I have worked retail for ten years, though, and I'm a fast learner. I'm good with customers, enjoy working with people, and I can provide several references."

Her disappointment at Marie's lack of experience came as a surprise. Had she really expected she wouldn't have to train someone? That they'd fit right in as if they belonged there already. That's exactly what she was hoping, since it had happened that way with both Willow and Cole. She reminded herself the most rewarding things in life were those you worked the hardest for. "Why do you want to leave retail?"

"Actually..." Marie hesitated. "I don't want to leave my full-time job; I just want to add hours. I was hoping I could work here part time on my days off, or the early shift, before my shift at the mall starts. My fiancé and I are saving up for our wedding next year."

"Oh, congratulations." She bit back her first instinct to ask if they'd chosen a venue. If she'd picked any of the ones Savannah had discarded, she might need more than one part-time job.

"Thank you."

Hmm…part-time might be a good way to start. Then, if she didn't work out, Gia could simply reduce her hours until she left. Of course, Marie probably didn't plan to work two jobs indefinitely. And her full-time retail job most likely provided her benefits. So, was it worth training her to have her only work part-time and then most likely leave after she got married?

She checked the time. Savannah would be there in a few minutes. Time to wrap things up. She shot the woman a few more questions for the sake of appearing like she knew what she was doing.

She liked Marie. Her answers were short and to the point, honest from what Gia could tell, and seemed to jibe with what Gia was looking for. Even the part-time hours could work out okay. But she really hoped to find someone with at least some waitressing experience. "How are you with multitasking?"

A warm smile spread across her face. "I am a multitasking genius."

Okay, that might trump experience. Gia nodded. "I would definitely consider hiring a part-time waitress who is a multitasking genius, and I don't even mind offering training, but I do have a few more interviews scheduled. I plan to finish interviewing within the next few days and make a decision by the end of the week, say Friday. I will contact you either way, though, so you don't have to sit around wondering what's going on."

"Thank you." Marie stood. "I appreciate that. I do hope to hear from you. I think I'd enjoy working here."

Gia thanked her and said good-bye.

Cole passed behind Gia and hefted a bus pan full of dirty dishes from beneath the counter. "How'd it go?"

Gia shrugged, checking the time on the clock above the cut-out to the kitchen. Five after two. Savannah was late. She checked her phone for text messages, missed calls, new voicemails. Nothing. "Not as bad as I expected. I actually kind of like the woman, but she only wants part-time hours, and she has no waitressing experience. Plus, she's looking to earn extra money for her wedding, so she'll probably leave once she's married next year."

"Hmm…"

"That's it? Hmm?" She'd been hoping he'd offer at least a few words of wisdom.

He scooted behind her with the dishes to load into the dishwasher, which meant he'd already cleaned up in the kitchen from the lunch rush. "I figure you'll decide what's best, but it's not that hard to train the right person, so I'd say go with your gut, and pick someone who will work well with your current staff. It's not like you won't have help training her.

Willow's very patient. And a year is a long time. You never know what will change within a year."

"That's true enough." A year before her move to Boggy Creek, Gia would never in a million years have anticipated Bradley's deceit, the destruction of her marriage, the trial, the death threats. Nor could she have foreseen her move to Florida, or the joy she'd feel each time she walked into her very own home and the café she'd dreamed of for so long. All feats she'd never have been able to accomplish without Savannah's help.

She flipped her phone over and over, checking the clock each time it came around.

Cole paused on his way to the kitchen. "Something wrong?"

"Savannah's late." She could call, but she didn't want to interrupt if she was in the middle of a sales pitch. Maybe she'd shoot her a text.

The front door opened, and she breathed a sigh of relief. It didn't last long.

"Hey there, Gia." Trevor Barnes waved as he crossed the room.

"Please, let me know as soon as you hear from her." Cole glanced at the clock as he resumed his trek toward the kitchen, his concern clearly mirroring her own.

Trevor pulled a stool out from the counter and sat. "What's up?"

"Not much. What's going on?" Distracted, she shot off a quick text message to Savannah, asking how much longer she'd be. She had gotten a late start, after all, so it wasn't surprising she might run a few minutes late.

"I don't know. You texted me and asked me to stop by. So, here I am." A shock of his too long in the front brown hair fell across his eye, and he shook it back. "Did you want something?"

"Oh, Trevor. I'm sorry." How could she have forgotten that? She needed to get her head back in the game. "I'm just a little distracted today."

"No worries." He grinned his boyish grin. "So, what's up?"

Gia's gut unknotted the slightest bit, and some of her former excitement returned. "I was thinking about something, and I wanted to run it by you and see how you'd feel about it."

"Sure thing."

She poured him an iced chocolate macadamia nut latte, a new recipe she was trying as part of her summer specials menu, and set it in front of him. "Tell me what you think of it while we talk."

She rounded the counter and sat on the stool next to him.

He sipped his latte. "Oh, man, this is delicious. My new favorite."

"Thanks." Gia laughed.

Trevor was a great boost to her ego, since he greeted each new recipe with the same level of enthusiasm.

She had to wonder if he'd ever admit he didn't like something. She had a feeling he wouldn't. Trevor was too sweet for his own good and had a hard time saying no to anyone, especially a friend. She hesitated. Maybe asking him to host Savannah's wedding at his house wasn't a good idea. She didn't want to put him on the spot, and he didn't often, or ever, invite people to his home.

If it was for anyone other than Savannah, she'd refrain. But the memory of Savannah's earlier disappointment prodded her forward. "This was just an idea, a brilliant one, mind you, but just one idea, so please don't feel obligated to agree. You can totally say no."

Trevor's expression turned serious as he swiveled his seat to face her. "O-kay."

"You know we've been working on planning Savannah's wedding."

He nodded.

"And she's been trying to find the perfect venue, but with her extensive guest list, everything is turning out to be too expensive. So, Earl suggested having the reception at a beach or a park, but that would limit what we could do for food."

Trevor's eyes widened. A slow grin inched in to replace his somber expression.

"And I was thinking..." When she'd first seen Trevor's house, she'd been both shocked and amazed at the beauty of the grounds and the size of the mansion. Even now, all these months later, she couldn't fathom boy-next-door Trevor living there. "Your house and grounds are absolutely gorgeous, more beautiful than any park, and—"

"Yes."

"And I thought maybe...Wait. What?"

He nodded enthusiastically, bouncing a little in his seat. "Yes, I'd be thrilled to have Savannah's reception at my house. I can even give her and Leo and the bridal party all rooms for the night before the wedding. We'll have a big dinner, and everyone can hang out together, maybe have dessert in the great room by the fireplace. It will be perfect. And everyone can stay the night of the wedding too, if they want, so no one has to worry about driving home."

"Wow." She didn't know what to say. She'd been hoping she could talk him into having the wedding there, and even had her arguments in favor of all ready, but she'd never expected him to so fully embrace the idea. "That's awesome, Trevor. Thank you so much."

"Of course. Savannah's a good friend, and so is Leo. I'd love to share my home with them." A blush crept up his cheeks. "It's not often I have company out there and, truth be told, it'll be nice to have a house full of guests for a change."

She jumped up off the stool and flung her arms around his neck. "Thank you so much, Trevor. You're the best."

He hugged her, then sat back, blushing all the way to his hairline. He waggled his eyebrows. "Hey, does that mean you'll dump the cop and go out with me?"

She laughed. Though she and Trevor had become very close friends, there was no romantic spark between them, on either end. "Not right now, but I'll keep you in mind just in case things don't work out."

He swallowed hard and pulled at the neck of his T-shirt, then looked around and stage-whispered, "Just don't let Hunt hear you say that. And don't tell him I asked. I've been on that man's bad side, and I am not going there again. Ever. He's scary."

She couldn't argue that fact, even though, despite a rocky period of time between them, Trevor and Hunt got along well enough. She pulled an imaginary zipper across her lips. "No worries. My lips are sealed."

Now that Trevor had agreed to host the reception, at least she had a direction to move in. "Okay, then, I'll need to figure out what to do about food."

"No problem. I have a fully stocked kitchen with a commercial stove, two ovens, and an industrial-size refrigerator. And I know a great catering company if you're interested. They even have servers for during the event, and their prices are very reasonable, and they clean up afterward."

Gia's mouth fell open. She promptly snapped it closed and kissed Trevor's cheek. "You never cease to amaze me, Mr. Barnes."

"Hey, what's going on out here?" Cole carried a clean bus pan behind the counter and slid it underneath.

"Trevor has agreed to let us have Savannah's wedding at his house. He's even giving the bridal party rooms for the night before and the night of."

"That's great, man. Savannah's going to be thrilled." Cole frowned. "Speaking of, have you heard from her?"

Gia checked her text messages. Still nothing. And it was two thirty already. Could be she hadn't answered the text because she was driving.

She dialed Savannah's number.

After four rings, her voicemail picked up.

"Hey, Savannah, it's me. I just wanted to check in with you since it's getting kind of late. Give me a call."

Picking up on the tension, Trevor frowned. "Is something wrong?"

Cole answered before Gia had a chance. "Savannah was taking Buster Clarke out to look at the Oakley Manor House, and everyone was a little uncomfortable about her going out there alone with him. He doesn't have the greatest reputation."

"She was supposed to be back at two, and it's already half past." Gia checked her phone for messages. Still nothing.

Cole pointed toward the clock. "Maybe you oughta give Hunt or Leo a call and let them go take a look."

"Are you kidding me? Do you know what Savannah would do to me if I sic those two on her when she's in the middle of selling a house? Especially that house." But she had to do something. It wasn't like Savannah to run late without calling, even if she was working.

"Do you want to take a ride out there? At least drive past and see if her car is still there?" Trevor finished off his latte and stood. "I'll go with you if you want."

Gia glanced at Cole.

He was already nodding. "Go ahead. If she shows up, I'll let her know you guys went out to the house to look for her and tell her to wait here."

"You'll call me the minute she walks in?" Gia was torn between waiting for Savannah to get there and going to check up on her. If she did get back and Gia wasn't there, they might not still have time to go shopping.

"I will," Cole said.

"All right. Come on." Gia grabbed her bag, fished her keys out, and headed for the door with Trevor. "I'm sure everything's okay, but I didn't have a good feeling about her going out there after Earl was so worked up about it this morning, and my anxiety level is through the roof now that she's running so late."

Chapter Three

"Make a right here." Trevor pointed to a dirt road that led deeper into the forest they'd been driving through for the past ten minutes.

Gia turned onto the narrow, rutted road that seemed more like a path through the woods than any kind of actual road. "Are you sure this is the right way?"

Trevor double checked the GPS he'd opened on his phone. "Yup. When you come to the end, make a left, and it'll take you straight to the Oakley Manor House."

Gia followed his directions, scanning the woods for Savannah's convertible in case she'd broken down or gotten stuck, as she bounced and rocked over the bumpy path. "Do you think this is the way Savannah would have come?"

"It's the only way in and out. All of the roads in this area are dirt." He braced himself against the dashboard as they bounced through a pothole.

The road widened a little, and they passed several walls and gates. Whatever houses lay behind them were hidden from view. When they came to the end of the trail, Gia turned onto another dirt road.

This one was smooth, hard-packed dirt, easy enough to drive over. Palm trees lined the road on both sides. At the end of the road, a brick wall surrounded a huge expanse of land. A set of wrought iron gates with the words Oakley Manor House spelled out in an arch above them stood open.

Gia crept up the curved cobblestone driveway, which was lined on either side by enormous moss-covered oaks. Their branches gently swayed in the soft breeze, sending a ripple of shadows skittering across her path.

Two cars sat side by side in the circular courtyard in front of the house: Savannah's blue Mustang convertible and a dark gray sedan that Gia didn't recognize. She assumed it belonged to Buster Clarke.

"I guess she's still here." Trevor flipped up the sun visor, leaned forward, and looked around. "What do you want to do?"

Savannah would probably have her head if she walked in and interrupted her while she was working. At the same time, she was almost an hour late already. Even though Gia was sure she'd have rescheduled their shopping date to make this sale, she was equally sure she'd have called or texted to let her know.

She switched off the ignition, torn between the need to check on Savannah and the desire to respect her privacy. "I'm going to take a look around. You can wait here if you want."

"Like that's happening." Trevor opened the door and got out, then rounded the car to stand beside her, gazing up at the old house. "I feel like I've stepped back in time."

"No kidding." A park-like yard surrounded the house, an abundance of flowers overflowed everywhere. Multicolored butterflies flitted from one plant to the next. Large moss-draped oaks provided shade to an assortment of seating areas, giving the illusion of privacy to each. "This is incredible."

"Do you want to walk around the grounds?" Trevor asked.

"I don't know. Savannah said there were five acres of land out here. If Buster wanted to walk all of it, that would definitely take a while." Gia pulled out her cell phone. "I have five bars, and Savannah has the same cell phone service I do, so she shouldn't have had a problem calling to say she was going to be late."

"Yeah, but you know as well as I do the cell phone service in this whole area is hit or miss. Three feet to the left, and you probably have no bars."

She didn't bother to argue, since he was right. The area was not known for great service.

Silence surrounded them, but instead of the sense of peace Gia would expect in such incredible surroundings, her gut knotted. Determined not to put off finding Savannah any longer, she strode toward the wide wrap-around porch and up the three stairs to the double front doors.

Trevor stumbled over the top step and plowed into her back, knocking Gia against the front door, which creaked inward. He blushed as he smoothed his T-shirt. "Sorry."

"No problem." She was too used to his clumsiness to pay it much mind. "At least you saved me the trouble of deciding whether to ring the bell or just walk in."

She wiped her feet on the doormat before stepping onto the foyer's marble floor. "Savannah?"

Silence screamed back at her.

"I don't like this." Trevor swiped a hand over his mouth, then propped it on his hip and turned to Gia. "Let's split up and search for her. I'll look down here. Do you want to check the upstairs?"

"Hello!" Goosebumps dotted Gia's arms, despite the summer afternoon heat. She glanced up the dramatic grand staircase that turned twice before finally emerging onto a loft-style landing that overlooked the foyer. Tall windows filtered an abundance of natural light into the rooms. "Yeah, come on. I don't know why, but this place gives me the creeps."

When she started up the stairs, Trevor grabbed her arm. "If anything seems off to you, even the slightest bit, yell for me, and we'll call Hunt and Leo to come check things out. Promise?"

She nodded. Truth be told, that was starting to sound like a good idea to her anyway. No matter how upset Savannah got over it. This whole thing seemed off. If a quick search of the house didn't offer any clues to her whereabouts, she'd call Hunt.

"Savannah!" She hurried up the stairs. When she reached the top, she turned to the left. She'd start at one end of the hallway and work her way to the other end. She pushed open the first door she came to, and stepped back into the early nineteenth century.

Calico wallpaper, yellowed by time, had turned brittle and peeled in several spots, the once beautiful crown molding dulled by age and dust. A canopy bed sat in the center of the room, surrounded by dressers and chests that would probably be worth a small fortune if they were authentic. Brick fireplaces stood sentinel on either side of the room. A thick coat of dust covered their mantles.

Gia ran across the room and peeked into a bathroom. Rust stains filled the sink, and a crack ran from one end of an ornate mirror to the other.

Since the bathroom stood empty, and the bedroom had no closets, Gia returned to the hallway and pulled the door shut behind her. Once she checked all of the rooms on that side of the hallway, she leaned over the railing beside the stairway and called to Trevor.

He appeared instantly. "Did you find her?"

"No, nothing. How about you?"

He was already shaking his head as he strode to the front door and looked out. "Her car's still here, though."

Gia returned to her search, heading the other way down the hallway. She opened the first door she came to. Renovations had been done on this room already. The ivory paint was pristine. The moldings had been refinished and polished to a brilliant shine. She checked the bathroom, which hadn't yet benefited from a makeover. Since there were no closets and no furniture, it was easy enough to see it was empty. She moved to the next room.

Unlike the other rooms she'd checked, which were either not started or fully restored, this room was in the middle of renovations. Tools littered the floor in a chaotic array. Paint cans were stacked haphazardly in one corner, a couple of which had fallen over and rolled away from the pile. What appeared to be a brownish-red colored paint or wood stain had splattered to the right of the doorway. Since none of it was smeared, apparently no one had bothered trying to clean it up.

The detached bathroom door stood against one wall, and plastic sheeting had been tacked up between the bedroom and bathroom.

"Savannah?" Careful not to step on any of the nails protruding from scattered pieces of two by fours and plywood, Gia crossed the floor to the bathroom, shifted the plastic aside, and peered inside.

"Hello?" She stepped into the spacious room.

A deep claw foot tub sat in front of another brick fireplace in the center of the bathroom. Two things struck Gia at exactly the same instant; the arm hanging over the side of the tub, and the nails, while well-manicured, were short and free of polish.

A scream welled in her chest, but she couldn't suck in enough air to let it out. She panted, her breath coming in ragged gasps as she backed away from the tub. She had to get a grip. Had to get help. Had to find Savannah.

"Savannah!" She stumbled backward, got caught in the plastic blocking the doorway, and pulled it down with her as she fell. "Savannah!"

"Hey!" Strong hands gripped her arms through the plastic. "Gia! Stop fighting me and stay still."

The heat, combined with the plastic covering her face, threatened to suffocate her. "Trevor?"

"Yeah, it's me." He managed to untangle her from the plastic, despite her frantic efforts to free herself from his grip. "What's wrong?"

"Ah, man." She shoved her sweat-soaked hair out of her face and took a good look around the bedroom. No sign of Savannah. She scrambled to her feet and stumbled back to the bathroom, then skidded to a stop in the doorway.

She had to check the tub. Had to make sure. She couldn't think about what might have happened to Savannah. If she could just stay calm and focused on getting help, she might get through this. She had to, if she was going to be of any help to her best friend. She sucked in a breath and sobbed. "Call Hunt. Now. Hurry!"

"What's wrong?" Trevor already had the phone in his hand and began scrolling through his contacts.

Gia edged toward the tub. If Savannah was lying somewhere in need of help, there's no way Gia would fail her. Holding her breath, she peeked over the side.

Buster Clarke lay on his back in the deep tub, one arm hanging over its side, his formerly immaculate business suit a rumpled mess. His other hand clutched a nail gun that apparently hadn't done a thing to save him. A blood-covered piece of two by four with nails sticking out from one end at all different angles had been thrown on top of him.

It only took a second to determine he was alone in the tub and definitely beyond saving.

Gia whirled away from the scene and ran into the bedroom. No closets. No furniture to hide under or in. Construction debris cluttered the floor. She made her way through the room, intent on searching the rest of the house as quickly as possible. Maybe Savannah had fled when someone attacked Buster. Maybe she was hiding somewhere in the mansion. Or maybe she'd run into the woods in an effort to escape whoever had killed him. Either way, she had to find her. Fast.

"Gia."

She turned to find Trevor staring at her, tears streaming down his face as he gripped his phone. "Hunt and Leo are on their way. He said don't touch anything."

"I have to find Savannah."

"Gia." His hand shook wildly as he pointed to a pair of mangled sunglasses amid the debris. Savannah's sunglasses: the same ones she'd been wearing when she left the café. "Hunt said you have to wait out front. He said you wouldn't want to, would try to refuse, but he wanted me to tell you it would do more harm than good and that you might mess up evidence pointing to a way to find Savannah."

She couldn't take it. Why did he have to be right? She sucked in a breath and screamed at the top of her lungs, finally releasing the pent-up emotions that threatened to choke her.

Trevor laid a hand on her arm, but she shook him off, couldn't have anyone touching her when her nerves were so raw.

"We have to find her, Trevor."

Chapter Four

Every inch of Gia's body vibrated with nervous energy and raw pain as she stood beside Trevor in the circular courtyard, feeling completely useless. The sun's intense rays and the thought of someone hurting Savannah boiled her blood.

Walking out of that room had been the most difficult thing she ever had to do, but she'd gone to wait out front, as Hunt insisted, without picking up the broken sunglasses, her only link to Savannah. No way would she risk a chance of tainting evidence that might lead to Savannah's whereabouts.

Approaching sirens shattered the menacing quiet.

Trevor cried softly at her side but made no further attempts to talk to Gia or offer comfort.

Hunt's official SUV fishtailed as it rounded the last curve in the driveway.

Leo was out and running toward them before Hunt had even finished skidding to a complete stop at the far end of the courtyard. "What happened, Gia?"

Keep it short. Don't waste time. "Savannah left to show Buster Clarke this house. No one was that comfortable with it, so when she wasn't back when she was supposed to be, we went to look for her."

Hunt ran toward them, barking orders into his phone.

Leo glared at her. "If you weren't comfortable, why'd you let her go in the first place?"

The exact same question she'd been torturing herself with for the past hour.

Trevor stepped in front of her and stood toe-to-toe with Leo. "That's not fair, and it doesn't matter right now. Gia tried to stop her, so did Cole and Earl. Savannah insisted she was just doing her job."

"There's no time for casting blame." Hunt grabbed Leo's arm and yanked him back, away from any further confrontation with Trevor or Gia. "Where'd you find Buster?"

Sirens tore through the afternoon as police vehicles barreled into the driveway and blocked off the crime scene.

"I'll show you." She started forward.

Hunt held out a hand to block her path. "Just tell me."

Gia nodded and gave him directions, then watched him and Leo take off through the front door, which neither she nor Trevor had bothered closing when they left.

"It's not your fault, Gia." Trevor laid a hesitant hand on her arm. "You tried to stop her, and you went looking for her long before the police would even consider an adult missing and long before anyone else would have realized there was a problem."

Gia's breath hitched. Unbearable pressure squeezed her heart. "And yet, she's still missing, isn't she?"

"Ah, Gia." He squeezed her arm, then released her.

Gia's phone rang, and she fumbled it out of her pocket, desperate to see Savannah's name on the display screen.

Trevor leaned over her shoulder. "Is it—"

"It's Cole." She took a moment to rein in her out-of-control emotions and wipe the tears from her raw cheeks before answering. "Hey, Cole."

"Hey, I just wanted to check in. Did you guys find her?"

Gia opened her mouth to answer, and a sob tore free. She lost her battle for control and fell to her knees on the cobblestone.

"Gia?" The concern in Cole's voice only made her cry harder. "Gia! What's wrong?"

Trevor leaned over her and pried the phone from her hand. "Cole, it's me. We found Buster's bo...uh...found Buster in a tub out at the Oakley Manor House, and Savannah is missing. Hunt and Leo are already here, as is most of the rest of the Boggy Creek Police Department."

Cole's muffled voice carried to Gia, but she couldn't make out anything that he said, only his sense of urgency.

"No. I don't think it would do any good to come out here," Trevor said into the phone. "But I'll ask as soon as I see someone I can talk to. Everything seems kind of chaotic right now, though they probably all know what they're doing. I'll let you know if they set up a search party."

Gia should have thought of that. She should be doing something other than kneeling in the middle of the courtyard crying.

"I doubt the twenty-four-hour rule will apply when there's obviously been foul play." Trevor laid a hand on Gia's shoulder, offering comfort as he worked out a plan with Cole. "Why don't you start getting people together at the café, or at least put them on alert? That way, if they ask for volunteers, we're ahead of the game."

Would that help? Probably. Unless it interfered with the investigation in some way. Gia sucked in a shaky breath. "Tell him not to mention Buster Clarke's murder to anyone. I'm not sure Hunt would want that to get out yet."

Trevor nodded and relayed the message. "As soon as I'm sure the police are done questioning me, I'll be there."

Gia looked around. There had to be some kind of clue. Grown women didn't just vanish into thin air.

Trevor handed her phone back and helped her to her feet.

She sniffed and wiped her face again, then started walking a slow circle around the courtyard. When she reached Savannah's car, she stopped and peered inside. The convertible top had been left down, so Gia could see the entire interior. Nothing lay loose, not surprising when she'd driven with the top down. Usually, she stuffed any important papers in the center console, since the glove compartment was already packed full of what she deemed essentials—things she might need in a hurry.

Gia quickly looked around to make sure no one had a problem with her looking in the car and then leaned over and reached for the center console.

"Wait." Trevor grabbed her arm. "You're not wearing gloves, and you don't know for sure no one else was in her car, either with her or after…"

Gia nodded slowly, her gaze still riveted on the console as if it held the answers to where Savannah had gone. But Trevor was right, no matter how badly she didn't want him to be.

Hunt emerged from the front door and stopped to talk to a man in a Boggy Creek Police Department T-shirt. He gestured toward the back of the house.

The man nodded, called to someone, and jogged around the house with a handful of officers.

With his mouth set in a grim line, Hunt strode toward Gia and Trevor.

Gia held her breath, praying fervently.

As soon as he reached them, he pulled out a notebook, his expression hard, unreadable.

"Did you find her?" Trevor asked.

He shook his head, and Gia breathed a sigh of relief. As much as she wanted to know Savannah's whereabouts, as long as she was missing there was hope that she was safe.

Trevor used the heels of both hands to wipe his cheeks. "Are you setting up a search party?"

"We will, and we'll ask for volunteers."

Trevor nodded. "Cole's working on it now. He'll gather as many as he can at the café, and I'm headed there as soon as we leave here."

"Good. I'm sending officers over there anyway, so they'll let you know what to do and where to go." He shook Trevor's hand. "Thank you."

"Of course." He laid his free hand over their clasped hands for a moment. "We'll find her, Hunt."

Hunt wiped his forehead with the back of his wrist but didn't say anything.

Gia thought back to the state of the room Buster had been found in. Construction debris littered the floor in a completely disorganized way throughout the bedroom and bathroom. The condition they'd found Buster in, as well as the equipment that could have been, and surely had been, used as weapons and left in the tub with him all pointed to signs of a struggle. But Savannah was smart, resourceful, and athletic. If there had been a fight, as the evidence indicated, at least to Gia's untrained eye, she'd have run.

There's a good chance she could have escaped into the forest. But why would she run into the forest when her car was sitting unlocked in the driveway—right in front of the house? With her keys, more than likely, in the center console where Hunt and Leo had both told her repeatedly not to leave them?

Maybe she'd hidden somewhere in the house.

So why hadn't she called or texted?

Cell phone service in the area was spotty at best. Just because her phone worked right there in the driveway didn't mean it would work five feet toward the tree line. Or in the yard, or in the house. Gia often lost her signal, usually at the most inopportune moments, in the forest surrounding the Haunted Town Festival, which had taken place right up the road. So that theory held.

But what if she'd hidden in the house? Why hadn't she come forward when Gia and Trevor had called out, and then a small army of detectives and crime scene techs, including Savannah's cousin and fiancé, had stormed the house?

"Gia!"

"Oh, huh?" She wrestled her attention back to Hunt.

"Could you please pay attention? Savannah needs your help right now."

Heat crept up her cheeks, and she lowered her gaze. "I'm sorry. What did you ask?"

"What time did she leave? Do you know?"

She couldn't think. It had been before the lunch rush started; she remembered that much. "I'm pretty sure it was around eleven. I remember thinking it would only be three hours and she'd be back."

"What time was she supposed to meet you?"

"Two. To go dress shopping." That time she was certain of, as she'd spent the better part of that three hours watching the minute hand creep toward it.

He jotted that down. "When did you get here?"

"Uh…" She shook her head, trying to clear her mind of the images threatening to crush her.

"Around three," Trevor said. "She started to get concerned, then texted Savannah. A little while later, after she didn't answer the text, Gia called. When she still didn't answer, she decided to risk Savannah's wrath by coming out here and checking on her."

Hunt squeezed his temples between his thumb and fingers and dropped his gaze to the mostly empty notebook page.

Gia wanted more than anything to reach out to him, to offer some kind of comfort. She'd give anything to take the pain away. But she was probably the last person he'd want comfort from, since it was her fault Savannah was missing. "I'm sorry, Hunt."

He sucked in a few ragged breaths and nodded. "I know. It's not your fault. I can't…"

She waited while he clenched and unclenched his jaw.

"There's no time for this. I have to find Savannah. And I have to work this case as long as I can before I'm removed from it. And to do that, I have to keep my head on straight."

Gia's gaze shot to his. "Removed? What do you mean, removed?"

"There's no way Savannah's cousin and fiancé are going to be allowed to continue working this case, and there's even less of a chance I'm going to be left in charge."

They couldn't do that. Hunt had to be the one in charge. He was the only person Gia trusted with Savannah's fate hanging in the balance. It wouldn't matter, though. He just needed to gather as much information as possible as quickly as he could. No way would he walk away from Savannah, no matter what anyone ordered. "What are you going to do?"

"I'm going to maintain my focus and do everything I can to find my cousin."

Gia nodded, determined to find that same strength.

"I'm sorry I can't be there for you right now. I know you need someone."
He glanced at Trevor.

Trevor nodded. "I'll take care of her, man."

"I'm fine, Hunt." She should be his last concern right now. "What do
you need us to do? Cole is already looking for volunteers to search."

"Trevor said." He blew out a breath. "That's good. Now, I need you to
get back to the café."

"What? Why? I want to help. I can't just sit at the café and wait, Hunt,
I have to do something to help her."

"This is a small town, Gia. Everyone knows how tight you and Savannah
are. If there's going to be a ransom demand, there's a good chance it will
come to you, though we will have family members and officers at her dad's
house as well. Since the café is where most people would know how to find
you, and it would be much more difficult for someone to find your cell
phone number, I need you to stay there for now. I've already sent officers
ahead and I'll tell Savannah's father and some of her brothers to meet up
there. I'll be there as soon as I can."

"But—"

"That's the best way you can help." He stuffed the notepad back into
his pocket. "I have to go."

"Come on, Gia." Trevor put an arm around her shoulder and guided
her toward the car.

She whirled out of his arm and back toward Hunt. "Wait."

He stopped and looked over his shoulder.

"Have you searched her car?"

He frowned and turned more fully toward her. "Not yet, why?"

"If she drove with the top down, she usually stuffed all of her important
papers in the center console. There might be a clue in there."

He looked back toward the house, then at the car, and swiped a hand
over his mouth. Changing direction, he pulled a pair of gloves out of his
pocket as he approached the vehicle. He used one finger to open the car
door, leaned in, and took a stack of papers and a key ring out of the center
console, then closed the top and moved away from the little convertible
Savannah loved so much, had worked so hard for.

He shuffled through the pages.

Gia tried to look over his shoulder, but she couldn't make out any of
the small print. "What is it?"

"Just information on the house." He held the keys out in his open palm
and stared at them, then shifted his gaze to the trunk. "No matter how
many times Leo and I reprimand her, she still insists on leaving her keys

in the console whenever she parks locally. Why bother carrying around those suitcase-sized tote bags she uses if you're just going to leave the keys in your unlocked car?"

Gia shrugged, having witnessed the argument more times than she could remember.

"She said it didn't matter if you locked a convertible." Hunt laughed, a soft, pained sound. "Of course, she did the same thing before she bought the convertible too."

Truth was, Savannah was the most trusting person Gia knew. She always saw the best in everyone, always believed people would do the right thing in the end. Unfortunately, Gia had learned from experience that wasn't the case. Sometimes, even those closest to you, those you thought you knew best, couldn't be trusted.

Hunt rounded the car to the trunk. He only hesitated an instant before opening it.

Empty.

Gia's knees went weak. If not for Trevor's arm around her, she'd have gone down.

Leaving the trunk open, Hunt stepped back. "I have to get back inside and get men started investigating Buster Clarke's murder."

"What are you talking about?" Gia bristled. "It's too late to save Buster, but Savannah's still out there somewhere."

His jaw clenched so tight she thought his teeth might crack, and he pinned her with a glare. "And finding Buster's killer may be the only clue we have to figuring out her whereabouts. So, if you don't mind, I'm going to do my job."

Rooted in place, Gia just stared at him. How could he be so cold? So calm? When Savannah was missing?

"Come on, Gia." Trevor tugged her closer to him. "We should go."

She turned and let him lead her to the car. Fighting with Hunt wasn't going to solve anything, only waste time. And she already knew she owed him a tremendous apology, but her anger and fear were running too high right now to force it out. He had more important things to worry about, anyway.

"Do you want me to drive?" He held his hand out for the keys.

"Nah. I've got it." She needed to have something, anything, other than Savannah's disappearance to focus on. She opened the driver side door, then looked over the roof at Hunt.

He stood staring into Savannah's empty trunk, tears streaming down his cheeks as he lost his battle for control.

Chapter Five

Gia hit the turn signal and slowed, then hesitated before making the turn onto Main Street. As much as she wanted to get back to the All-Day Breakfast Café and see if Savannah had called, she knew in her heart there'd been no word. If anyone had heard anything, they'd have called immediately.

Holding her cell phone in a death grip while she drove, checking the screen every other second to make sure she hadn't missed a call, Gia eased off the brake and accelerated, passing her turn.

Trevor, who'd been silent and lost in thought since they left Oakley Manor House, straightened and looked around. "Where are you going?"

"I need to check something." At least it would feel like she was doing something, anything, to help find Savannah.

Trevor flipped his hair out of his eyes. "Hunt said to go straight to the café."

"I know, and I will. As soon as I'm done." And she'd never forgive herself if a call came in while she wasn't there, but the police and her staff were all at the café, along with whomever Cole managed to rally for the search party. They could reach Gia in an instant if need be, and she could get there in less than ten minutes.

"Can I ask where we're going?" Trevor shoved the sun visor down, laid his head back against the seat, and closed his eyes.

"There's ibuprofen in my bag if you need it."

He nodded but made no move to look for it.

Gia sighed. She at least owed him an explanation. And if he didn't want to accompany her, she should drop him off somewhere—no sense both of them earning Hunt's wrath. "I'm going to the real estate office where

Savannah works to see if any of her coworkers have heard anything or if I can find out anything. I'll drop you off somewhere first, if you want."

"No. It's fine. I'll go with you."

"But Hunt—"

"I know what Hunt said." Still resting his head against the seatback, he turned to look at her. "And by the time you're done begging forgiveness for going against his order to go directly to the café, maybe he'll forget about my involvement."

If only that were true. "You know that's not likely?"

"Yeah." He massaged his temples. "I know. Don't worry about it."

Lacking the energy to keep up a conversation, Gia left Trevor to whatever he was thinking about. She tried to fill her mind with ways to help Savannah, but each thought brought an image of what might have happened to her. She shifted her thinking; she had to if she was going to function.

She pulled into the small gravel parking lot, where only three other cars remained, and parked beside a white split-rail fence. A quick glance at the clock told her she wouldn't have much time before they closed. "Would you mind waiting here, Trevor?"

"I don't know if you should really go in there alone right now." What he didn't say was that she was acting irrationally and liable to blurt something inappropriate or accusatory, especially if that weasel Ward Bennet was lurking around. He didn't have to. And she appreciated it, since they both knew it was true.

"I'll be all right." Now that she was there, she had to admit, to herself if not to him, this might not be a good idea. The receptionist, Tempest Brooks, was dating Savannah's brother, Michael, and if Hunt hadn't notified him yet, word would certainly spread if she walked in there and announced Savannah was missing. Plus, she had no clue if Buster's family had been contacted, or if Hunt wanted word of his murder to get out yet. "I'm just going to go in and ask if they've heard from her. I won't mention anything else."

Trevor looked at her and raised a brow. "Have you looked in a mirror?"

She flipped the visor down, opened the mirror, and cringed. He was right. She wasn't going to fool anyone. "I have a scrunchie in the glove compartment; would you get it for me, please?"

She smoothed her hair as best she could, took the scrunchie Trevor handed her, and tied it in a sloppy knot at the back of her head. After wiping the mascara and eyeliner that had run down her face, she gave up on being able to do anything with her eyes and slid her sunglasses on to cover them, then left the car running with the air conditioner on for Trevor and got out. "I'll be right back."

She slammed the car door, then headed across the lot before she could change her mind. Or come to her senses. Whichever. When she reached the front porch, she paused, argued with herself over whether or not to just turn around and go to the café, then gave up and went in.

Tempest sat at the reception desk, her dark brown eyes red and puffy, a box of tissues beside her computer. So much for them not knowing what was going on.

"Hey, Tempest."

She looked up and sniffed, then tucked her dark, curly hair behind her ear. "Oh, hey, Gia."

"I guess you already heard. Is there any news?"

She frowned. "News?"

Uh oh. "Oh, um…"

Tempest lurched to her feet. The chair rolled behind her and crashed into a filing cabinet. "Has something happened? Is Michael all right?"

"Michael? Why wouldn't Michael be all right?"

"Oh, I don't know. I just assumed…Never mind." She pulled the chair back to her desk and flopped onto it. "What's happened?"

"Nothing, I wanted…" She was messing this up. She needed to pull herself together and act normal if she was going to get any information. "Are you okay? You look like you were crying."

With a quick glance around the office, she yanked a tissue from the box and blew her nose. "Allergies. Or maybe a cold. I'm not sure."

The tear tracks running through her makeup belied the excuses, but Gia let it go. "I was supposed to meet up with Savannah to go shopping. I thought we were meeting at the cafe, but she hasn't gotten back from showing the Oakley Manor House yet, and I was—"

"The Oakley Manor House?" A man stood from his desk, where a nameplate read Ward Bennett, and strode toward her. "She was showing that today?"

Ah, man. Clearly, showing up at the office had been a mistake. She was blurting out all kinds of top-secret information inadvertently. In her defense, how was she supposed to know that people who worked in the same office kept secrets from one another? She needed to find out if they'd heard from Savannah and get out of there before she stuck her foot so far into her mouth that it would never be pried out. "Um. I think that was the one she was showing, but I could be mistaken. Either way, I thought maybe

I was supposed to meet her here instead of at the cafe, so I just wanted to check if she's called."

Tempest shook her head. "Nah, haven't heard from her at all today, actually. But she doesn't always come into the office if she's showing a house."

"What's going on?" Angelina Lombardo, owner of the real estate office and Savannah's boss, stuck her head out from an office at the back of the large room. She was an imposing woman, tall, broad-shouldered, more handsome than pretty, with short black hair, sharp features, and dark eyes that could bore right through you. Power oozed from her.

Ward shot her a glare, his barely-there lips rolling into his mouth until he looked like the weasel Savannah was always comparing him to. He shoved his glasses up his hawk-like nose. "Savannah's friend just stopped in to see if she was back from showing the Oakley Manor House."

Angelina's already pinched features puckered even further as she stepped into the room on four-inch heels. "What are you talking about?"

"You're saying you didn't know?" Ward ripped off his sports jacket and slammed it onto his seat, then loosened his tie and ran a hand over his already perfectly sculpted brown hair.

With a glance out the corner of her eyes at Gia, Angelina shook her head once then ignored him.

Gia backed toward the door. "Look, I'm gonna go. I'm sorry to have bothered you."

"When did you last speak to Savannah?" Tempest asked.

"She was at the café this morning." She had to try to salvage this somehow. Obviously, Savannah hadn't shared where she was going with anyone in the office, and she'd mentioned being worried about weasely Ward trying to steal her sale. That's probably why she'd kept her prospective buyer a secret, and now Gia had gone and let the cat out of the bag. "I know she was saying something about that house, but I'm not sure that's where she said she was going. I don't know the area well, and I was kind of busy, so I may have misunderstood. Probably did, since I apparently missed where we were supposed to meet as well."

Ward leaned against his desk, folded his arms across his chest, and scowled at Angelina.

"Anyway..." Gia fumbled behind her for the doorknob. "I'm gonna run, but thanks. Sorry, again, to have bothered you."

"If I see her, I'll tell her you were looking for her." Tempest smiled.

"Sure, thanks." She fled before any of them could stop her and practically ran to the car.

"What happened?" Trevor asked before she'd even climbed all the way in.

"I should have listened and gone straight to the café." Although she'd clutched her phone in her hand through the entire encounter with Savannah's office staff, she still checked for any missed calls. No calls. No texts.

"Why am I not surprised?" Trevor pressed his thumb and forefinger against his eyes, then massaged the bridge of his nose. "I take it no one's heard from her?"

"No, nothing." Although Tempest's reaction still seemed off. Did she know something more than she was saying? There was no way to find out with Angelina and Ward standing there. Maybe later.

Trevor looked out the window. "I called Cole."

"And?" She held her breath.

"No one's heard anything."

Okay. No news meant they hadn't found her. View it as a good thing.

She drove the rest of the way back to the café in silence. Cars lined both sides of Main Street and filled the small parking lot by the park at the end of the road. Gia had never seen the town so crowded. Though she still wasn't completely comfortable parking in the lot behind the café, she turned the corner and pulled as close as she could get to the back door, and parked.

She rested her elbows on the steering wheel and clutched her head in her hands. Now what? She wasn't sure she could go in and face all of their friends and still maintain any semblance of control.

Trevor opened her door and held out a hand. "Come on, Gia. You can do this. You don't have a choice; you have to."

She nodded. He was right. She wiped the tears, even though they'd just pour down her cheeks again in a few minutes, and climbed out of the car.

Trevor held the café door for her and gestured for her to precede him.

"Thanks." With one last deep breath, she walked inside.

She peeked into the kitchen on her way past, but it stood empty. Cole had already cleaned up and turned off the grill. When she reached the dining room threshold, she stopped short. Every inch of space was packed full of people, none of them eating, though many held coffee cups or soft drinks. Every coffee pot behind the counter was either full or brewing.

Hushed conversations stopped as people caught sight of her, and silence descended on the room. Anticipation hung heavy in the air.

Cole hurried toward her, pulled her into a warm embrace, and whispered, "I'm sorry, Gia. I had to close about an hour ago. First, we were all too distraught to work, and then it just got too crowded to seat customers."

Gia held on tight. "It's okay, Cole. You did the right thing. All that matters right now is finding Savannah."

When Cole stepped away from her, Earl took his place. He wiped tears from his swollen eyes before hugging her. Soft sobs racked his thin frame. "I should have done more to stop her from going."

"It's not your fault, Earl." She rubbed a hand up and down his back, offering what comfort she could. "It's nobody's fault. You did everything you could to stop her, but...as much as I hate to admit it, showing houses was Savannah's job. And she wasn't wrong. She needed to work, so let's not dwell on the past. Let's just concentrate on finding her."

Though she spoke honestly and from her heart in the hope of easing Earl's pain and guilt, she doubted she'd ever find that forgiveness for herself.

A sea of both familiar and unfamiliar faces stared at her, all waiting for news that she didn't have.

Estelle Bailey waved to her from a seat at the center of the room, where she and her twin sister, Esmeralda, would be sure to hear everything that went on. They must have come in as soon as they heard the news to have gotten such a prime position. No surprise, really. The elderly women were a force to be reckoned with when it came to gossip. Gia swore they often had news before it happened.

She bit back a sigh and approached their table. "Good afternoon, ladies."

"Oh, dear, we came as soon as we heard." Estelle patted her perfectly coiffed blue updo. "It feels like we've been here forever awaiting news. Have they found her yet?"

"No, ma'am, not yet."

Esmeralda reached out and squeezed Gia's hand with a firm grip. "Don't you worry, dear, they'll find her."

Gia nodded. "Thank you."

"And what about Buster Clarke?" Estelle's voice carried over the mostly hushed conversations among the crowd. "Is he really dead?"

All conversation ceased.

"Um..." Gia had no clue whether or not she was supposed to comment on Buster's death. Obviously, word had begun to spread, but if it were any more than a rumor, Estelle wouldn't be asking for confirmation; she'd simply nod knowingly as she blurted out the information loud enough to be heard from the park at the end of the street.

"It's okay, dear; you don't have to answer that." Esmeralda winked and shot her twin a warming scowl. "We understand, don't we, Estelle?"

"Yes, of course, we do, but things are going to get pretty ugly around here if those rumors turn out to be true."

"What do you mean?" Despite her best intentions to shut the two women down before they could create a stir, she couldn't miss the opportunity to learn something that might help Savannah. Gia took a seat at the table with the women and lowered her voice, hoping they'd get the hint and do the same.

"Well." Estelle leaned toward Gia. "The Clarkes are a very well-known family around these parts."

Thankfully, the conversation around them picked back up again, giving them some semblance of privacy.

"And their feud with the Esposito brothers is common knowledge," Esmeralda added.

"Feud over what?" Despite the café having become quite a gossip hot spot over the past year, Gia wasn't aware of any feud.

"Well, pretty much everything." Estelle finally puckered her features into an all-knowing expression, obviously back on familiar territory. "Neither family boasts the most upstanding citizens, and when they go at it, people usually end up hurt."

"Or worse," Esmeralda finished.

"Does that happen often?" Gia hadn't heard either name until that morning when Savannah had mentioned Buster. But Earl had picked up on the name Buster right away, as had the Bailey twins, apparently.

Esmeralda shrugged a slim shoulder. "Not often, but occasionally. The last time was maybe a year and a half, two years ago, when one of the Esposito cousins was killed by a hit and run driver out by the springs. The driver was never apprehended, and no one knew for sure who it was. One of the Clarkes ended up having a tragic accident soon after."

"Coincidentally, that crime was never solved either." Estelle lifted a brow and dipped her chin. "Everyone assumed the brothers had retaliated, and the matter was closed."

And this was the kind of person she'd allowed Savannah to leave with this morning? Nausea churned in her gut. "And was it? Closed, I mean?"

"No one else died if that's what you're asking, though the police kept the case open as far as I know." Estelle lifted her coffee to take a sip, then looked inside and lowered the empty cup back to the table.

"Let me get you another cup." Gia used the excuse to escape the two. While they were nice enough and had an abundance of knowledge about what went on in Boggy Creek, nothing they shared would help find Savannah. And, at the moment, that's all that mattered to Gia.

She asked Willow to refill the sisters' cups. Cowardly, maybe, but she didn't want to get roped into another gossip-fest with the two.

Cybil, an older woman who'd become a good friend, a woman who often walked the woods alone despite Gia's discomfort with the idea, offered a warm hug. "If there's anything I can do, just let me know."

"Thank you, Cybil."

"I'll be heading out to search with Cole and Earl as soon as they'll allow." Gia doubted anyone in Boggy Creek knew the woods in the area as well as Cybil did. "Thank you."

"No need to thank me." She rubbed a hand up and down Gia's arm. "Savannah is a sweetheart. And a friend. We'll find her, Gia. Have no doubt."

She didn't doubt they'd find Savannah. She just prayed she'd be okay when they did.

Chapter Six

Gia moved through the room, stopping to speak to those she knew, introducing herself to those she didn't, many of whom offered words of encouragement and spoke fondly of Savannah. Some shared stories of how they'd met her, things they'd done together, how Savannah had helped make their lives better in some way. It was humbling to realize the impact she'd had on so many people over the years. The mood in the room was somber, yet anxiety sizzled like a live wire as people awaited word or a call to help. Gia's mind whirled with possibilities. Possibilities she didn't dare contemplate.

Savannah's father sat at a table in the far corner, with two of her brothers, Michael and Joey. If her other brothers, James, Luke, and Ben, had been notified already, they must have either waited at the house in case a ransom demand came or gone out to the crime scene with Hunt.

Gia paused. If Michael was already there, how had Tempest not known Savannah was missing? And why had she been crying? Had Michael contacted her but told her not to say anything? Had Hunt been hoping to keep her disappearance quiet until he could question the other agents in the office? She swallowed hard, hoping she hadn't messed anything up by going there. Especially since she hadn't even learned anything.

She approached Mr. Mills tentatively, not knowing what to say to a man who had already lost so much. Assurances that they would find his daughter seemed somehow inappropriate, nowhere near enough to ease his suffering.

Joey noticed her first and jumped to his feet. "Gia. Have you heard anything?"

"Nothing yet, I'm sorry."

Joey opened his arms, and she went to him.

She clung tightly, taking comfort from the love surrounding her, desperately wanting to convey her love and support, though she had no words.

Joey had been the first to welcome her as part of the family when she moved from New York to Boggy Creek. He had helped Savannah set up the café before Gia was able to move down, helped move all of her belongings into her new home, and often doggie-sat Thor when she needed him to.

She couldn't stem the flow of tears, even as guilt hammered her for indulging in them. They would find Savannah. Her father, her brothers, her friends, her community; they would all work together and not rest until she was found. Knowing that didn't ease the pain threatening to consume her.

Gia lay a hand on Mr. Mills' shoulder and squeezed. "We'll find her, Mr. Mills."

He reached up and patted her hand, then nodded but didn't look up at her.

She knew the words rang hollow, but what more could she say? Unfortunately, he already knew the cruelty of having violence take the love of his life. Leaving him to find whatever peace he could, she held a hand out to Michael.

He stood and shook her hand. "Thank you for allowing our family and friends to gather here. It means a lot."

"Of course. There's nothing I wouldn't do for Savannah." Though she'd met Michael, along with Savannah's other three brothers, numerous times over the past year at various family functions, Joey was the only sibling who still lived at home. Because of that, Gia hadn't become as close to the others as she had to Joey. "Anything any of you need, just let me know, please."

Michael nodded. "Thank you. Right now, if you'll excuse me, I need to get up and walk around."

"Of course." She could certainly sympathize; staying still was driving her crazy. Gia turned back to Mr. Mills. "Is there anything I can get you?"

He shook his head and waved her off, keeping his gaze averted. His shoulders shook, and tears dripped onto the table.

Gia hesitated, but in the end, there was nothing she could do. Mr. Mills had largely withdrawn from life after the death of his wife; she couldn't imagine how he'd hold up with his daughter missing. But, if Savannah had inherited any of her strength from him, he'd get through it.

When she started to walk away, Joey grabbed her arm and turned his back to his father. He glanced at a small group of police officers sitting at a table in the front corner of the room in case a ransom call came in and leaned closer to her, keeping his voice low. "I can't just sit here doing nothing. Do you have any ideas? Anything. It doesn't matter how far-fetched, I'd be willing to check it out."

She shook her head. "I know it's hard, Joey. I'm going crazy myself, but if I could think of any way to help Savannah, I'd already be out there doing it. Right now, as difficult as it is, the best way for me to help her is to wait here. Hunt will get a search party organized soon, I'm sure, and then we'll be able to help."

"I don't understand why we can't just form our own search party."

"I know, but Hunt said it could contaminate evidence. He's already got the professionals searching; he just wasn't ready for civilians yet." No matter how much she disagreed.

He nodded, his expression grim.

"Excuse me, Ms. Morelli?"

"Yes?" Gia turned to find Angelina Lombardo standing behind her. "Oh, Ms. Lombardo, how can I help you?"

"Might I have a word?" She gestured across the room to where Ward the weasel stood with an elbow propped on the counter, glaring daggers at her.

"Of course." There was no denying Gia already knew about Savannah's disappearance when she went into the real estate office earlier. Surely they'd heard enough gossip to realize that, since she was the one to have found Buster's body and report Savannah's kidn—disappearance. Five minutes in the café with the Bailey twins rambling on would have told them that much and more.

"It seems you lied to me." Angelina stuck to Gia's side as they weaved through the crowd. The cloying scent of her overly applied perfume made Gia's eyes water as she leaned close.

She refused to make excuses. And she certainly wouldn't compound the first lie with another. "I did, and I'm sorry. I was aware we couldn't find Savannah, but I didn't want to say anything before her family was notified, especially since Michael's girlfriend works in the office."

Narrowing her eyes, Angelina studied Gia for a moment, then nodded. "Understandable."

Gia relaxed a little as she rounded the counter and stood across from the two, glad for the opportunity to put some space between her and Angelina so she could breathe again. "We're not open right now, and the grill is turned off, but would either of you like something from one of the cases or a cup of coffee or something else to drink? It's on the house."

Ward shook his head, then looked over his shoulder before returning his attention to his boss.

"No, thank you," Angelina said. "What I would like is information."

"Okay, but I don't know what I can tell you. I don't know much." And what she did know, she planned to keep to herself as much as possible.

Ward pointed a finger at her. "You can start by telling us when Savannah set up the appointment to show Buster Clarke the Oakley Manor House."

"Ward." Angelina shot him a warning glare as she gripped his wrist and lowered his hand. "That's enough."

He yanked his hand away.

"Ms. Morelli." Her smile didn't reach her cold, gray eyes. "Gia. Do you know when Savannah scheduled the appointment with Buster?"

"I don't. I'm sorry. The first time she mentioned the house to me was this morning, and only to say that she was showing it." She'd already spilled those beans when she stopped at the real estate office earlier, not that they couldn't assume as much from the events that followed. "Why do you ask?"

"Because it was supposed to be my sale," Ward blurted out, like a spoiled child who hadn't gotten his way.

Gia had no patience for that nonsense, and she opened her mouth to blast him.

Angelina intervened before she could go off on him in the packed dining room. She stepped between them and turned her back on him. "Excuse us, please, Ward."

Gia snapped her mouth closed, letting the words burn their way back down her throat. They would do nothing to help Savannah.

Leaving him to stew over whatever his problem was, Angelina pointed toward the far end of the counter. "Could I speak with you more privately?"

Gia followed. "I'm not sure what I can tell you, Ms. Lombardo."

"Angelina, please. And forgive my agent for his insensitivity—the Oakley Manor House is an expensive piece of property that's expected to bring a large commission."

"Well, if you ask me, no amount of money is worth ending up in whatever position Savannah's in right now. And it's certainly not worth what her family is suffering."

"You're right, of course, and I apologize for Ward's behavior, but I am trying to help figure out what could have happened to Savannah, and the more information I have, the more I might be able to help."

A glimmer of hope surfaced. "What do you need to know?"

"While Ward's outburst was completely inappropriate given the circumstances, he's not wrong. The owner listed the house with Ward, which means he'll get part of the commission regardless, but all appointments should have been booked through our office. Yet, I can't find any record of a call coming in from Buster Clarke, and Tempest doesn't remember taking a message from him."

Gia tried to remember exactly what Savannah had said that morning. It seemed so long ago, and so much had happened since, it was difficult to pull up the memory. "I believe she said Buster Clarke came into the office and sought her out."

Angelina frowned. "Are you certain of that?"

Was she? It seemed important to Angelina, but was that because she was annoyed Ward would have missed out on the sale or because it pertained to Savannah's disappearance? Who could have known such an insignificant statement, made in passing, might come to mean the difference between life and death? "I'm pretty sure that's what she said. That Ward was the listing agent, but Buster had come in and specifically chosen to speak to her."

Angelina snorted and muttered under her breath, "Of course, he would have, that snake."

Gia's head began to pound. It was starting to feel like she was hurting Savannah more than helping her. "Savannah's not going to be in trouble, is she? I thought anyone could sell a house."

"Oh, yes, of course, they can. And if Buster sought her out, rather than calling the office, where his call would have been directed to Ward, that's not Savannah's fault. Though, she might have mentioned it, as professional courtesy would dictate."

The woman's attitude was getting on Gia's last nerve. "Is there some reason Buster wouldn't have wanted to work with Ward?"

Angelina dismissed the question with a wave of her hand. "Not that I'm aware, but it is odd that Buster would have sought her out directly. Even if he didn't want to work with Ward, there are other real estate offices in Boggy Creek. Someone might want to look into what Savannah's connection to someone like Buster Clarke might have been."

The sound of chatter from a police radio in the corner pulled Gia's attention from Angelina to a small group of officers, none of them familiar to Gia, who'd commandeered two tables by the front window. Not that she understood the burst of numbers and codes, but the urgency in the tone was unmistakable.

An officer walked out front with his radio.

"If you'll excuse me…" Gia was past done with this conversation anyway. "I have customers to attend to."

"Thank you for your time." Angelina returned to Ward, and after a brief conversation, Ward stormed out with Angelina on his heels.

Gia grabbed an order pad and approached the officers who remained.

The radio remained eerily quiet after that burst of chatter. A map lay spread across the table, with several officers leaning over it.

One pointed to a large blue patch Gia assumed was a lake. "...found here."

Another of the officers marked the spot she'd pointed to. "Are we holding off now?"

The first officer glanced up, noticed Gia, and frowned, though her pale blue eyes held only kindness and sympathy. "Ma'am. I'm Officer Kenney. Can I help you?"

"I'm sorry, officer, I, uh... I'm Gia Morelli." She held out her hand.

Officer Kenney took it. "It's good to meet you, Gia. I've heard a lot about you. Please, call me Regina."

Gia nodded, her gaze fixed on the mark on the map. Bearing the weight of every set of eyes watching her, and knowing each person was probably trying to hear any exchange that might occur, Gia lifted the order pad, held her pen ready, and lowered her voice. "Did you find her?"

Regina glanced at the officer who'd drawn the mark then back at Gia. She laid a hand on her shoulder and leaned close. "Is there somewhere we can talk more privately?"

Unable to speak, dread clutching her in an iron grip, Gia nodded and led the woman through the sea of people, careful to keep her gaze averted. When she reached her office, she closed the door behind them and turned to face Regina. Since she couldn't force any words past the lump blocking her throat, she simply waited.

"I know we haven't met before, but Savannah and Hunt are my second cousins. We grew up together; we're a tight family." Tears shimmered in Regina's eyes. "Though we were very close growing up, life happens. I got married, joined the police force, had two kids, and Savannah went to New York for those years, then came back and started working, helped you with the café, got engaged. We catch up often by phone, e-mail, text, but don't have much time to get together. Because I work for the police department, I see Hunt more often. I'm telling you this because I want you to understand that this is extremely difficult for me, and yet, in a couple of minutes, I'm going to pull myself together and walk back out there and do my job. And not a single person in that room is going to know how torn up I am. And I'm going to need you to do the same if you want me to be honest with you. Can you do that?"

Gia closed her eyes, then sucked in a shaky breath and nodded. She would keep control of her emotions, no matter what it took, so she'd be able to help Savannah. She blew out the breath and opened her eyes. "I can."

"Hunt called a few minutes ago." A single tear tipped over Regina's lashes and rolled down her cheek. She wiped it away. "We have no word yet on who it is, so please hold onto hope and pray."

Panic squeezed every ounce of breath from her lungs.

"A woman's body was just found in the lake behind the Oakley Manor House."

Chapter Seven

Gia's hands shook as she lifted a coffee mug from the counter to place it on a tray for the two police officers who'd stayed behind when the rest had gone out to search, taking most of the café's customers with them. At least they hadn't called off the search after the woman's body was found. That had to be a good thing. She prayed.

The mug slid from her hand and shattered against the floor. Hot coffee splashed her feet and ankles.

Willow grabbed her arm and yanked her back. "Are you all right? Did you get burned?"

"I'm okay." Thankfully, most of the coffee had spilled in the other direction.

"Here, let me get that." Willow's mother, Skyla, who'd spent the afternoon helping out, wet a dish towel and wiped Gia's ankles and shoes.

Willow grabbed another towel, soaked it in the sink behind the counter, wrung it out, and then handed it to Skyla. She rounded on Gia. "Are you sure you're okay?"

She was far from okay. It had been close to an hour since they'd found the woman's body in the lake, and there was still no word on who it was. "I'm fine. Thank you."

Regina had already left, along with most of the people who'd gathered, to set up search parties. She said they didn't want to waste time if Savannah was still out there, but it would be getting dark soon, and she hadn't sounded that optimistic.

"Sorry, there's nothing I could do with your capris." Skyla tossed the towels into a bus pan beneath the counter.

"Don't worry about it. Thank you." Splatter marks stained her pale yellow capris, but there was nothing she could do about that. She bent to help Skyla pick up the glass while Willow mopped up the spill.

Regina had begged Gia to stay behind, arguing she needed to wait in case a ransom call came in. Willow had stayed with her, as had Skyla. Mr. Mills had also stayed behind, but he'd gone home a little while after the searchers had left.

Willow poured another mug of coffee and placed it on the tray.

When Gia reached for the tray to bring it to the remaining officers, Willow lay a hand on her wrist. "I've got it, Gia."

She nodded. "Thanks."

A woman and a man she'd never seen before walked into the café, then paused and looked around.

"I'm sorry, but the café is closed for the day." She'd turned the closed sign, but it hadn't made sense to lock up with so many people coming and going, seeking news of Savannah, offering to help search. She didn't want to shut anyone out.

"Are you Gia Morelli?" The woman strode toward the counter. She was a petite woman with long, curly wheat blond hair and a killer smile that didn't quite reach her hazel eyes but did accentuate her dimples. Her gray skirt and light pink blouse fit perfectly, tasteful jewelry accentuated her long, slim neck, and she moved with catlike grace on her spiked heels. Gia decided she'd probably be considered cute if not for the no-nonsense attitude that would either prove refreshing or intimidating. Gia hadn't yet decided which.

"I am. Can I help you?"

"I'm Paige Clarke, Buster's sister, and this is my brother, Robert." She gestured to the short, stocky man standing next to her. "I understand you were the one to find my brother's body."

How had she found that out so quickly? Surely, Hunt wouldn't have revealed it. Neither would Leo. At least, she didn't think they would have. Of course, the gossip had already spread through the café, so why would she think it wouldn't have reached Buster's family. "Yes, I did. I'm so sorry for your loss."

"Thank you." Though Paige approached the counter, she didn't sit.

Her brother remained where he was, behind and to the side of Paige, his muscular arms, accentuated by a thin black T-shirt, folded across his thick chest. He kept his head on a constant swivel as he surveyed the room. His expression remained unreadable, and his mouth pressed tight in a grim line. Not that she blamed him for being protective of his sister; they'd already lost one brother. Though neither seemed too broken up over it.

Paige tapped the counter for emphasis or, perhaps, to refocus Gia's attention on her. "I need you to tell me everything you saw."

"Uh..." She had a very strong suspicion Hunt wouldn't want her revealing anything just yet.

"That wasn't a request, Ms. Morelli." Paige leaned forward, rested her forearms on the counter, and clasped her hands together. She smiled and peered from beneath long, thick lashes, a confident woman, used to getting her way. Spoiled? Maybe. Powerful? Perhaps. Either way, the expression on her face held no doubt. She fully expected Gia to answer the question.

It didn't seem to matter to her that Skyla and Willow stood on either side of Gia, staring open-mouthed. She didn't acknowledge either of them. Nor did she pay any attention to the officers sitting at the table by the window, whose attention she'd also attracted, though neither of them intervened. "Please, Gia. Tell me what you know."

Gia's initial assessment had been accurate. While Paige's direct approach was somewhat refreshing, she was an intimidating woman, despite her pixie-like appearance.

This was not an enemy Gia wanted.

Earl's warning about Buster wailed like a siren in her mind and extended to his siblings. She could definitely see this woman asking her thug nicely to break someone's legs. She huffed out a breath. "I um..."

"I'm sorry. I understand your friend is missing." Paige tilted her head and lifted a brow.

Gia nodded, taking a moment to compose herself.

"Then I'm sure you can understand my need to look into my brother's death. Not that I don't trust the police, mind you. I do, and I'll cooperate with them as best I can. But I'm not the type to sit around and do nothing while depending on other people to solve my problems."

Gia could certainly understand that. Staying behind at the café instead of searching for Savannah was the hardest thing she'd ever had to do. If not for the possibility of a ransom demand, she'd be out investigating Savannah's disappearance herself, even if it meant wading through every square inch of swampland in Florida.

Paige leaned farther across the counter and crooked a finger at Gia to do the same, bringing them face to face, then whispered, "The best way to help your friend return safely is to give me the information I'm asking for."

Gia gasped. Was that a threat? Did this woman have something to do with Savannah's disappearance? Was this the ransom demand they'd been hoping for? Or was she just stating fact? Certainly, there was a good chance that finding out who'd killed Buster would lead to Savannah's whereabouts, which Gia prayed were anywhere other than the lake behind the Oakley Manor House.

Paige straightened, but still spoke quietly. "I command resources the police don't. Have ways of investigating that the police can't indulge in."

Gia would comply. She'd do whatever was necessary to secure Savannah's safe return. Aware of the attention they were drawing, Gia gestured toward the back of the café. "Why don't you come into my office where we can sit down and talk?"

Paige smiled. "Of course, thank you."

"Would you like coffee or anything?"

She held up a hand. "No, thanks."

Robert followed them to the office but, thankfully, remained in the hallway when Gia and Paige entered and closed the door.

Gia took a seat behind the desk, Savannah's desk, the one her Pa had made her and she'd put in the small office for Gia until she could afford to get one of her own. Paige perched on its edge, as Savannah often did when Gia was doing paperwork. Though when Savannah did it, it felt like she was trying to be close. Paige stared down at her, her expression hard, meant to intimidate.

Gia needed to be rid of her so she could call Hunt and tell him about the visit and ask him about the woman they'd found. "What do you want to know?"

Settling more comfortably on the desk, Paige crossed her legs and waited. Obviously, not going anywhere quickly. "Just walk me through what happened. Tell me what you remember. Every detail you can think of."

Gia told her about getting nervous when Savannah didn't return when she was supposed to, leaving out the warning from Earl and the fact she'd been scared Buster had done something to her. She walked her through the search and finding Buster's body. She tried to gloss over some of the more disturbing details, but Paige would have none of it, insisting on hearing everything.

"And the nail gun, it was in his hand?"

"Uh…yes, I believe it was."

"The two by four, was he holding that?"

"I…" Gia closed her eyes and tried to envision the scene. She remembered thinking at the time that it looked like the two by four had been tossed on top of Buster's body. "It looked more like someone else dropped the two by four on top of him after they put him in the tub. Whether or not he was holding it or using it at any point before that, I don't know."

Paige pounced. "What do you mean, put him in the tub? Why do you say that?"

"Oh, I don't know." What had given her that impression? She shook her head; she couldn't put her finger on any one thing that made her feel that way, and yet, the scene felt somehow staged. Was someone trying to send a message? One Paige Clarke was trying to piece together and interpret? The last thing Gia needed was to land smack in the middle of some kind of deadly family feud. "I guess it just didn't look to me like he landed there accidentally, though, I suppose he could have fallen in. I'm sorry, I'm not sure what gave me that impression. I shouldn't have phrased it that way."

"No, no, please, I want you to tell me exactly what your impressions were. You seem like an intelligent woman, and even though you can't put your finger on exactly what made you think it, it's obviously the conclusion your subconscious mind settled on from viewing the scene. And since I haven't yet seen it for myself, I have to rely on your interpretation."

If this woman was making decisions based on that kind of thinking, Gia vowed to be more careful about what she said.

When she completed her interrogation, Paige nodded and stood. "Thank you for your cooperation."

"Wait." Gia stood as well, tired of this woman looking down at her, and met her gaze. "Please, Savannah is my best friend, my sister, really. Is there anything you can tell me about her disappearance or where to find her? Anything you tell me will remain between us. I won't breathe a word of it to anyone."

Paige studied her, looked her up and down as if sizing her up, then sighed. "The only thing I can tell you right now is that she's not the woman they found in the lake."

The breath shot from Gia's lungs, and tears sprang into her eyes. Her legs turned to rubber, and she dropped onto her chair, no longer caring if she had to look up at Paige. "You're sure?"

"I am." She shifted her hair behind her shoulder. "Thank you for cooperating. I trust I can contact you again if I need any further information."

Gia nodded, though it hadn't been a question. "Of course, thank you."

"And in return, I will keep you updated on any information I find. A fair trade, yes?"

"Yes, yes, thank you."

"I'll be in touch, then." She dropped a business card in the center of Gia's desk. "You will find all of my contact information there. I am reachable on my cell phone any time of the day or night. Do not hesitate to call."

When Paige left, Gia lowered her head to the desk and cried deep, racking, painful sobs. She had no reason to believe Paige, no reason to think she had any information on Savannah's whereabouts, and yet, she was certain Paige had told her the truth. She didn't strike Gia as the kind of woman who spoke without knowing what she was talking about, though Gia wasn't sure she'd call her honest, exactly.

As grief eased and common sense returned, doubts about Paige's sincerity crept in. She jerked upright. While Gia relayed the details of the crime against her brother, Paige remained perfectly calm, giving no outward indication the specifics bothered her. Gia had figured she was just cold. But what if Paige had already known the details and was just looking to confirm? What if she was trying to determine what, if anything, the police would decipher from the crime scene? Even the Bailey sisters didn't have the level of knowledge Paige seemed to possess.

Only a few explanations made sense. Either Paige Clarke had informants in the police department, which was possible given the officers in the café hadn't interfered when she'd approached Gia. Although, in all fairness, Paige hadn't done anything wrong to warrant their intervention. Or, Paige knew Savannah wasn't the woman found in the lake because she knew exactly where Savannah was. Or, she was well aware of the woman's identity, and that knowledge could mean she'd had something to do with her ending up there.

She had to call Hunt.

He picked up on the second ring. "Hello."

"Was it her?" The words blurted out before she could stop them, and she slapped a hand over her mouth.

"Ah, Gia. I'm sorry."

"Oh, no!" she sobbed.

"No. No, Gia, wait, it wasn't Savannah. It wasn't her."

She cried harder.

"I didn't mean…uh… when I said I'm sorry, I meant, I didn't realize you knew we found a woman. It was supposed to have been kept quiet. If I knew someone had told you, I'd have called right away, as soon as we confirmed it wasn't her."

"It's okay." She laughed through the tears. "It's all right, really. As long as it wasn't her, that's all that matters."

"Was that why you were calling?"

"No, I um, no. Well, yes, that, and…Listen, Hunt, I need to tell you something, but you have to at least try to keep it between us." The last thing she needed was Paige finding out she'd repeated everything she'd promised not to. But with Savannah's life on the line, she didn't much care about anything else.

"Fine, Gia, what's going on?"

She needed to get a grip and get to the point. Every second she kept him from searching pushed the chances of Savannah being recovered before nightfall further away. "A woman and a man just came in, Paige and Robert Clarke. Paige wanted information on what I saw when I found Buster."

"Yeah, those two are going to be a problem. Hang on…" His muffled voice came through the line as if he'd covered the phone to talk to someone else. "Sorry. What did you tell her?"

"I just told her what I saw."

"That's fine. It's nothing they wouldn't have been able to find out anyway."

"But Hunt…"

"Yeah."

"Not only did she seem to know an awful lot about the crime scene, she also told me the woman in the lake wasn't Savannah." She relayed the conversation as close to word for word as she could remember.

He was silent for a moment, probably running through the same possibilities Gia had run through herself. "Did she say who the woman is?"

"No. You haven't identified her yet?"

"Not yet. But I saw her myself, Gia. I'm a hundred percent certain it's not Savannah."

She nodded, even as she realized he couldn't see her through the phone. The phone. "Wait, Hunt, can't you find Savannah through her cell phone, like with her GPS or something?"

"It won't work."

"Why not? I thought they could do something like that. I know I've heard of it before."

"We found her purse on the back lawn. Her phone was inside it."

Gia wanted to scream. She refrained. "So, now what?"

"Now, you wait. I don't know what is going on with Buster's family or if their visit was anything more than a fishing expedition, but I need you to stay there, Gia. Just in case. I will send a few more officers, though."

"No, don't. I'm fine, Hunt." Paige hadn't threatened her in any way. If anything, she'd seemed to want to work together if necessary. "Please, don't. I'm fine here, and I don't want you taking anyone else away from the search."

She didn't have to remind him it was getting dark out, and Savannah could be anywhere, lost, alone, hurt, frightened.

Chapter Eight

Gia sat at the counter, cradling her head in her hands. It had been hours, and still no word. Hunt had just told her to go home, but she'd refused. Zoe, who owned the doggie daycare center Gia used, had been kind enough to drop Thor, Gia's Bernese Mountain Dog, off at Gia's house. She'd fed both him and Klondike, the little black and white kitten she'd adopted after Thor had rescued her and her siblings from a coyote attack, only after a piece of Klondike's ear had been bitten off, and walked Thor. They'd be okay until morning. There was no sense sitting there doing nothing. If Hunt was okay with her leaving the café, she'd head out to the Oakley Manor House to join the search.

She stood and called to the remaining officers, "I'm going to lock up and head out to join the search party."

One of the two officers still posted at the café nodded. "We'll pack up and head out there with you."

She started to argue but thought better of it. It would only waste time, and the end result would be the same; those two officers would remain in position to protect her until this was done. "It'll take me about half an hour. Would you like anything?"

"No, we're good, thank you. We'll meet you out front whenever you're ready."

Gia should really have started closing up sooner, hadn't been doing anything but sitting there thinking about Savannah and speaking to the scattering of people who'd stopped in during the evening to see if there was any word or to offer help. She should also have eaten something, since she hadn't all day, but the knots in her stomach would have made it impossible.

She opened the register to remove the drawer and put it in the safe until morning. The drawer was still in place, but all of the cash was missing. Maybe Cole or Willow had put the money in the safe already. She went to her office and opened the safe. Empty, but for the bag of extra change she kept in there just in case she ran low.

This wasn't the first time money had gone missing from the register, but she still hadn't implemented any kind of access codes to know who had opened the drawer. While she had no doubt none of her employees had stolen from her, she also didn't know who to call and ask.

They'd stopped serving before Gia had returned to the café from the Oakley Manor House and hadn't charged for coffee or drinks or even the pre-prepared food they'd offered throughout the day, so she had no clue when the register had last been opened. With the number of people who'd been packed inside when she returned, and the steady stream in and out all day, anyone could have taken it.

She dialed Cole's number.

"Hey, Gia." He panted, clearly winded.

"You okay, Cole?"

"I'm fine. Just not as young as I once was."

"Any news?"

"Nothing yet. But we're still searching."

At least, they hadn't called off the search until morning. If Hunt had his way, she was sure they wouldn't. And if they did, some wouldn't give up anyway. "I just had a quick question, and then I'm going to be heading out there. Did you take the cash out of the register?"

"No, why?"

"The drawer is empty."

"You might check with Willow or Skyla. I only cleaned up the kitchen. I never checked the register. Sorry."

"No, no, don't worry about it." She would check with Willow and Skyla, but if it was gone, there was nothing she could do about it, anyway. There had been too many people in and out all day. Gia and her staff had been moving throughout the café, so anyone could have accessed the register if they'd gone behind the counter or even just leaned over. The money was the least of her concerns right now, but knowing if someone had robbed her seemed important, especially if it had anything to do with Savannah's disappearance. What if someone had stolen the money to pay a ransom? Had her father or one of her brothers been contacted? Surely, if they had, they'd have just asked for the money, knowing full-well Gia would hand over every penny in a heartbeat.

Cole coughed, interrupting her thoughts, then cleared his throat. "Did you remember to make Harley's dinner?"

"Oh, no. I forgot. Thanks, Cole." How could she have forgotten that? Hopefully, he hadn't been by yet. "I'll do it now."

"I'll let you know if I hear anything. Otherwise, give me a call when you get out here, and I'll meet you in the courtyard; I need a quick break and something to drink anyway."

"Thanks, Cole. I'll throw a few cases of water in my trunk before I head out." She hung up and called Willow, who had gone home with her mother.

She answered immediately. "Did they find her?"

"No, nothing, I'm sorry." Gia asked about the cash, but neither Willow nor Skyla had removed it, nor had they noticed anyone behind the counter.

"The last time I opened the register was before we closed. When I rang up the last customer, the cash was still there."

"Thanks, Willow."

"I'm really sorry, Gia." Her breath hitched.

"No, please, don't worry about it. I've been here all evening, and I couldn't tell you if anyone went behind the counter. We were all distracted. I'm just locking up, and I wanted to make sure it wasn't laying around somewhere before I left." She didn't mention her ransom theory. If the kidnapper had demanded a ransom and insisted it remain quiet, Gia wasn't about to open her mouth and possibly do something to hinder Savannah's safe return.

"Are you going home?" Willow asked.

Gia dumped whatever coffee was left in the pots and rinsed them. "No, I think I'll head out and see if I can join a search party."

"Mom and I were thinking about doing the same, so maybe I'll see you out there."

"Sounds good." After making sure they were all turned off, she set the coffee makers up for the morning, so she'd just have to flip the switches when she came in. If she came in. If Hunt didn't need her to be there, she probably wouldn't even open.

"You'll call if you hear anything before we get there?"

"Right away, I promise."

"Thanks."

Gia hung up and headed to the kitchen. She wouldn't bother prepping any food. If Savannah was found safe and sound before morning, she could always come in early and take care of it or just open late. But she had to make Harley's dinner.

She'd been leaving dinner out back for the homeless man since she opened. Harley had become a good friend, but he had issues and wasn't comfortable entering buildings, so Gia had set up a small table and chairs in the lot behind the café, and she left him dinner every night. Sometimes his friend Donna Mae even joined him, but she always let Gia know ahead of time if she would be there.

The grill had already been turned off and cleaned, and she was starting to get anxious about getting out to search, so she took a meat lover's breakfast pie out of the refrigerator and warmed up two slices, along with an order of home fries. She packed it into a bag along with a couple containers of orange juice, flipped the back light on, and shoved the door open. Keeping her gaze focused fully on the table, she set out Harley's bag, then turned to go inside.

A woman lay crumpled against the back of the building. Long blonde hair was strewn across her face, one arm flung over her head. The spotlight reflected off rhinestone-studded, salmon-colored nails.

"Savannah!" Gia ran to her. She dropped to her knees at her side and shoved the hair away from her face. "Savannah, please, answer me."

She was completely limp.

"Please, be breathing." Tears streamed from Gia's eyes, impeding her vision. She swiped them away with the back of her wrist and felt for a pulse. A strong, steady beat fluttered beneath her fingers. "Oh, thank you. Thank you. Thank you."

She lowered her forehead against Savannah's for one brief moment.

She had to get help. Where had she left her phone? No idea. She couldn't remember. She'd spoken to Hunt from her office. Hunt. She had to call him. And Leo. And Mr. Mills.

Cradling Savannah's head on her knees, Gia leaned over her and sobbed. "Oh, Savannah. Wake up, please."

No response.

Gia rocked back and forth, clutching Savannah tightly against her. "I'll get you help. I will, I promise. But I can't leave you here alone. I won't."

She looked around the empty lot. Hers was the only car there. The two officers had gone out front. Surely they'd realize she hadn't come out and search for her at some point. But Savannah was unconscious. She needed help now.

Gia sucked in a breath and screamed, "Help! Somebody, help me, please!"

Smoothing Savannah's hair away from her face, she searched for injuries. No sign of any. She felt through her hair for bumps on her head, squinted in the dim light for any signs of blood. Nothing. "Come on, Savannah. You have to wake up so I can—"

A man emerged from the woods, running toward them with a steady limp. "Gia?"

"Harley! Harley, I need help. Please!"

"What should I do?" He skidded to a stop beside her. "Is that Savannah? You found her? She's okay?"

"Yes, yes. She is, but she's not waking up, and I need help. I don't have my phone. There are two police officers out front; can you go get them, please?"

He turned and started running, then disappeared into the dark alleyway around the side of the building.

Gia's gut cramped. What if whoever had left Savannah there was still lurking around, and she'd just sent Harley into danger? She strained her ears for any sign of a struggle.

The pounding of running footsteps started a moment later, too many footfalls for just Harley.

A bright light shot from the corner of the building, blinding her for an instant.

She lowered her gaze to Savannah's too pale face.

"Gia? Is she all right?" One of the officers ran toward them, Harley keeping pace at his side, while the other spoke frantically into his radio.

"She's breathing, but she won't wake up."

"Let me see." The officer dropped down next to her and examined Savannah. "There's an ambulance on the way."

"Call Hunt. You have to call Hunt, please."

"Hey." The second officer gripped her shoulder. "We called him. He's already on his way. Just hold tight. She's safe now."

Gia nodded, crying harder, hugging Savannah against her.

Harley paced back and forth in a steady path, like a guard dog putting himself between them and harm, sobbing softly.

"You're safe now, Savannah. You're safe now. Nothing can hurt you." She spoke quietly, trying to get her breathing under control, so Savannah wouldn't sense her fear if she could hear her. Tremors shook her voice, but she couldn't help it. "It'll be okay now. I won't leave you, I promise."

She held Savannah's head against her chest while Harley stood guard.

One of the officers had disappeared and returned a few minutes later, pulling his cruiser into the back lot. They strung crime scene tape across the parking lot entrance. Gia figured they'd need it once people heard Savannah had been found back there, at least, they would if they wanted to preserve any kind of evidence that might have been left behind.

The thought stopped her mid-rock. What if she was messing up evidence by holding her? She hoped she wasn't, but no way was she letting go. She stroked her hand over Savannah's hair, over and over again, smoothing the tangles as best she could.

"Gia." The softest whisper of a sound.

"Savannah?" She looked down to find Savannah's huge blue eyes open and staring up at her. "Oh, Savannah. Thank God you're safe."

"'s, okay." Her words slurred, but at least she was starting to wake up. Sirens wailed in the distance.

Gia kissed the top of her head. "It's okay, Savannah. Everything's okay now. Help will be here any minute."

"Gia." Savannah gripped her wrist for an instant; her hold surprisingly strong, then her hand fell limp at her side.

"I'm here, Savannah." She leaned closer.

"Tell 'em. 'Bout the clown." Her eyelids fluttered closed, and her head dropped to the side. "Clown."

Gia held Savannah close while chaos reigned around her. Emergency vehicles barreled around the corner, then parked haphazardly across the road before officers flooded the taped off lot. Sirens screamed. Flashing lights pierced the night in a dizzying stream. Voices encroached on her peace as word spread, and people began to gather.

"Savannah!" Leo fell to his knees sobbing softly.

Hunt squeezed in next to him.

Gia wanted desperately to hold her friend tighter, cradle her, and protect her. Take comfort in knowing she was alive. Instead, she released her to Hunt and Leo and scooted back. She remembered all too well the need to hold her when she'd first seen her, as it still raged through her. But Hunt and Leo had just arrived, and they needed that comfort as well.

Gia scrambled back out of the way.

A strong hand reached out to her, and she looked up into Harley's eyes. She gripped his hand and let him help her to her feet.

"They asked me to wait. To tell what I saw." Harley was the only other civilian amid a crowd of first responders inside the taped off area.

Gia kissed his cheek. "Thank you, Harley."

"Protecting you is getting to be a full-time job." He smiled as he patted her hand. "It gives me purpose."

"You're a good man, Harley." She hooked her arm through his and rested her head against his shoulder.

Familiar faces began to appear among those lining the barrier. Cole, Earl, and Cybil stood together, looking on anxiously. She didn't see Willow or

Skyla yet, though she was sure Cole would have called them as soon as he heard Savannah had been found, nor did she see Savannah's father or any of her brothers. No doubt, Hunt had told them to go ahead to the hospital.

Gia returned her gaze to Savannah as Hunt and Leo each clutched one of Savannah's hands while the EMTs started an IV line. She understood that need to hold on, to never let go.

Another familiar face popped up; Ward Bennett. His hair stood up in all directions and a pajama top peeked from beneath his crookedly buttoned shirt. Apparently, he'd gone home to bed rather than join the search for his colleague.

She scanned the faces for Angelina but didn't see her. Nor did she find Paige or her brother. Surely, they would have heard, given the speed with which Paige had learned everything else that had happened. Gia wanted to let it go, to step back, be grateful Savannah had been found safe, let the police or the Clarke family or anyone else find out what had happened.

But she couldn't. She searched through the sea of faces, cataloguing who was there and who was absent, determining who she'd need to call with the news of Savannah's safe return. Cold seeped through her, straight to her bones, and she shivered, despite the thick heat of the summer night.

Because there was no way she'd rest until whoever had taken Savannah was found, punished, and no longer posed a threat.

Chapter Nine

The steady beep, beep, beep of Savannah's heart monitor, combined with the soft sound of her breathing, finally allowed Gia to rest. Though the doctor hadn't found any sign of injury, he'd insisted on keeping her overnight for observation. The strong sedative she'd been given hadn't worn off completely yet, and Savannah was severely dehydrated but, thankfully, that was all. It could have been so much worse.

Gia let her head fall against the seat back and closed her eyes. She'd lost track of time hours ago, but it had to be getting close to morning, though darkness still peered through the gaps surrounding the blinds Hunt insisted remain closed.

Without opening her eyes, Gia reached through the railing and gripped Savannah's hand, the need to know she was close a constant ache. The doctor had assured them she'd be fine, just needed to sleep off the sedative used to keep her unconscious, but the contact offered reassurance.

"Gia?" Savannah whispered.

Gia jerked upright. "I'm here."

Savannah gripped her hand. "Thank you."

"For what?"

"Staying with me."

Tears gathered in her eyes, but she did her best not to let them fall.

"No tears." A small smile formed, though her eyes remained closed. "You promised."

"You're right, I did." Gia sniffed and shifted to sit on the edge of the seat, beating back exhaustion. "Can I get you anything?"

She rubbed her throat. "Water would be good."

"Sure thing." She jumped up and poured a small amount of water from the pitcher on the tray into a cup. "Do you want a straw?"

"Please." Savannah tried to sit up.

"Hang on a sec." After dropping a straw into the cup, Gia used the remote to lift the back of the bed, then helped Savannah scoot up more comfortably and handed her the cup. "Better?"

She took a tentative sip, then hesitated. "Much, thanks."

"Do you feel like you could eat some crackers? I had them leave some."

Savannah winced and waved her off. "No, not yet, thanks."

"Do you feel up to talking to Hunt and Leo yet?" They'd battered Gia relentlessly on the importance of calling them as soon as Savannah was awake enough to talk, but if she needed a few minutes, Gia would give her that.

She frowned. "They're not here?"

"Not now. They stayed until they knew you were okay, but you were sleeping, so they didn't want to lose time investigating. I promised I'd call, though, when you woke up."

"Yeah, I think I'll be awake for a little while, but I have a bad headache." She pressed a hand against the top of her head.

"Do you think…uh…Sorry. I'm not allowed to ask you anything. Hunt said he and Leo had to be the first to talk to you, so I told them I'd stay with you, but I promised not to ask any questions."

Gia took a quick minute to call Hunt and let him know Savannah was awake and up to talking, keeping Savannah's hand in hers while she spoke. Though she'd been gone less than a day, she seemed somehow more fragile since her return.

"It feels like someone hit me over the head."

Gia turned on the light at the head of the bed and leaned over to look. "I'll take a look at your head, but the doctor didn't find any injuries."

Savannah lowered her hand to her lap and took another sip of water.

Parting her hair carefully, just in case she was hurt, Gia searched through the long, blond strands. "I don't feel a lump or see anything, but your hair is so tangled it's hard to tell. Could be it's pulling from the tangles. I have a brush in my bag if you want me to brush it out."

"Could you please? It's annoying me."

She grabbed the brush from her bag and sat on the bed beside Savannah. "Can you turn a little?"

Moving slowly, Savannah held onto the rail and scooted around until her back faced Gia, then took one more sip of water and put the cup on the tray. "My Pa left?"

"He did. He would have stayed, but your brothers and Hunt insisted he go home and sleep for a little while. They promised to bring him back first thing in the morning if you haven't been released." She lifted Savannah's hair behind her shoulders and separated a small section, then started at the bottom and brushed gently through the tangles, unknotting the worst of them before moving up the strands. "All of your brothers were here and, of course, Hunt and Leo. I don't think either of them would have left if they weren't racing against the clock. Now that you've been found, Hunt's pushing to be kept on the case, but they're not sure what'll happen."

Her voice hitched, but she couldn't help it.

Thankfully, Savannah ignored it. "Did they find out anything?"

The urge to question her, to ask if she knew who'd abducted her, was almost impossible to fight. If Hunt and Leo didn't get there soon, she might lose that battle. "Not that I've heard, but I haven't talked to them in a few hours."

Savannah looked over her shoulder at Gia. Deep, dark circles ringed her eyes. They were made more prominent by the pastiness of her usually tan complexion. "Will I be able to go home soon?"

Gia shifted the smoothed hair in front of Savannah's shoulder and went to work on the next section, careful to avoid the top of her head. "Hopefully, when the doctor comes in, she'll release you."

"That would be good. I'm achy and uncomfortable, and I just want to be out of here. I hate the smell of hospitals, you know?"

The unmistakable scent of disinfectant clung to everything, but instead of smelling clean, it reeked of sickness. "I do."

With a deep sigh, Savannah lowered her head.

When Gia finished brushing out all of the tangles, she smoothed her hair back and weaved it into a loose French braid, then tied it with a band she kept wrapped around the end of her brush. "Does that feel better?"

"Yeah, thanks."

Gia helped her turn back around and arranged a pillow behind her to lean against. "Do you want a cool rag for your head?"

"I'll be—"

The door to the room opened, and Leo rushed through with Hunt on his heels.

Gia stood and stepped back to allow him room to get to Savannah.

He pulled her into his arms and held on for dear life.

Hunt put his arm around Gia and kissed the top of her head. "How are you holding up?"

"I'm fine." The exhaustion that had nearly overcome her earlier had abated. "I'll feel better once we can take her home, though."

He nodded.

"Is there any news?"

"Nah, nothing new. There were no fingerprints found on the piece of two by four, and the only prints on the nail gun belonged to Buster and three of the workers on the construction crew, all of whom have alibis for the time in question and no connection we've been able to find to anyone involved."

"And you didn't find any witnesses?" Though it was a long shot, since the construction crew had the day off while waiting for inspectors, they'd hoped to find someone who'd seen the suspect enter or leave the house.

"We found one man who'd been fishing on his boat on the lake behind the house at the time, but he didn't see or hear anything."

"Did you hear any more from Paige Clarke?"

"Surprisingly, no, but I have a feeling silence might be worse with that one. I have no doubt she's launching her own investigation; I just hope it doesn't turn into an all-out war with the Espositos if she finds something before we do."

"Do you think they're responsible for killing Buster?"

Hunt stayed quiet, seeming to mull over whatever information he had. "I really don't know. It's just too early to tell. We've found no motive for them to have killed him other than the fact that they don't like each other, so why now?"

True enough. If the Bailey sisters were correct, which they usually were, the feud between the families had been ongoing, so why suddenly kill Buster?

Leo stepped out of the way, and Hunt hugged Savannah. "You okay?"

She nodded against his chest.

"Gia." Leo stood in front of her, his cheeks red. "I owe you a huge apology."

"For what?"

"I had no right to speak to you the way I did when we arrived at the Oakley Manor House. I have no excuse other than that I was out of my mind with fear when I found out Savannah was missing. You had nothing to do with that. I know you'd have moved Heaven and earth to find her, and I am sincerely sorry, and I should have said so sooner."

"Ah, Leo, you don't owe me an apology at all. Truthfully, I don't even remember what you said. Besides..." She glanced at Hunt, remembering all too clearly her willingness to dismiss Buster's murder in favor of searching for Savannah. A fact she wasn't proud of. "I have a feeling I owe Hunt the same apology."

"I'm sure I have apologies of my own to make." Hunt grinned. "Why don't we just chalk it up to people sometimes react poorly when family is in danger?"

Warmth rushed through Gia at the idea of being included as family, something she cherished and had been too long without. "That works for me."

Hunt held Savannah another moment before kissing her head and stepping back. "Are you okay to answer a few questions?"

She nodded. "I think so, but can Gia stay?"

He rubbed a hand up and down her arm. "Of course, if it makes you feel better."

"It does, thank you."

Gia returned to her spot on the bed next to Savannah, and Hunt and Leo sat in chairs on either side of the bed.

Hunt set a small tape recorder in the middle of the bed. "I'm going to record this, okay?"

"Uh huh." Savannah glanced at Gia, her bottom lip caught between her teeth.

Gia took her hand. "I'll be right here the whole time."

"Okay." She grabbed her water from the tray beside the bed, took a sip, then set the cup down. With her free hand, she reached out to Leo and entwined her fingers with his. "I'm ready."

Hunt started the recorder and dictated the date and time. "First, what can you tell me about what happened? Just walk me through from the time you met up with Buster."

Clutching Gia's hand so tightly her knuckles turned white, Savannah frowned. "I was supposed to show Buster the Oakley Manor House. We took separate cars because Earl was nervous about us riding out there together, said he didn't trust Buster Clarke."

To Hunt's credit, and Leo's, they managed to remain silent.

"When we got there, everything was fine. I showed him the downstairs, and he seemed really interested. He spent a long time in the kitchen, opening and closing cabinets, commented how much he loved the fireplaces in the kitchen and dining room, and he was pretty impressed with the pantry. I was getting excited, you know? I thought there was a good chance he was going to make an offer." She sniffed and lowered her gaze to their intertwined hands.

Gia handed her a napkin from the tray.

"I don't remember much after that. We went upstairs, and I started to walk down the hallway, figuring I'd start at one end and work my way down the hall showing him all the rooms. But he didn't walk with me. He just stood there on the landing, frowning about something."

Realizing how tightly she was squeezing Savannah's hand, Gia loosened her hold.

"I asked him if something was wrong, and he didn't answer at first, then he asked what was in one of the rooms and pointed to a door not far away. I told him it was a bedroom, and he said he wanted to see that one first, so I opened the door."

She sniffed again and wiped her eyes.

Gia jumped up, grabbed a box of tissues from the counter beside the sink, and handed them to Savannah.

Leo patted her hand. "It's okay, hon, just take your time."

She nodded and blew her nose. "When I opened the door, someone grabbed me from behind, and I felt a sting in my arm, like a shot. Then everything started to get hazy, and I got…like…tunnel vision, ya know?"

Hunt nodded and inched closer to the edge of his seat. He rested his elbows on the bed and clasped his hands beneath his chin.

"And then everything went dark." She laid her head back against the pillows. "And I don't remember anything else until I woke up in the hospital."

Hunt pulled out his notebook and started jotting notes, even though the recorder was still running. "When things were hazy, before you blacked out, do you remember anything? Anything at all?"

She squeezed her eyes closed. "I…kind of. I remember someone yelling. A man's voice, but I don't know if it was Buster or someone else."

Leo lifted her hand and kissed her knuckles. "Could you tell what he was saying?"

She stayed quiet for a minute. "No. I…don't know if I didn't hear it or if I don't remember."

"What about the person who grabbed you? Was it a man?" Hunt asked.

She nodded, then winced and released her hold on Gia and Leo to rub her temples. "I think so. He felt big. Strong. He wrapped one arm around my waist and pulled me against him, then clamped his other hand over my mouth. I didn't see him, but I'm very sure it was a man."

Hunt clenched his teeth and worked his jaw back and forth. Then he took a deep breath and continued. "If he had one arm around you and one hand over your mouth, how did he inject you? Was there a second person in the room? Other than Buster?"

"Umm…" Her eyes narrowed. "I don't know, but I think there must have been. I just don't know. I'm pretty sure he kept holding me until I blacked out. The last thing I remember is my vision tunneling and his firm grip on me. I don't remember falling. And I was never able to scream, though I did try. I also tried to fight back and get away from him, but he was too strong. Maybe if he hadn't caught me off guard?"

"It's okay, Savannah. You're safe now." Leo rubbed his thumb back and forth over her knuckles.

She nodded and lifted his hand to rub against her cheek.

"What about Buster? Do you know where he was when you were attacked?" If the increased pace of the questions was any indication, the interview was beginning to take its toll on Hunt.

"I… No, I can't remember. I opened the door and stepped into the room ahead of him. I never saw him again after that. Is he missing too?"

Gia's gaze shot from Hunt to Leo. How hadn't she realized Savannah didn't know about Buster?

Leo scooted closer to her. "I'm sorry, Savannah, Buster didn't make it."

"He…?" She shook her head. "What do you mean he didn't make it?"

"He was murdered and left in the house."

All the air rushed out of her lungs in one big whoosh, and she slumped against the pillows. Tears trickled from the corners of her eyes and ran down her cheeks. "I'm sorry I can't remember more that would help you find his killer."

"Do you remember anything else?" Hunt asked. "Anything from the time you were moved or held captive? You had to have been transported from the house to somewhere else, then again from wherever you were held to the café lot. Did you wake up at all?"

"Not that I remember."

"Okay, that's enough for now." He turned off the recorder and started to stand.

"Wait." Gia grabbed his arm and turned to Savannah. "What about the clown?"

"Clown?" Her expression remained blank. "What do you mean?"

"When I found you outside the café, when I first ran over to you, you said 'tell them about the clown.' At least, that's what it sounded like at the time." She tried to turn her attention to the past. Tried to bring the moment back. "Yes, I'm pretty sure that's what you said."

"I don't know. I don't remember waking up at the café. I only remember waking in the hospital, in the emergency room, and you were already there, and the doctor and nurse were there." She shrugged and shook her head. "I'm sorry, I just don't remember anything else."

Hunt patted her hand. "That's okay. More might come back to you over time. For now, you just worry about resting and feeling better. If you do remember anything else, have Gia call us right away, okay?"

"Sure."

Savannah might not remember now, but Gia was positive that's what she had said. Not only once, but twice. Maybe there was some kind of circus or traveling carnival in town, or even in a nearby town. Was that where they'd held her? Maybe an abandoned fairground. She'd let it go for now, but as soon as she could get a few minutes free, she'd find a way to look into it.

Chapter Ten

Gia pulled into her driveway, careful to take the turn slowly so as not to inflame Savannah's headache, then shifted into park. "You okay?"

"I am, thank you." Savannah offered a shaky smile and cuddled her gray and white tabby, Pepper, closer against her cheek. They'd stopped at Savannah's to spend some time with her father and pick up Pepper before heading out to Gia's, where Savannah had claimed the spare bedroom and all but moved in even before her disappearance.

Savannah tilted the air conditioning vent to blow on her face and closed her eyes.

Gia shifted into park but left the car running. "Do you want to sit for a minute before we go in?"

She started to shake her head, then winced. "That's okay. We can go in now. I just want to feel like I'm home, you know?"

Tears threatened, but Gia held them back. She'd spent all night and half the day sitting at Savannah's bedside in the hospital, watching how upset she got every time someone else started crying. Especially her dad and Gia. "Sure thing. Are you hungry?"

"Actually, I am." Nausea had kept her from eating anything at the hospital, courtesy of whatever drug her assailants had used to knock her out.

Gia smiled, surprised to realize she didn't have to force it as she had in the hospital. Joy flowed through her. Savannah was home, and she was healing. Nothing else mattered right now. But it would. Once Savannah recovered and didn't need Gia at her side, Gia would honor her vow to find whoever did this. "Well, it's a good thing because Cole made enough homemade soup to feed a small army. He didn't know what you'd be able to eat, so there's a variety. He said he'd drop it all off whenever you're ready."

Savannah laughed, and tears streamed down her cheeks.

Gia laid a hand on her arm and looked out the driver's side window until she could get her emotions in check. "Come on. Let's go in and get you something to eat. The doctor said you'd feel better once you can get something in your stomach and keep it down. Maybe Hunt and Leo will get here in time to eat something too. They said they'd be by as soon as they finished following up a lead."

She nodded and rubbed a finger over Pepper's head, just between her eyes. "Thank you, Gia. So much. For everything. I was so scared in the hospital, afraid whoever took me would come back again. I'd never have gotten to close my eyes for an instant if you weren't sitting at my side."

"Ah, Savannah." She gripped her hand and held tight. A stream of tears escaped. Savannah would just have to forgive her this once. "I will never leave your side."

"I know." She lowered her gaze for a minute, then looked back up at Gia and breathed in deeply, and smiled. "Okay. I'm ready to eat."

Gia laughed through her tears. "Yeah, but are you ready for the enthusiastic greeting you're going to get from Thor and Klondike, especially when they see you've brought Pepper to visit."

Savannah opened her mouth to say something, then hesitated.

"What?"

She shook her head.

"Do you think Thor will be too much? I could go in ahead of you and try to keep him calm, maybe put him in the garage for a few minutes and settle you in your bedroom instead of the living room, if you'd prefer before I let him back in?"

"No, no, it's not Thor. I love Thor. And Klondike. It's just…" She sniffed and wiped her nose with a tissue. "Could I stay, Gia? Me and Pepper?"

"What do you mean? Of course, you can stay. For as long as you want."

"That's just it. I want to move in permanently. At least until after Leo and I get married." She sat up straighter. "I'd pay my share, of course, contribute to the bills and everything. We could split everything fifty—"

"Stop." Gia held up a hand to stem the flow of words. "Savannah, you are my sister, in every sense imaginable. I don't know where I'd be right now if not for you always standing at my side. There is nothing on this earth I wouldn't do for you. You are welcome to stay forever—you and Pepper—if that's what you want. And don't worry about contributing. That shouldn't even be a thought in your head. Let me take care of you. At least, for a while. I need that, Savannah. Please."

She grinned, and for the first time, a semblance of her former self shined through. "Thank you."

"What are friends for?" Gia hit the button on the garage remote. "Now, let's go eat something. We'll go into the garage so we can close the door behind us. Then you can put Pepper down and have your hands free to deal with Thor."

"Are you kidding me? I can't wait to get my hands on Thor. I'm hoping he'll take pity on me and snuggle with me on the couch, especially since you know Pepper and Klondike are going to take off running as soon as they see each other. I'll apologize for the curtains ahead of time."

Gia laughed as she collected everything that needed to be taken inside. The last time the two kittens had been together, they'd found them clinging from the top of Gia's living room curtains, where their claws had left run marks all up and down. "You just sit in the car with Pepper for a minute while I put your bags and stuff in the garage."

She grabbed Savannah's oversized purse and the duffel bag she'd packed with Pepper's food and toys and an extra bag of litter and put it right inside the garage door, then returned for her two suitcases from the trunk. When everything was inside, she helped Savannah out of the car, keeping a firm grip on her arm in case she got dizzy again.

She waited until the garage door was closed completely. "Okay, go ahead and put Pepper down, and brace yourself."

Savannah lowered the kitten to the floor and patted her head. "You be good and stay out of trouble, you hear me?"

Pepper purred softly and weaved back and forth between Savannah's feet.

Gia turned to go into the house, but there was a round hole where the doorknob should have been. The doorknob lay on the garage floor beside the step, the door closed over, but the latch was gone. She froze. "What the…?"

"Is something wrong?"

Where was her cell phone? In her bag. Which she'd forgotten in the car when she'd brought Savannah's bags in. "Savannah, listen to me right now, and do exactly what I say."

"What's wrong?"

She held her keys out to Savannah. "Take Pepper and get back in the car. Lock the doors, and call Hunt and tell him to get out here. Now. My cell phone is in my bag on the floor behind the driver's seat."

"Gia, tell me what's going on." She took the keys and scooped up Pepper, who thankfully hadn't strayed far.

"There's no time." Urgency beat at her. Where were Thor and Klondike? Klondike tended to be a bit aloof when she came in, at least for a few minutes, but Thor always greeted her. She shifted so Savannah could see the hole. "Someone broke in."

Savannah gasped and lurched back. She hugged Pepper close as she backed away. "Don't go in, Gia."

A quick scan of the garage found the side window broken and shattered glass on the floor. "I have to. I have to get Thor and Klondike, and I'll meet you in the car."

Thankfully, Savannah gave up arguing, hit the button to open the garage, and ran out, leaving the door open.

Careful not to open the door far enough to let Klondike escape, Gia squeezed through into the kitchen and shut the door behind her.

Cabinets stood open, their contents strewn across the counters and floor. The refrigerator and freezer had both been left open, and a puddle spread from beneath the fridge. One chair lay on its side, while the others still stood in place at the table.

She grabbed a knife from the block on the counter and clutched it close. She didn't dare call out, just in case someone was still in the house.

She tiptoed through the mess and peeked into the living room. Furniture had been overturned. Cushions lay torn apart amid the debris; their foam spilled out onto the floor. With a quick glance down the hallway toward the bedrooms, Gia crept across the room to the foyer.

Silence tormented her.

In the foyer, the side table stood empty, the drawers and their contents scattered across the floor. Maybe whoever had broken in had locked Thor in the bedroom. Though he was the friendliest dog she'd ever met, she doubted he'd have let a stranger come into the house without putting up a fuss. She held onto that hope with all of her might as she made her way down the hallway, peeking into Savannah's room and the spare room she'd made into an office, only to find the same state of disarray as in the rest of the house. But no Thor and no Klondike.

She listened intently for any sound: nothing but the hum of the air conditioning unit.

A quick peek in the bathroom yielded no better results.

When she reached her closed bedroom door at the end of the hallway, she opened it carefully, hoping it wouldn't squeak and alert anyone to her presence.

A big black ball of fur lay on the dog bed at the foot of Gia's bed.

"Thor!" She ran to him, quickly feeling to make sure he was breathing.

"Is he okay?"

Gia squealed and whirled toward the voice.

Savannah stood in the doorway, a baseball bat clutched in both hands. "Sorry, I didn't mean to startle you, but I didn't want to make any noise in case anyone was still in here."

"It's okay. He's breathing. I'm guessing he was drugged just like you were." She stroked his long fur. "The only place I didn't check was the bathroom in here."

Savannah crossed the room and disappeared inside the master bath, then emerged a moment later. "Empty."

"Klondike," Gia called quietly. "Psst, psst, psst."

"Shh…" Savannah held a finger to her lips and frowned, deep lines furrowing her brow. "Do you hear that?"

"What?"

"Purring." Savannah knelt and peered under the bed. "It's okay, girl, you can come out now."

"She's there?" Keeping one hand on Thor's side, Gia leaned over to look under the bed.

"She seems fine, just frightened. She probably hid when whoever it was broke in." Savannah reached under and pulled the kitten out, then petted her and kissed her head before handing her to Gia. She sat down next to them with her back against the footboard, her bat held at the ready, and her stare riveted on the doorway. "Thor would have put up a fight, even if they'd managed to get in and get him sedated pretty quickly. Klondike probably got scared and hid before they could get ahold of her."

"They?"

"It would have taken more than one stranger to subdue a dog this size without, well, you know…."

"You're okay, baby, Mama's here now." Gia nuzzled Klondike close for another moment, kissed her head, and then handed her back to Savannah. She ran her hands along Thor's sides and legs, reaching underneath him to do a thorough search for any bumps and breaks. "You don't think they hurt him, do you?"

"I hope not." Finally releasing her death grip on the bat and laying it across her legs, Savannah weaved her fingers into Thor's thick fur.

As Gia slid her hand out from under Thor, it brushed something that felt like paper. She pulled it out. "A note. He must have rolled over on it."

"Don't touch it any more than you have. What does it say?"

Gia pointed to the pink paper with the All-Day Breakfast Café logo emblazoned across the top. "It says, 'don't call the police.'"

Savannah went white. "Too late."

"You already called?" Great. Now what? What if whoever did this was watching when they pulled up?

"I called Hunt." She chewed on her bottom lip. "He and Leo are on their way."

"What did he say?"

"What do you think he said?" She rolled her eyes. "He said, 'wait out in the car until we get there.'"

"Of course, he did." She figured it was okay, though, because he'd never in a million years expect her to sit in the car if she had reason to believe Thor and Klondike might be in danger.

Savannah lifted a brow. "Did you expect anything less?"

"Yeah, well, I hate to tell you this, but right now we have a bigger problem than Hunt."

"Of course, we do." She lifted her hands to the sides, then let them drop into her lap. "What is it now?"

Something creaked in the hallway.

Gia turned, throwing herself in front of Savannah, Thor, and Klondike.

"What are you doing in here? I thought I told you to wa—" Hunt glanced around the room before turning his attention to her and catching sight of Thor. He ran to him and laid a hand on his side. "You found him like this?"

"Yes. Do you think he'll be okay?"

"I think he was probably sedated, but we'll take him to the vet and have him checked out anyway." He examined the big dog quickly, running his hands over him with care. "Do you know if anything's missing?"

"I have no idea." Nor did she care at the moment. "But I did find this."

He held up a finger when she held the note out to him. "Where'd you find it?"

"Kind of next to but partly under Thor. I think whoever broke in left it next to him, and he must have rolled onto it."

Hunt took a plastic evidence bag from his pocket and held it open for Gia to slip the note inside. He read it through the plastic.

"I was just telling Savannah, before you came in, we have another problem." She pointed to the logo on the top of the page. "I don't have this paper in the house. It came from a pad I keep beside the register at the café. Which means someone took it from there and left it here."

Hunt ran a hand over his face as he studied the note. His dark, shaggy hair was disheveled, as if he'd run his hand through it a million times. Frown lines bracketed his mouth, and he was developing a permanent scowl. "Could you take a quick look around for me? It would help us figure out if someone was looking for you or Savannah or if they took anything."

"Yeah, sure." She didn't bother questioning him; it would only waste time. If it wasn't important, he wouldn't ask her to search right now.

"I'll call Cole and ask him to put a glove on and put the pad in a plastic bag, and I'll pick it up as soon as I can."

"You don't want to have an officer pick it up?"

He stayed quiet for a moment, brows drawn together, then shook his head. "No, I'd rather pick it up myself or have Leo do it."

She wasn't sure what was going on with Hunt. Maybe he was afraid of getting removed from the investigation now that Savannah had been found and wanted to keep a hand in everything. Whatever his reasons, she trusted him and figured he knew what he was doing, so she dropped it and turned her attention to the task at hand.

She kept what little jewelry she had in a case in her nightstand drawer. She didn't do an inventory, but a quick glance showed most of what she did own scattered across the floor and under the bed.

But the manila envelope full of cash she kept in the same case, the money she'd been saving for Savannah's wedding, was nowhere to be found. "I had an envelope with cash in it, a few thousand dollars I'd been saving. It's gone."

Hunt nodded. "All right."

Leo returned from searching the house and helped Savannah to her feet. "Can you put a bag together for Gia?"

"A bag? For what?" Gia had a pretty good idea of what was coming, and she wasn't opposed. Not when everyone's lives could be at risk.

"There's no way the two of you are staying out here until we catch whoever did this and figure out if it's the same person who kidnapped Savannah." Hunt squatted beside Thor and scooped him into his arms, then hoisted him up.

"Go. Get in my car, and we'll take him to the vet. Leo can follow with Savannah in your car." Hunt waited for Gia to go ahead of him down the hallway, then hefted Thor higher and followed.

Savannah and Leo came behind them.

"You'll get Thor's things and bring Klondike?" Gia called over her shoulder. "Her carrier's in the garage."

"Of course." Savannah still held Klondike close.

"Where's Pepper?"

Savannah hurried after her with Leo glued to her side. "I put her in the carrier in the car when I got your phone and called Hunt. Where do you want to stay, though?"

"We'll go to the apartment over the café if you want. There's only one entrance, and Hunt can post guards out front if it makes him feel better. Unless you want to go to your dad's?"

"I'd rather stay with you. My family tends to hover, in case you hadn't noticed." She shot Hunt a dirty look filled with affection. "I'll take care of everything and then meet you at the vet with your phone and purse."

Leaving Savannah to deal with everything else, Gia ran across the lawn to Hunt's Jeep.

Hunt placed Thor on the back seat, and Gia jumped in beside him and cradled his head in her lap. "You'll be okay, baby. I'm sorry someone hurt you."

The wail of sirens once again shattered the silence as several police cars barreled down the road toward her house. Hopefully, whoever wrote the note was long gone and not watching the house.

Chapter Eleven

The next morning, Gia sat at the café counter, sipping her second cup of coffee, her eyes burning with exhaustion.

"Hey, there." Cole flicked a towel at her. "Why don't you go upstairs to the apartment and take a nap?"

"I'm fine." She sat up straighter. "Between keeping watch over Savannah and checking on Thor all night, I didn't get much sleep. And the busier than normal breakfast shift, thanks to all the new gossip, has only tired me out more."

"He's doing okay, though? Thor?" Earl broke a biscuit in half and soaked it in gravy.

"The vet said he'll be fine. Someone injected him with a sedative." He woke up about an hour after they got to the vet, and the vet had estimated the sedative would have lasted somewhere between six and eight hours. That meant whoever broke into the house did so after Savannah was found and taken to the hospital...sometime during the night before she was released.

So, what had they been searching for? Cash? Since that's all that had been taken, maybe. Gia didn't have anything else in the house worth stealing. Maybe kids broke in looking for a place to hang out? While she'd like to believe that, the chances were probably less than zero, considering the note was left by someone who'd most likely anticipated breaking into the house while they'd been in the café. Otherwise, why take the paper for the note? Unless...unless someone used the pad to write on and had taken more than the first sheet off the top.

Savannah sat on a stool next to her, chin resting on her hand, eyes drifting closed. "The kittens chasing each other around their new environment all night didn't help either. That apartment is not big enough for that."

"Hey." Trevor lowered his fork onto his plate. "I have an idea. Why don't you guys stay with me? Just think how much easier it'll be to prepare for the wedding if you're living in the venue."

Savannah's eyes shot open, and she jerked upright in her seat. "Wait. What?"

"Oops." A blush crept up from Trevor's cheeks all the way to his hairline. "Sorry, Gia, I didn't mean to spoil the surprise."

"No, don't worry about it. With everything going on the past two days, I forgot all about it." Gia swiveled her stool to face Savannah. "Remember the other day, before we were supposed to go shopping, when I said I had an idea for your wedding venue?"

"Uh huh." For the first time since she'd been found, Savannah's eyes shone with delight.

"Well, I was telling Trevor about the park idea, and he offered to have the wedding at his house. Said the bridal party could even stay over for a couple of nights."

Savannah clapped her hands together and squealed. "That would be perfect. Oh, Trevor, thank you."

His blush deepened until it was almost purple. "No problem. I'm happy to have you. And you and Gia are welcome to stay out there now too. For as long as you need to."

Savannah jumped off the stool and threw her arms around Trevor's neck, then gave him a big kiss on his cheek.

"Hey, hey." Leo walked in with Hunt. "Don't make me go shootin' anyone now."

Savannah kept her arm slung around Trevor's neck. "You can't shoot the man who's hosting our wedding reception. At least, not until after the wedding."

She shot Trevor a wink.

He kissed her cheek, then wagged a finger at Leo. "Uh. Remember, no shooting until after the wedding."

Leo shook Trevor's hand. "Thank you, man, I don't know what to say."

"No problem. You guys are friends, and I'm happy to have you." He returned to his breakfast as Leo and Hunt took seats with him at the counter. "And I was also thinking, the one-bedroom apartment upstairs is kind of tight for Gia, Savannah, a hundred-pound dog, and two rambunctious kittens. So, if you want, they are welcome stay out at my house."

Hunt took a blueberry muffin from the cake dish on the counter. "I appreciate the offer, Trevor, but—"

"Think about it. I have Zeus and Ares, my two trained guard dogs, out there, even during the day, plus you can post as many guards as you'd like. I'll even hire security if you want." He looked around the café, which was mostly empty but for one couple at a table in the far corner of the room. They seemed completely captivated by one another, but he lowered his voice anyway. In Boggy Creek, two people were enough to have the rumor mill up and running in a matter of minutes. "And as long as we keep it quiet, for the time being, that Savannah and Leo are having their wedding there, who would ever think to look for them at my house?"

He had a point. While they were good friends and often went kayaking and hung out together, Gia had only been to Trevor's house once, and she hadn't been invited.

Cole placed coffee cups in front of Hunt and Leo, then topped off everyone else's.

Hunt chewed slowly, then swallowed, shrugged, and looked at Leo. "It's not really a bad idea."

Leo lifted a brow. "You're only saying that because you didn't walk in and find him hugging your girlfriend."

Hunt grinned. "He knows better."

Trevor hooked a thumb toward Hunt. "Hunt's actually right about that, Leo."

"Um, excuse me, boys." Savannah held up a hand. "But don't Gia and I get a say in where we stay?"

"No," Leo said.

"Not really," Trevor agreed.

"Hush now," Hunt added. "The men are talking."

Savannah slapped him in the back of the head.

"What?" He winked at Gia. "Too much?"

Savannah held up her thumb and forefinger, the tips of her nails a fraction of an inch apart. "Maybe just a little."

Hunt's expression sobered too soon.

It hurt Gia to see the moment of normalcy pass so quickly.

"If everyone's okay with it, I'll go along." Hunt clapped Trevor on the back. "Thanks, man. I'll have a car sit out front. Between the guards and your two Akitas, then Brandy and Thor being there at night, I think it should be all right. Do you get good cell service out there?"

Trevor nodded. "I've never had a problem. And I do have a landline as well, just in case."

Savannah and Gia stood on either side of Trevor and each kissed one of his cheeks. Savannah used her cell phone to snap a selfie. "My very first picture of our wedding preparations."

"You'd better watch out, Trevor." Cole laughed. "If this keeps up too much longer, your face might just stay purple."

Trevor laughed but then changed the subject. He was not one to enjoy being the center of attention. "Do you have any clue who broke into Gia's house?"

Not wanting to embarrass him further, Gia let it drop.

"No, nothing." Hunt tossed his piece of muffin back onto the plate and brushed the crumbs off his hands. "Whoever it was broke the garage window and climbed in, then used a screwdriver to take the door knob off the door between the garage and the house. We boarded up the window and replaced the knob, but we found nothing. Not even one print."

"What about on the note?" Gia had hoped they'd get at least something off the note since whoever took the paper had carried it around with them for a while. "When I pulled it out from under Thor, I thought it was wrinkled because he'd rolled over on it, but what if it wasn't? What if whoever wrote it crumpled it up and stuffed it into their pocket or purse, then took it out and smoothed it to write the note?"

Hunt tapped a finger against his lips. "Do you have the pad it was taken from?"

Gia jumped up, pulled on a glove from the back counter, and handed Hunt a glove and the bag Cole had put the note in.

He lifted the pad out of the bag, tilted it back and forth, studying the top page intently. Then he laid the pad on the counter. "Do you have a pencil?"

"Aren't you going to take the pad as evidence?"

Hunt shot a quick glance at Leo. "Yeah, right after I see what was written on it."

Gia dug a pencil out of the drawer beneath the register and handed it to him.

With a very light touch, Hunt scribbled back and forth on the page. As he did, a number emerged. "It's a phone number."

Gia's breath caught. "I know that number."

Hunt frowned. "How?"

She ran into her office and took Paige's card off the desk where she'd left it, then returned and handed it to Hunt. "It belongs to Paige Clarke."

"So, someone wrote down Paige's number, then ripped off the top page and at least one other page with it, and then it somehow ended up in your house." He swiped a hand over his mouth, then rested his elbow on the counter and leaned his face against his hand.

"Was anything stolen from the house, or did they just break in and sedate Thor to leave the note?" Trevor asked.

She'd gone back home with Hunt after they'd finished at the vet's office and searched the house more carefully. She didn't find anything missing, other than the money she'd noticed in the first place. "Just some cash I'd been saving."

"I'm sorry to hear it, but I guess it could have been worse," Trevor said, and he wasn't wrong.

Gia nodded, but something niggled at the back of her mind. The cash that was missing. She frowned. "You know what's weird?"

"What?" Hunt asked absently, still frowning down at the note.

"Cash went missing from the register the other day too."

Hunt's gaze shot to her, and he sat up straighter. "When? Why didn't you say anything?"

"It was the day Savannah was missing. I went to close up and the drawer was empty. I checked the safe, and it wasn't there. I called Cole and Willow to see if either of them had put it somewhere, but they hadn't." She shrugged it off, uncomfortable with everyone staring at her. "What? There were a million people in and out of here that day. Anyone could have taken it. Besides, Savannah was missing, and then I found her out back, and she was all that mattered."

"It's all right, Gia." Hunt ran a hand up and down her arm. "Don't worry about it. I'll take a look at the register and dust for prints, but chances are we're not going to find anything at this point."

"Do you think it had anything to do with what happened to Savannah?" Guilt crept in. If saying something sooner might have helped them find who'd hurt Savannah, she'd never forgive herself.

"Probably not. Like you said, there were a lot of people in and out of here that day. Someone probably just saw the opportunity and grabbed the cash."

She had a feeling he wasn't being completely honest, but she didn't push it. While Hunt would often discuss cases with her, there were always some things he kept to himself. Especially when they weren't alone and were sitting in a public place. She'd ask him more about it later.

Gia's brother Michael and his girlfriend, Tempest, entered and headed straight for Savannah.

Michael hugged her tightly, then set her back, still holding onto her arms. "How are you feeling, sis?"

"I'm doing okay. Just a little tired."

Gia stretched her back, then rounded the counter. "Would you guys like something to eat?"

"Sure, thanks." Michael took a seat at the counter with the others.

Tempest sat beside him, her eyes bloodshot and swollen almost shut. She was either having a terrible time with allergies, had a wicked cold, or there was trouble in paradise, and she spent most of her time crying.

Gia handed each of them a menu.

Cole refilled the coffee pots and readied them for the lunch crowd. "Do you want me to fill this order before I leave?"

"Nah, I've got it, thanks, though, Cole." Maybe once she got back in front of the grill, she'd wake up a little.

"You bet." He pulled off his apron and tossed it in the hamper in the back. "I'll be here to open in the morning if you're tired and want to come in a little late."

"Thanks, Cole, I appreciate it."

"No problem." He squeezed her arm and said his good-byes.

Gia grabbed an order pad. "What can I get you guys?"

Michael browsed the menu, rubbing circles on Savannah's back as she stood next to him.

Tempest left her menu closed on the counter in front of her. "Do you have something light? Maybe toast and fruit?"

"Sure thing. I could do oatmeal with fruit if you want."

She nodded. "That sounds even better, thank you."

Michael pointed to the vegetable omelet with salsa. "Could I get this with home fries, please?"

"Sure thing. Do you want anything, Hunt? Leo? Savannah?"

Savannah wanted oatmeal and fruit, and Hunt and Leo both asked for vegetable omelets with salsa. Easy enough. She didn't bother writing it down. Even with no sleep, she could remember that much. Leaving the order pad beside the register and Savannah with her family, Gia went to the kitchen to start cooking.

She dripped a bit of oil onto the grill, let it warm for a moment, then added pre-cut onions, bell peppers, mushrooms, zucchini, squash, tomatoes, and spinach. While that cooked, she scrambled the eggs with salt and pepper and set them aside. After stirring the vegetables, she added oats and water to a small pan and put it on the stove.

With everything set up and cooking, she peeked through the cut-out at Savannah. Though Gia was fully confident she'd be fine with Hunt and Leo and even Michael, the need to keep checking on her wouldn't let up.

"Gia?"

She whirled toward the woman's voice.

Tempest stood in the doorway. "I'm sorry. I didn't mean to startle you."

"No, no, that's fine. I guess I'm just a little on edge."

"I don't blame you." Tears shimmered in her bloodshot eyes, then tipped over her bottom lashes.

"Come in and sit." She gestured toward a stool beside the center island. "Are you okay, Tempest?"

Refocusing her attention on the grill, she waited for Tempest to sit. She obviously wanted something, so Gia would give her the time she needed to get around to it. Though she'd met the woman several times, they'd only hung out in groups. They weren't close, and their brief conversation in the real estate office was the most individual interaction Gia had ever had with her.

Gia poured the eggs over the vegetables, stirred the oats, spooned home fries onto three plates, and then set them on the counter.

"I don't know who to talk to." Tempest rested her elbows on the butcher block countertop and cradled her head in her hands. "Michael will be so upset with me if I say anything, but I need help. And…well…"

As difficult as it was not to grill Tempest, Gia waited her out. She sprinkled cheddar cheese over the eggs, poured the oatmeal into bowls and added sliced bananas, strawberries, and blueberries over the top, then sprinkled it with shredded coconut and drizzled honey over the coconut.

After setting the two bowls of oatmeal aside, she dropped bread into three of the toasters, plated the omelets, and grabbed a bowl of homemade salsa to pour over the top.

"I can't go to the police," Tempest said.

Gia froze halfway to the counter, fumbling the bowl of salsa but catching it at the last minute. "The police?"

She'd figured Tempest was having some kind of relationship issues with Michael, and she'd been willing to lend an ear or even a shoulder to cry on. But if Tempest was hiding something from the police that involved Savannah's disappearance, that was a different story.

"Michael said he'd take care of everything, but I'm afraid. He's already in over his head, and I don't want him to end up getting hurt…" She paused and stared into Gia's eyes. "Or worse."

She set the salsa aside and went to Tempest, giving her full attention to the distraught woman. "What's going on, Tempest?"

She took a deep, shuddering breath, then nodded, as if convincing herself to go ahead. She pulled a folded piece of paper out of her pocket and held it out to Gia, her hand shaking wildly. "I found this."

"What is it?" Gia pulled off one glove, took the Post-it note from her, and opened it. Scribbled in black ink were the letters OMH followed by a space, the letter M and the number 1. She turned the note over, but the back was blank. "I don't understand…"

Tempest pointed out the letters one at a time. "Oakley. Manor. House. Monday at one."

While it was definitely possible that the note contained an abbreviation of that message, it could also mean a million other things. "Where did you get this?"

She chewed on her thumbnail for a moment, and Gia was afraid she might not answer. "You have to promise you won't say anything. Michael doesn't want me getting involved, but I can't just let it go either. If I go to Hunt and Leo, they're going to have to ask questions, and the person involved will know it came from me. Besides, it's not like there's any proof that's what it means, and it couldn't be used as evidence, anyway, because I removed it…well, stole it, really, if the person wanted to push the issue, so—"

"Hold on, Tempest." Gia laid the paper on the counter and held up a hand to stop her. "Why are you coming to me with this?"

"Because I don't know who else to go to. Savannah is still not feeling her best, Michael has forbidden me to get involved. As it is, he thinks I threw the note out. And Hunt and Leo will spook the person involved if they talk to hi…" She winced, realizing she'd inadvertently given something away. "I don't know you well, but I do know Savannah and Hunt and even Leo a little, and they all trust you, so I'm figuring I can too. And I need someone to talk to, someone who loves Savannah enough to help me get to the truth of what happened to her. No matter what it takes."

The smell of something burning intruded on Gia's thoughts. "Oh, no."

"What?"

She ran to the toasters, popped the toast, and dropped it all into the garbage. After she washed her hands and put new gloves on, she started over. What was she supposed to do? Tempest was clearly upset, but if she had information that would help apprehend Savannah's kidnapper, Hunt and Leo needed to know about it. At the same time, Michael wasn't saying anything, and he'd obviously seen the note and knew Hunt and Leo as well as anyone.

"I'm sorry, Gia." Tempest stood from the counter and pushed the stool back underneath. "It was a mistake for me to say anything. I shouldn't have involved you."

"No, it's okay." If she let Tempest leave without finishing what she was saying, she might never find out the truth. If she pushed the issue with Hunt or Leo, Tempest would certainly never trust her again, even if she learned something else. Plus, she'd be causing a problem between Michael and Tempest. "Tell me where you found the note."

"You won't say anything?"

"No, I won't tell anyone." At least, not yet. If they found something that could lead to Savannah's attacker and Buster's killer, then she'd... Well, she had no idea what she'd do, but she could cross that bridge when she came to it.

She popped the toast, buttered it, and set it on plates.

"Ward got a phone call just after lunch the other day, and he was out of the office, so I took a message. When I went to put it on his desk, I saw this note stuck to his calendar. I thought it odd, since Ward usually writes everything out, but other than a passing 'hmm…that's weird' I didn't give it any thought. Then, later, after you came in and Michael called and told me Savannah was missing, I started thinking about the note, so I swiped it off his desk."

Gia loaded everything onto a tray.

Tempest kept her gaze fixed on her hands. "And if that is what it means, and Ward had an appointment at the Oakley Manor House at one, he could easily have run into Savannah and Buster out there."

Gia had to admit, the idea had merit. And the timing did work. "I don't remember exactly what time I came into the office, but I remember thinking you'd be closing soon."

Tempest was already nodding. "And Ward had only just returned not long before you showed up."

"So, what? You think he could have gone out there with a client, or to meet someone, and killed Buster and the woman who was found in the lake, then kidnapped Savannah?" Far-fetched? Maybe, but she didn't have any other explanation, and Hunt and Leo seemed fairly confident they were looking for more than one person of interest. Savannah had said as much when they'd interviewed her. Who knew, maybe the woman they'd found in the lake was the person he was supposed to meet out there?

Tempest sighed. "When you say it like that, it doesn't sound likely, right?"

Buster had been killed with something that had most likely been lying around the construction site, so it wouldn't have involved any premeditation.

He could have found out Savannah was showing the house, been irate over it, gone out there to confront her, and had it out with Buster. But could Ward have killed him and a woman, sedated and moved Savannah, then returned to the office before Gia showed up?

Possibly, but why? And what of the sedative? The two by four might not require any premeditation, but the medication certainly would. Unless he just happened to carry around enough sedatives with him to render a full-grown woman and a hundred-pound dog both unconscious.

Tempest still avoided looking directly at Gia, keeping her gaze focused downward. "Maybe he knew Savannah was showing the house to Buster Clarke and went out there purposely to kill him."

"But why would he do that?"

"Jealousy. Greed. Who knows?" Tempest shrugged and glanced through the cut-out into the dining room. "But he and Angelina have been acting weird about the Oakley Manor House ever since the listing came in. We've gotten a few calls on it, but as far as I know, they haven't shown it once."

Gia stuck the Post-it note in the pocket of her jeans and hefted the tray. That didn't seem all that unusual to Gia. While people might be interested in the beautiful old home, not too many could afford the better than a million-dollar price tag.

Tempest finally met her gaze. "The house belongs to one of the Esposito cousins, and they wouldn't sell to one of the Clarkes if their lives depended on it. Buster should never have been in there, and that's a fact."

"What would that have to do with Ward?" Gia balanced the tray on her shoulder. If she didn't get this food out there, it was going to get ice cold.

"Nothing. Maybe." Tempest held the door open for Gia. "I don't know about Ward, but Angelina would certainly have had a vested interest in knowing Savannah was showing the house to Buster Clarke."

"Oh, why's that?" She started through the doorway, careful not to hit the tray into anything.

"Because her maiden name is Esposito."

Gia stopped and faced Tempest.

"And because not long after Ward left the office that day, Angelina disappeared too. She showed up about a half-hour before him, and from what Michael said about Savannah's attack, it seems likely it would have taken two people, one to hold her and one to administer the sedative."

Chapter Twelve

Gia served everyone breakfast, then stood behind the counter to think for a minute while Willow took orders from the customers that had begun to trickle into the dining room. It wouldn't be long before she had to return to the grill as the lunch rush picked up. She wanted to talk to Hunt and Leo, and even Savannah, but how could she bring up Ward Bennett or Angelina Lombardo without pinging Michael's radar when she'd just spent the better part of fifteen minutes alone in the kitchen with Tempest?

She couldn't. Unless she could think of a roundabout way to do it.

Learning Angelina was part of the Esposito crime family, so technically the sworn enemy of Buster, Robert, and Paige Clarke, had come as a shock, but did it matter? Did it mean anything as far as Buster's death or Savannah's kidnapping were concerned? Probably not. It wasn't likely Angelina had killed him or kidnapped her. Plus, she said she didn't even know Savannah was showing Buster the house, and she had seemed surprised when Gia had slipped and told her. Still… Tempest said Angelina had disappeared during that time frame, so it wasn't impossible either.

Tempest fidgeted with her spoon, glancing back and forth between Gia and Michael.

Savannah swirled her spoon through her oatmeal, scooped out a thin slice of banana, and then dropped the spoon back into the bowl without taking a bite.

"Do you want something else, instead? Toast, maybe? Or—" Gia asked.

"No, thanks. I'm okay. I'll eat it in a minute." She turned to Hunt. "Have you found out anything more about the woman who was found in the lake?"

While Savannah drifted in and out of consciousness in the emergency room, the only two questions Hunt and Leo asked were who attacked her and if there'd been a woman present at the house. The answer to both had been no.

"No, why?" Hunt narrowed his eyes and set his fork aside. "Do you remember anything?"

She shook her head. "I just...she's been on my mind a lot. Did you find out who she is?"

Hunt put an arm around her shoulders. "Not yet, but we will."

Tempest's statement about there being more than one attacker played through Gia's mind. Hunt had said the same thing at the hospital when he questioned Savannah, and Savannah thought there might have been a second person in the room. "Do you think the woman you found dead in the lake could be the second attacker?"

Hunt cut a piece of his omelet without even pausing, not at all surprised at the question. Clearly, they'd already considered the possibility. "It's possible. We have to get a positive ID before we can even start to figure it out."

"You're sure you didn't see anyone else out there, though, right?" Leo asked Savannah.

She thought about if for a minute, but her response was still the same. "No. I don't remember seeing or hearing anyone...else...but..."

"What?" Leo put his fork down, wiped his mouth, and turned to face her.

Savannah stared into her bowl and frowned. Keeping her head down, she closed her eyes. "I remember...something...a smell. Not bad. But cloying, like when you walk into a funeral parlor and the scent of flowers, which would normally smell good, overwhelms you.'"

"Do you think it could have been—" Tempest started.

Hunt held up a hand to cut her off. "Just wait. Let her think about it on her own without leading her at all. Savannah, take as long as you need. If you remember anything, anything at all, just call one of us."

The group continued to eat their breakfast in silence, Savannah picking at her food rather than eating.

Willow had already tacked three tickets above the grill.

Gia wasn't going to be able to wait. "I have to get back to the kitchen. We're starting to get busy."

Savannah stood. "I'll help you in back for a bit. I need something to do, or I'm going to be sleeping on your counter soon."

Gia pulled an apron over her head. "Enjoy your breakfast, guys."

Savannah took her bowl and stood, then turned back to Hunt and Leo and lowered her voice. "I'm not a hundred percent sure, but I think it could have been perfume or lotion or something. But a floral scent, one that reminded me of real flowers."

"There are a lot of flowers around the house. Is it possible someone came in and left the front door open, and the scent of flowers drifted up to you?"

She considered Hunt's question before answering. "Yeah. It could be possible. I'm sorry, I can't tell you more."

"Don't worry about it. You never know what might come to you as time goes on and your head clears more." Hunt patted her arm and returned to eating.

Gia left them to finish their breakfast. She'd already kept her customers waiting too long. "Is there anything special you feel like doing?"

Savannah set her oatmeal on the center island and pulled out a stool. She sat and took a bite. "First, I'm going to eat my breakfast. I'm hungry, but I'm tired, and I don't feel like sitting with everyone right now."

To make up for the time she'd waited out front, Gia started all three tickets at once. Thankfully, one was just breakfast pies and home fries, two things she had already prepared. She'd just heat them quickly and get one order out of the way.

"If you want to be alone, you're welcome to sit in my office and eat."

She quickly shook her head and jammed the spoon into her oatmeal. "Thank you, but I don't want to be alone. I just…I feel like I'm letting everyone down because I can't remember anything."

Gia abandoned the orders and went to her. "Oh, Savannah, you're not letting anyone down."

"No?" She shoved her bowl aside. "What about the two people who were murdered, most likely by whoever attacked me? I know it's too late to save them, but they might at least get some justice, their families get some peace, if I could just remember what happened."

"It's not your fault you can't remember. That blame lies with whoever drugged you. You're doing the best you can, and if you remember anything more, which you might once you get some sleep and are able to relax a little, you will let Hunt or Leo know right away." Gia pushed the bowl back in front of her. "Now, eat something. Who knows? Maybe getting some food in your stomach will help clear your head a little."

"Thanks, Gia." She smiled, a shaky smile, but still a smile. "You're right."

She studied Savannah for another moment, but she seemed okay, so Gia started ladling pancake batter onto the grill. "Maybe you're trying too hard. Sometimes, when I'm trying to remember something and I can't, it comes to me when I finally let it go."

"That's true." Thankfully, she started eating again.

"Can I ask you something?" Somehow, Gia needed to find a way to look into Tempest's information without alerting anyone to a problem.

"Sure, what?"

Gia added bacon to a couple of plates and sausage to another, doled out home fries and grits, and finally started shoving orders onto the cut-out for Willow. "When you were waiting for Buster the other day, you said you didn't want to lose the sale to that weasel Ward Bennett. Is there a problem between you and him, or you just didn't want to lose the sale?"

Her eyes widened. "Are you thinking Ward had something to do with this?"

She should have known better than to try to question Savannah, even discreetly. Her thoughts ran so similar to Gia's own it was sometimes scary. "Not necessarily, but, as much as I hate to admit it, everyone seems suspicious to me right now."

When Savannah didn't say anything, Gia let the matter drop. No way did she want to upset her. Allowing Savannah whatever space she needed, Gia continued cooking, filling order after order. If the growing line of tickets was any indication, they were quite crowded for a weekday, even during the lunch rush. A quick peek into the dining room confirmed her suspicions.

Savannah ate most of her fruit and some oatmeal, then scraped the rest into the garbage and loaded the bowl into the dishwasher. When she finished, she slid into pace with Gia, adding whatever was needed to plates, making and buttering toast, filling any orders that didn't require cooking on the grill and setting them up for Willow.

When the bulk of the orders were served, Savannah stepped aside, leaned against the counter, and wrapped her arms around herself. "I've been thinking about what you said about being suspicious of everyone, and I could see that happening, even in myself. But I don't want to be that way. One person did this to me. Well…possibly two. I refuse to live my life in fear of every person I come across, constantly looking over my shoulder, jumping at every little sound."

Gia stopped and turned at the conviction in her voice.

"And I don't want you letting that happen to you because of me. When everything first went on with he-who-shall-not-be-named…" She rolled her eyes to accentuate her point about Gia's ex-husband, who Savannah had never liked. He'd swindled so many people out of their fortunes that Gia'd had to deal with a steady stream of stalkers throughout his entire trial and her divorce. "You were a mess, jumping at everything, spooked by your own shadow, withdrawn. I don't want to see that happen to you again, Gia. And I will not allow anyone to do that to me. Ever."

Gia threw her arms around Savannah and hugged her tight. Compared to Gia's five foot seven, Savannah was petite. Her slim build made her seem even more so, but the woman was a force to be reckoned with. While events from her past—including her mother's murder and growing up in a houseful of overprotective men, had shaped her, they had also given her an inner strength Gia admired. And yet, she was the most forgiving person Gia had ever met. "You're amazing, you know that, Savannah?"

She laughed and stepped back. "And you're just saying that because you think I'm vulnerable right now."

"No, you're wrong. Actually, I was just admiring your strength."

"Well, thank you. And you're right; I am strong. And do you know what strong people do when someone has done something wrong to them?"

Uh oh. The sneaking suspicion that she was about to be played crept in. She narrowed her eyes at Savannah and waited.

"They find whoever wronged them and make sure they go to jail." She plopped onto the stool, crossed one leg over the other, and grinned. "Now. We can start with why you're asking about Ward."

"Ugh… What am I going to do with you?"

Savannah shrugged. "Well, right now, I'm assuming you're going to help me figure out who kidnapped me and why."

She shouldn't. Her mind screamed at her to take Savannah out to Trevor's house and hide her away. She could call Cole and ask him to man the grill for a few days while she took some time off and helped Savannah plan her wedding. They could try on gowns, pick out flowers, and find the perfect music. Surely, Trevor had a pool at that mansion. The urge to stretch out on a lounge chair with a cold drink and soak up some sun battered her. But, was she going to do that? Of course not. Because she was going to be too busy finding out who had hurt her best friend and making sure whoever it was could never get near her again.

Chapter Thirteen

"So," Savannah scraped dishes into the garbage pail and loaded the dishwasher. "Spill it. What makes you think Ward might have had anything to do with abducting me?"

As much as Gia wanted to be forthcoming with Savannah, she'd promised Tempest she wouldn't say anything. Torn, she avoided the subject. For now. "I asked you first. What was the deal with you and Ward? Professional jealousy?"

"Oh, please." She rolled her eyes. "You should know me better than that. I sell houses fair and square. If I help another agent out, which I often do, it's still their sale, and I never take a portion of the commission."

Gia did know that. She also knew Savannah was very well-liked among agents, not only in her own office, but others. "I didn't mean on your end, silly. I meant he was jealous of you."

"Oh, right. Umm…" Savannah worried her bottom lip for a minute, her brow furrowed in concentration. She finished loading the dishes, turned on the dishwasher, then washed her hands, and turned to face Gia. "No, I don't think he's jealous of me. He has no reason to be. Angelina favors him, and whenever a big client comes in, Ward always gets the listing. And I've never given him a hard time about it like some of the other agents have. Why bother? It's not going to change anything. Plus, like I said, he's a weasel. He has no problem undercutting people and thinks nothing of outright cheating other agents, seeking out clients they'd spent months working with and convincing them he'd be a better choice."

"So, he's sneaky?" Gia asked.

"Oh, absolutely. And devious. And outright mean. I've seen him bring more than one person to tears over the years. He doesn't have a compassionate bone in his body. But, all that said, while I still think he's a weasel, and I wasn't willing to give up such a big sale to him if I could help it, he and I have never had a disagreement. When we've had to work together in the past, it hasn't been a problem."

That didn't come as a surprise. Savannah was one of those rare people who got along with almost everyone. Even so, the thought of her returning to work with that man didn't sit well. She might just have to go to Hunt and Leo with the information before Savannah returned. Hopefully, she still had some time to decide. "Have you given any thought to when you'll go back to work?"

"I..." She hesitated and lowered her gaze. "I don't want you to say anything to anyone yet, but I'm not sure I'm going back. Not to real estate sales, anyway. I'll have to do something, but...I just don't know."

The surge of relief was short-lived. If Savannah didn't want to go back to her job, it most likely meant she was more traumatized by what happened than she was willing to admit. "I thought you liked your job."

She shrugged. "It serves a purpose; we all have to work. And there are aspects I enjoy. I love working with people, and I do enjoy their excitement when I can help them find just the right home. Especially when it's their first."

"Maybe you should go to a different real estate office." One where Ward Bennett doesn't work. "Or even better, open one of your own."

"It's not the office. I have friends at work, as well as friends among the mortgage brokers and inspectors I work with regularly, but I'm not sure I want to walk into an empty house with a stranger any time soon."

Gia wasn't sure what to say. On the one hand, the thought of Savannah being alone with strangers after what happened gnawed at Gia's gut. On the other hand, Savannah shouldn't have to give up something she enjoyed because of the experience either. "Why don't you just take some time to think about it? It's not like the Oakley Manor House is going anywhere right now, at least not until Hunt and Leo, or whoever ends up in charge of the investigation, releases the crime scene."

"It's funny, but that sale that seemed so important the other day no longer matters to me. All I care about is spending time with family and my pets, and being grateful I survived."

Gia started toward her.

Savannah held up a hand to stop her. She was going to have to stop babying her. "Besides, I'm having my reception at Trevor's house, so it won't cost anywhere near what some of the venues would have charged us."

"That's true." Gia busied herself peeling potatoes for home fries. "Have you given any thought to when you'd like to get married?"

"Nah, not yet. But I don't want to wait too long." Savannah grabbed a peeler, sat across the island from Gia, and dug in. "Do you think I should offer to pay Trevor for the use of the house? I wouldn't feel right not paying him something, but at the same time, I don't want to insult him."

Trevor had been so quick to offer; Gia hadn't thought about it. "I'll talk to him about it and see what he says. If I know Trevor, he won't take any money."

"You're probably right, but still, let me know. Either way, I'm going to do something super special for him." She pointed the peeler at Gia. "And you can help me figure out what."

"Of course." When the potatoes were done, she left Savannah to wash and cut them while she started covering the bins of vegetables she hadn't used with plastic wrap. "Have you given any thought to what kind of job you'd like to do if not real estate?"

"Not really. I know I want to work with people, but beyond that, I'm not sure." She waved off any further discussion. "Now, while that was a valiant effort to change the subject, I've answered all I'm going to until you tell me why you're asking about Ward Bennett."

Gia nodded. Fair enough. "I'm not going to say where I got this just yet, but you can't tell Hunt or Leo about it until I have a chance to look into it."

She shrugged. "Sure thing."

Apparently, Savannah's conscience when it came to keeping a secret from her cousin didn't bristle as much as Gia's did. She pulled the note from her pocket and laid it on the counter. "Do you think it's possible this means Oakley Manor House Monday at one o'clock?"

Savannah flipped the page over and looked at the blank back, then returned it to its original position and studied the markings. "I don't know. It could, I suppose, but it could mean a lot of other things too. It could be a doctor's appointment at Orlando Med Health."

Gia had to concede that point, even if it did belong to Ward, but still… It seemed a little too coincidental that the time on the note would have been exactly when Savannah was at the house with Buster. "Does the fact that it was found on Ward Bennett's desk make it more likely to mean the former?"

Savannah slowly lifted her gaze to meet Gia's. "Is that where this was found?"

Gia nodded, unsure what Savannah's reaction would be. Her expression was too neutral to read. Too neutral in general.

"Tempest brought this to you?"

Gia cringed but nodded.

"And asked you not to say anything?"

"I'm sorry. I wasn't going to keep—"

"Stop, it's okay. If Tempest had come to me with it, I'd have agreed to stay quiet too. I like Tempest, but she and Michael seem to be having some problems lately." She tapped her nail against the page over and over again.

"Do you think they're going to break up?" Gia didn't want to be the cause of that breakup.

"I don't know. Tempest and Michael have been together on-and-off since high school, longer this go around than any other, but the signs of an impending breakup are all there."

"The past couple of times I've seen her, it seemed like she's been crying a lot."

Savannah set the knife aside and washed her hands. "Yeah. I noticed that too. And I overheard an argument between them one night when they were at Pa's for dinner."

"Oh, yeah? About what?" Gia drizzled oil onto the grill and poured the bowl of cut-up potatoes onto it. She added chopped peppers and onions from the fridge, crumbled bacon she kept warming on the grill, salt, and pepper.

Knowing Gia's routine—after she cleaned up, she'd start prepping what they were running low on, and she'd just used the last of the peppers— Savannah grabbed a bag of green peppers from the refrigerator and started washing them. "I don't know exactly what the problem was, but it seemed they were arguing over money. Which I found kind of odd since they don't even live together."

"Hmm…"

"She was giving Michael a hard time about a loan, and he told her to mind her own business." Savannah piled the peppers in a bowl and took them to the counter. "I felt bad for her at the time because he acted like kind of a jerk, but I didn't see what business it was of hers what Michael chose to do with his money either."

"That's true. Unless it had a direct effect on her somehow." Gia washed down the counters and stirred the home fries. The aroma filled the kitchen, and her stomach growled. "Maybe the loan was in her name?"

"Maybe." Savannah started chopping, and the scent of green bell peppers filled the air, mixing with the rest. "I heard her say something about missing a payment, so that would make sense if it was in her name."

"Or if she's hoping to get married and buy a house, and he's wrecking his credit."

"I guess." She scraped the peppers from the cutting board into a stainless-steel bin. "But I think she's way off base. Michal has said numerous times, he's just not marrying material. And he's really not. Not now, anyway. He likes to play the field. She's got about as much chance of Michael marrying her as she does of getting kicked by a snake."

A chill crept up Gia's spine, and she shivered. "Did you have to say snake?"

Savannah grinned, enjoying Gia's fear of creepy crawlies more than she should.

Gia had gotten better since moving to Florida. Just the other day, she scooped up a lizard she found in her living room in the butterfly net Savannah had given her, covered it with a piece of junk mail from the counter, and ushered the poor little thing outside. Something she'd not have been able to do when she first moved there. Though, she still called for back-up when she found spiders.

"Anyway, back to the matter at hand," Savannah said.

After stirring the home fries again, Gia grabbed a bag of onions, washed them, and stood across from Savannah at the center island to chop them. "Ward Bennett."

"Exactly, and I would say yes, the fact that note was found on his desk makes it a little more suspicious than if she'd found it anywhere else, but I don't know..." She shook her head, the only sound in the room the thud, thud, of the knives hitting the wood counter. "I can't see why he would want to hurt me."

"Don't take this the wrong way, because whoever did this is absolutely guilty of hurting you, and I want to see them punished and be sure they never threaten you again, but—"

"But considering that Buster and an unknown woman were murdered, whoever it was really didn't hurt me," Savannah finished, saving Gia from having to utter her thoughts aloud.

Gia nodded, studying Savannah's expression to make sure she understood what she meant.

"And you're right. So, I have to wonder why. Why not just kill me and be done with it? That way, there's no chance I'd be able to give them away." Savannah swiped the peppers that clung to the knife onto the cutting board and transferred them into the bin.

Gia paused with the knife in mid-air. "Don't even say something like that."

"Don't get me wrong, I'm obviously glad they didn't, but it does seem weird, doesn't it?"

Gia refused to contemplate the idea or justify what had been done to Savannah. "Maybe not. If Buster was the intended target, maybe whoever did it just didn't have a reason to kill you."

"You mean a killer with a conscience?"

"Or a killer who was sending a message and wanted to make sure his point was understood." Somehow that felt more right, which led her back to the warring families.

She and Savannah worked in comfortable silence, each of them lost in their own thoughts, weighing what little information they had to make sense of what happened.

Gia wanted to cling to the family feud theory. If Savannah was no more than collateral damage, chances were, she'd be safe. As long as she didn't give anyone reason to believe she remembered anything or posed any kind of threat.

"Would you do something for me?" Savannah asked.

"Sure, what do you need?"

Savannah laid the knife aside and folded her hands on the counter. "Tomorrow, when Cole's here to work the grill, would you take a ride to the office with me at some point?"

"Of course, but why do you want to go into the office? I'm sure everyone will understand if you take a few days off to recover."

"Oh, I don't want to work."

Uh oh. "Then what are you going to the office for?"

Savannah pointed to the note still lying on the counter. She tilted her head and fluttered her lashes; her expression deceptively innocent. "To poke a stick in the bush and see what slithers out."

Chapter Fourteen

Willow stuck another ticket above the grill.

"Are you kidding me? What's going on out there?" Gia slid a finger over the order, quickly running through the ingredients she'd need in her head. While she had whole tomatoes in the fridge, no way could she stop to cut them in the middle of the busiest dinner hour she'd ever had. "I'm not sure I have enough tomatoes left to do the omelet."

Savannah hurried in and waved a ticket back and forth. "This is just for breakfast pies. I'll get it out to the customers at the counter, refill their coffees, then I'll quick chop some tomatoes."

"Thanks." Willow picked up her next order, saving Gia the few seconds it would take to stick it on the cut-out, and rushed back out to the dining room.

Gia scrambled eggs for French toast and added a few teaspoons of vanilla. "You're a lifesaver, Savannah, thank you. I don't know what we'd have done without you tonight."

"No problem, I enjoy doing it."

"Is something going on out there?" She dipped three slices of French bread into the egg mixture and set them on the grill. "My breakfast and lunch business has picked up considerably, but I've honestly thought about discontinuing dinner hours and going home earlier. No matter what I've added to the menu, dinner hours just didn't pick up."

Savannah shrugged. "I haven't heard anything, but I've been running pretty crazy. Willow has too. Pretty much every seat is full."

Cole poked his head through the doorway. "Need a hand?"

"Yes!" Gia and Savannah cried in unison.

He laughed as he headed for the sink. "Just give me a minute to wash my hands."

Savannah took the breakfast pie slices she'd heated and put them on a tray with toast and home fries and ran back out.

"What are you doing back here? You're supposed to be off tonight." Gia tossed bacon slices onto the grill to heat and flipped the French toast slices.

"Ehh. I was bored so I decided to take a walk in the park, but when I drove past and saw all the cars, I thought maybe something had happened. I just stopped in to make sure everything was okay." Though he made the comment in an off-handed manner, the concern beneath the gesture was unmistakable.

"Thank you, Cole. I don't know what I did to deserve you, but I sure am grateful."

"Believe me, hon, I appreciate you just as much." He laughed out loud as he dried his hands. "Turns out retirement doesn't really agree with me."

"Apparently not, since you're always here," she pointed out.

"That's because my friends are here." He waved a hand around the kitchen, gestured toward the dining room, and his expression turned serious. "It's a nice place, Gia. A real family place. That's what everyone's doing here tonight, you know."

She added cinnamon to a second bowl of eggs and scrambled them as she turned to face him. "What do you mean?"

"I stopped to say hello to a few people on my way through the dining room, and it seems word spread that Savannah was found and that she's been here all day." He slid his apron over his head and shrugged. "They wanted to come in and show their support."

A rush of love surged through her. This wasn't the first time her new community had come together in a time of need. And she had no doubt it wouldn't be the last. "The best thing I ever did was move to Boggy Creek. I can't even believe I ever second-guessed that decision."

Savannah had just run back in and started washing tomatoes. "Does that mean you've stopped making your mental list of good and bad points of living in Florida versus living in New York?"

Gia laughed. She'd forgotten all about her mental pros and cons list. She couldn't even pinpoint when she'd stopped adding to the con side of living in Florida. "Seems I have."

Savannah lifted a brow. "Does that mean I get to say I told you so now?"

"Ugh…I suppose." Gia dipped bread into the cinnamon egg mixture and lined them on the grill.

"Good." She smirked. "I told you so."

Gia took the vanilla French toast off the grill and sprinkled them with powdered sugar. She put the dish on a tray, added a couple cups of syrup, finished up the cinnamon French toast and bacon, and then added everything to the tray.

Savannah lifted the tray and hurried out to the dining room.

The three of them worked with incredible efficiency and coordination. It was as if every move had been choreographed. Even in the smallish kitchen, they never got in each other's way. Savannah jumped between the dining room and kitchen with ease. Everyone knew what needed to be done, and both Savannah and Cole were often a step ahead of Gia when she was running low on something.

Finding a new waitress who would fit smoothly into that rhythm wouldn't be easy. Unless...Careful to phrase her question so that she wouldn't alert Cole to their earlier conversation, Gia caught Savannah on her way in. "You know, Savannah, if you ever decide to give up real estate, I'd love to have you work here."

She stopped short and almost dropped the tray she was carrying. "Seriously?"

"Are you kidding me? You move at warp speed, know the job inside and out, and enjoy chatting with the customers, most of whom you know. I'd be a fool not to recruit you."

"In that case," she grinned. "I'd love to."

"Wait. Really?" Not that Savannah didn't hang around the café all the time anyway, always pitching in and picking up slack where needed, but having her there full time would be a dream come true.

"Yup. I was thinking about taking a break from real estate anyway." She winked at Gia. "And this would be perfect. I'd have a job I enjoy, and I'd be busy enough to keep my thoughts from wandering too far."

That was not the first time Savannah had alluded to having lingering effects from her kidnapping.

"And, best of all, I'd be surrounded by friends who love me, which would make me feel safe. It's perfect."

"Yes!" Gia pumped her fist in the air.

"In that case, welcome aboard." Cole saluted her, since he couldn't shake hands while cooking.

Savannah paused. "Are you sure you won't get tired of being around me all the time, Gia? Between me moving in on you and now encroaching on your workspace too..."

"Savannah, I could never get tired of having you around." A point that was driven home way too convincingly when Savannah was missing. "Besides, with everything that's gone on the past few days, I had to cancel all of the interviews I had scheduled for the week. So, you basically have to come to work with me."

"Yay!" She did a little happy dance as she hurried back to the dining room.

Now, Gia just had to remember to call Marie Winston and let her know the position had been filled.

Once Savannah was gone, Cole looked through the cut-out to the dining room. "How's she holding up?"

Gia followed his gaze to where Savannah stood behind the register with a big smile ringing someone up. "Okay, I think. At least, when she's here with everyone. Last night was a bit rough. She woke up more than once with nightmares. At first, I went to sleep on the couch so she could have the bed, but after the second time she woke crying, I ended up just laying down next to her so I'd be there if she needed me."

"I'm sure they'll ease over time. As long as she's surrounded by people she loves and who love her, she'll start to feel safe again." Cole moved away from the cut-out.

"It would help if they could figure out who abducted her and send them to prison." Until then, Gia doubted she'd ever feel safe. She couldn't begin to imagine how Savannah felt.

"I'm sure. No leads yet?"

"Not that I've heard."

"Listen…" Cole gestured toward the dining room with his spatula. "Why don't you take a break, get something cold to drink, and go socialize with your customers for a few minutes. I've got this now."

"You're sure?" The orders had begun to lighten up over the past few minutes, and only three tickets remained above the grill.

"Positive." He shooed her toward the doorway.

"Thanks, Cole. I could use the break." She found Savannah standing behind the counter talking to Michael, who was sitting in the same seat he'd been sitting in when she'd left him earlier. "Don't tell me you're still here?"

When he grinned, he reminded her of Savannah. She often forgot how alike the two looked, the same delicate features and slim build, same blond hair and blue eyes, but Michael wasn't as quick to smile as Savannah and, although his eyes were the same color as Savannah's, they didn't hold the same warmth and openness as hers.

"Nah, I went to Pa's and sat with him awhile, then I came back." He tapped a sugar packet up and down on the counter.

The rhythmic tap, tap, tap reminded her of Savannah's habit of tapping her nails. Apparently, another shared trait. "How's he holding up?"

"He's doing okay." The pace of the tapping increased. "Now that Savannah's back, at least."

"How about Joey?"

"Joey's Joey, ya know? Of all of us, he's the most like Savannah, always happy, always able to see the best in any situation, quick to forgive and move on." Michael tossed the sugar packet aside, sipped his latte, and opened the menu in front of him. "He was a wreck when she was missing, but now that she's back, he's ready to return to some semblance of normal, though he's sticking closer than usual to Pa."

"That's good. I'm glad neither of them is alone right now."

Michael nodded and squeezed Savannah's hand. Seemed Gia wasn't the only one needing constant reassurance that she was okay.

Gia sat down next to Michael. It might have been a mistake; the instant her bottom hit the stool, her eyes grew heavy. "Where's Tempest?"

Savannah set a Diet Pepsi in front of her.

"Thanks." She needed the caffeine.

"She went to work for a while." Michael closed the menu and slid it aside. "They gave her the day off, but she had a few things to catch up on that couldn't wait."

"Can I get you something?" Savannah returned the menu to its place.

Gia could definitely get used to having her around. With any luck, Savannah would decide she loved waitressing and stay on permanently. But that was selfish. Savannah needed a career she'd love, no matter how much Gia loved having her and would miss her if she left.

A short, stocky man approached the counter beside Michael and stopped, facing Savannah. "Excuse me, but are you Savannah Mills?"

Savannah stiffened. "Yes. Can I help you?"

Michael looked up at the man, and all the color drained from his face.

"I should have known; you look just like your brother." The man extended a hand.

Since all of the Mills siblings resembled one another, that didn't help narrow down which of her brothers he was referring to.

With a quick glance at Gia, Savannah reached out to shake his hand.

He deftly caught her fingers and brought her knuckles to his lips. "It's a pleasure to meet you, my dear. My name is Francis Esposito, but please, call me Frankie."

The name pinged Gia's radar instantly. She didn't know what she expected a member of a supposed crime family to look like, but Frankie Esposito wasn't it. He was young, maybe late twenties, and wore jeans, a blue T-shirt, and cowboy boots. He had an easy smile and warm green eyes.

"It's nice to meet you, Frankie." Savannah offered a tentative smile. "This is my friend, Gia Morelli, and my brother, Michael."

"I'm glad to meet you, Ms. Morelli." He took her hand and kissed her knuckles as well.

"Gia, please."

He covered their clasped hands with his free hand and nodded toward Michael before returning his attention to her. "Gia. I've heard wonderful things about your place, but I haven't yet had the pleasure. Perhaps my wife and I will stop in one day soon."

"That would be nice. Be sure to say hello if you do." If he was a friend of one of Savannah's brothers, she'd pick up the check for his first visit.

"However." He released Gia's hand and refocused his attention on Savannah. "Today, I've come to see Ms. Mills."

"Please, call me Savannah. And sit; make yourself comfortable." She gestured toward the free stool next to Michael. "Can I get you something to eat or drink? Coffee? Anything?"

When Savannah took an order, she made it sound more like she was inviting an old friend in to sit a spell and offering refreshments. No wonder so many customers loved her. Willow was the same way. Gia would have to remember that if she ever had to train someone new, which hopefully she wouldn't.

Frankie sat but held up a hand. "No, thank you. My wife will have dinner on the table by the time I return home, and she'll be upset with me if I've already eaten."

"I can sure understand that." Savannah leaned against the counter behind her, putting a bit of space between her and Frankie Esposito. "How can I help you?"

"Actually, I just stopped by to check on you and see how you're feeling. And to apologize."

She frowned. "Apologize? What for?"

"I am so sorry about what happened the other day and equally sorry I wasn't able to come by sooner to see you. As the owner of the Oakley Manor House, I should have come right away. You have my sincerest apologies, ma'am, as well as my assurance I'll get to the bottom of what happened."

"Oh, thank you, but it's no problem." Savannah smiled, but it held none of the warmth she usually greeted people with. "Thank you for stopping by; it was very kind of you but completely unnecessary."

Savannah, dismissive? Either something was up between her and the suave Mr. Esposito, or she'd been more traumatized by her ordeal than Gia had realized. She stood and went to lean against the counter beside

Savannah. She had no clue what was going on, but Savannah was acting out of character, so Gia would stand at her side and let her know she had her back no matter the situation.

"No trouble at all. I feel somewhat responsible, since it happened while you were showing my property."

Michael sat staring straight ahead, seemingly at the row of coffee pots on the counter behind Savannah and Gia.

Savannah started to back up, but there was nowhere to go with the counter at her back. "Of course, it's not your fault, but thank you for your concern. It was very kind of you to come see me."

"Oh, no bother at all, dear." He stood and checked his watch, a gold Rolex with a brown leather band.

Sweat sprang out on Michael's head and trickled down his hairline. He mopped his brow with a napkin. "Is that all you came in for?"

Frankie pinned him with a stare, and Michael all but slid off his stool into a puddle on the floor. Despite Michael's slight build, he'd never struck Gia as timid, and yet, he seemed ready to melt under Francis Esposito's intense scrutiny.

Savannah stepped forward, gripped Michael's hand, and squeezed. "Mr. Esposit...uh, I mean, Frankie, I didn't realize you owned the Oakley Manor House. Your name wasn't on the paperwork, at least, not that I noticed."

He stared at Michael another moment, then returned Savannah's smile. "No, I bought the house as a business investment years ago, through a company I own. But I never really found the time to renovate it or the interest to re-open it as a bed and breakfast."

"It's a shame. It really is a beautiful home, and the grounds are incredible." For the first time since Frankie walked in, Savannah sounded genuine.

"Yes, they are, aren't they?" Frankie took a business card from his pocket, laid it on the counter, and then tapped a perfectly manicured fingernail against it. "If there's anything I can do for you, please, don't hesitate to call."

"Thank you. That's very kind of you. But, please, don't feel obligated to help me. I'm fine. I actually don't remember any of my ordeal after going upstairs to show Buster the bedrooms."

Frankie offered a slight bow, then turned to go, but he turned back before taking a step as if he'd forgotten something. The move seemed a little too calculated. "By the way, speaking of Buster, do you mind if I ask how he came to be viewing that property?"

Why did it seem that everyone was more interested in how Buster got into the house than who killed him?

"I was at the office late one day, after everyone else had gone, and he came in. He apologized for coming in so late, but he was on his way home and saw the lights on and figured he'd stop. He said he was interested in the Oakley Manor house, but not as a business investment, as a private home."

While the excuse seemed legitimate enough on the surface, Gia was starting to wonder if Buster Clarke had sought Savannah out specifically. The thought he could have been lying in wait to find her alone in the office, or even stalking her to ascertain her whereabouts in an effort to get her alone, turned Gia's stomach. As soon as Mr. Esposito walked out the door, she'd call Hunt. Sooner if he didn't go quickly. This friendly little chat was beginning to have the feel of an interrogation.

Frankie's gaze skipped back and forth between Savannah and Gia. "Well, then, I'll be going. I have one more stop to make on my way home. Seems only right I should pay my condolences to Paige Clarke, even though it wouldn't surprise me one bit if she offed the old boy herself."

Gia gasped before she could catch herself.

"Or perhaps she had her lapdog do it. Either way." He shot Michael one last look. "It was nice to meet all of you. I'm sure we'll see each other again soon."

Savannah's posture relaxed, and she smiled. "I'm sure we will, and thank you again for checking up on me. I do hope you'll come in for breakfast one day. I look forward to meeting Mrs. Esposito."

"I'll be sure to pass along the invitation, thank you."

Savannah leaned forward on the counter, hands spread wide, and waited for Frankie to walk out and the door to close behind him, then turned a glare on Michael. "Spill it."

His gaze shot to hers. "Spill what? I don't know what you're talking about."

"Then why were you acting so weird?"

He scowled at her. "What do you mean weird?"

"As if you were terrified. And how do you know Frankie Esposito?"

"I don't actually know him, but his reputation precedes him. And that is one scary guy, no matter how debonair he pretends to be." He blew out a breath and shoved a hand through his hair as he lurched to his feet. "Look, Savannah, I'm not trying to scare you or anything; you've been through enough as it is, but I can't keep pretending nothing's wrong either. I understand Hunt and Leo want to protect you. So do I. But let's face it, you were on one of Francis Esposito's properties with Buster Clarke, one of Frankie's sworn enemies. Even you can't be naïve enough to think there won't be repercussions for that. No matter what kind of deals Hunt and Leo are running around trying to make in the background."

"Deals? What are you talking about?" Savannah whirled on Gia.

Gia shook her head. "I don't know anything about that."

Michael scoffed, then stormed out without another word.

Thankfully, there were no customers left to witness his tirade.

"Savannah." Gia laid a hand on Savannah's arm.

She yanked away from her grasp. "No, he's right. They're coming for me, and all anyone else can do is get in the way."

Chapter Fifteen

Gia pulled through the wrought iron gates, with Savannah in the passenger seat and Thor, Klondike, and Pepper in the back. She followed Hunt beneath the canopy of palm trees lining either side of Trevor's curved driveway. When Hunt stopped, she pulled beside his Jeep and shifted into park. "This really is amazing, even more beautiful than I imagined it would be, since the last time I saw it was in the dark."

"Can you believe the stonework?" Savannah blew out a breath. "Incredible. Far nicer than any venue I looked at."

"No kidding."

In the cobblestone courtyard center stood a large fountain surrounded by a circular garden overflowing with flowers. A stone wall surrounded the property, not only creating the feel of a private oasis but providing an extra layer of security Gia suddenly felt sure they needed.

Trevor held the driver's side door open for Gia.

"Thank you, Trevor." She climbed out and let him shut the door behind her.

"No problem." He started around the car with her. "Is Savannah okay?"

Gia peered in at her through the windshield. "I think so. It's just a lot to take in. Not that she didn't realize the person who kidnapped her was still out there, but I think she felt like whoever it was let her go so they wouldn't come back for her. Now, she has to accept that maybe they only let her go temporarily because they wanted something. She doesn't like being used as a pawn in a game she doesn't even understand, and she's convinced someone's coming for her."

Trevor slung an arm around Gia's shoulders in a companionable embrace. "Try to convince her not to worry about it, at least while she's here. She'll be safe, Gia. You both will."

Gia nodded, still not thoroughly convinced. Though Trevor's mansion rivaled a fortress, they couldn't hide there indefinitely. "Thank you, Trevor, for everything. You didn't have to leave Storm Scoopers and come all the way out here with us."

"Don't worry about it." He opened the passenger side door for Savannah. "Mathew's been working out great, and he'll be okay by himself for a little while."

Savannah climbed out of the car and stood gawking. "Trevor, I don't even know what to say. There are no words to tell you how thankful I am."

"Anything for a friend. Now, come on and let's get you guys settled." He took the keys from Gia and popped the trunk.

Hunt and Leo each grabbed a couple of bags from the trunk and started toward the house.

"Do you mind if I take a walk around the property once I get these bags inside?" Hunt asked.

"Not at all. Go anywhere you want, and just let me know if you need anything or if you think Gia and Savannah do." After shutting the trunk, Trevor took the two cat carriers from the back seat.

Gia hooked Thor's leash to his collar. "Where would you like me to walk him, Trevor?"

He used his elbow to gesture toward the side of the house. "The potty pavilion is around that side. There's a door right down the hall from your room, so it'll be safe if you have to take him out at night."

Gia followed his directions around the side of the house with Savannah sticking close at her side. A walkway led around the far side of the porch, through a clump of thick palms, and into a walled in area, which was a far cry from what Gia envisioned as a potty pavilion.

Savannah stopped short in the archway. "My dogs are severely neglected."

"You ain't kidding." Because the area was fully enclosed, except for the archway and a door that led to the house, Gia unhooked Thor's leash, hugged him, and let him run. "Trevor's dogs sure do have it made."

"Brandy, especially. She's like his child," Savannah agreed.

A large square of thick grass that had to be sod spread out before her, with a massive moss-covered oak providing shade in its center. A rack of plastic bags hung beside a covered garbage pail. A row of wood cabinets with a stone countertop ran along one wall and butted up against a large, stone-encased tub. Adjoining the potty pavilion was what appeared to be a doggie playground, of sorts, complete with obstacle courses and a range of activities designed to keep his dogs active and healthy.

Gia opened one of the cabinets beneath the counter and found dog shampoo, brushes, and various treats, including a bunch of the ones she made and sold at the All-Day Breakfast Café. Warmth rushed through her.

Savannah sat on a bench, pulled her feet up, and wrapped her arms around her knees. "I don't even know what to say. I come from a humble, modest home. But even selling real estate, I've never seen anything like this."

"I know, right." Gia had grown up in an apartment in New York City with a father who'd tossed her out the day she graduated high school. Even though her life with Bradley had been more luxurious, his condo couldn't even come close to this splendor. "Thor seems to be enjoying it."

He'd found the play area quickly enough and was jumping back and forth over a low gate, ringing a bell with his nose each time he reached the other side, an obstacle Zoe had taught him at daycare.

"What's not to enjoy?" Savannah asked.

"True." Keeping an eye on Thor, Gia sat next to Savannah. "Are you okay?"

"Yeah, I am. Michael's revelation really didn't come as a surprise. It's not like I didn't think of it the instant Frankie Esposito revealed he was the owner of the Oakley Manor House. I just can't believe Hunt and Leo didn't tell me."

Though Gia shared Savannah's feelings on the two of them keeping secrets, she understood they'd only been trying to protect her. She'd been through enough, and no threats were made. It's not like they hadn't been taking every precaution. "I know, but they didn't want you to be scared. It's not like you weren't already aware the killer was still out there."

She shrugged. "I guess."

When she got Hunt alone for a few minutes, she had every intention of finding out what kind of deals he was making and with whom.

Determined not to allow Savannah to dwell on things she couldn't do anything about at the moment, Gia changed the subject. "So, if this is the potty pavilion, what do you think the rest of the grounds look like?"

"I can't even begin to imagine." She grinned, and some of the moodiness left her. "But I sure do intend to find out."

The door at the far end of the courtyard opened, and Trevor stuck his head out. "If you guys are ready, I can show you to your rooms. The archway has a gate if you want to close it and let Thor play a while."

Thor barreled toward Trevor, apparently just as eager as them to explore.

"That's okay. I'll take him with us for now." Even though it did seem safe, and Hunt, Leo, and Trevor were all there, and guards had been posted out front already, she wasn't leaving Thor unsupervised after what someone already did to him. If not for how much Thor loved, and Gia trusted, Zoe at the doggie daycare center, she would have left him in the apartment above the café with Klondike and Pepper just to have him close while she worked.

The three of them followed Trevor into the house. "Hunt got a phone call, and he and Leo had to run out, but they said they'd be back later. I gave them rooms down the hall from you, so if they want to hang close, they can."

"That's awesome. Thank you, Trevor." For some reason, Trevor seemed out of place in such luxurious surroundings. He seemed much more at home behind the counter at Storm Scoopers.

"Your rooms are right down here." He led them down a hallway filled with light from windows set high in the walls, up a spiral staircase to the loft-style second floor, then stopped in front of a set of French doors. "I figured you'd want to stay together, so I gave you this suite."

They entered a comfortable, rustic style living room with a large stone fireplace and an entire wall of shelves packed full of books. Two kittens hung from their claws on the curtains. They whipped their heads toward the door as it opened but didn't bother to stop their game.

"Klondike, Pepper, you get down. Right now." Great. They hadn't been there five minutes, and already their pets were doing damage. She rushed toward them.

They continued to stare at her.

"I am so sorry, Trevor." She yanked Pepper off and handed her to Savannah, then grabbed Klondike. First, she looked her in the eye and reprimanded her, then she snuggled her close, running a finger over the spot where a coyote had bitten off a chunk of her ear before Thor had intervened. "I'll replace the curtains, Trevor."

Trevor laughed. "Don't worry about it. They're kittens. That's what they do. Besides, if not for you two staying here, this suite would just be empty. I'm happy to see someone enjoying it. Let them go play."

She kissed the top of Klondike's head and let her go. She scrambled straight back to the curtains. Gia added shopping for new curtains to her mental to-do list.

Trevor put a hand on her back and guided her toward a hallway at the far end of the room. "The bedrooms are down that hall and sit side by side. Each has its own bathroom with towels and whatever else you might need in the linen closets."

Their bags had been set aside next to the door.

"I don't have any staff, though, so you're on your own if you need anything." He handed Gia a key. "That's the key to the front door. I have to get back, but feel free to explore the house if you want. Find somewhere special you'd like to have the wedding and reception, take pictures, and whatever else you need. The kitchen is downstairs and toward the back of the house. Help yourselves to whatever's there."

Gia nodded. Words eluded her.

He petted Thor's head, kissed Gia's and Savannah's cheeks, and left them alone.

"So, what do you want to do?" Gia asked. "Explore?"

"Would you mind if we just have something to eat and go to bed? I'm kind of tired."

"Of course not. Why don't you go take a nice warm bath, and I'll see what Trevor has for dinner?"

Savannah looked down the hallway, then back at Gia. "That's okay. I'll come with you to the kitchen, and we can make something quick."

"Sure thing. Come on, Thor." Gia hooked one arm through Savannah's and lay the other hand on Thor's head as they walked down the hallway and, in that one moment, all was right in her world. "Cole is going to open tomorrow, so we can sleep in if you want. I'll wait here for you until you get up."

"You don't mind?"

"Not at all. I could use the sleep myself."

"And then we'll go to my office, right?" Savannah asked.

"Sure thing." Going to the office might not be the best idea, but there was no way Gia would leave Savannah on her own if she insisted on going in. Besides, who knew? They might even learn the note held a perfectly legitimate message that had nothing to do with the Oakley Manor House or Savannah's abduction.

Savannah pointed toward the kitchen. "Can you even believe this place? It makes the Oakley Manor House look like a hunting cabin."

She wasn't kidding. The place was a maze of rooms and suites, all decorated in an inviting rustic style. "How many rooms do you think there are?"

"I have no idea, but I wouldn't want to have to clean this place."

Gia laughed. Leave it to Savannah to think of the practical.

When they reached the kitchen, Savannah stopped short.

"Is something wrong?"

"Can you imagine what this place would look like decorated for Christmas?"

Gia's father never did much for Christmas, but when she was old enough, she always set up a small tree in her room. Bradley's Christmas plans had always been a long list of events he needed to attend with her on his arm. "No, I can't, but I bet it would look like something out of a movie."

"Exactly." Savannah moved into the room and looked around. She turned her gaze on Gia, mischief dancing in her eyes. "I know when I want to get married."

"Yeah?"

"If it's okay with Trevor, and it doesn't interfere with any holiday plans he might have, I want to get married at Christmastime. I want to decorate this entire mansion and have all of my friends and family together for the wedding and the holiday."

"That sounds perfect." But right now, she needed to get Savannah something to eat.

"I'll talk to Trevor as soon as I see him. Oh my goodness gracious, I could get married right here in this kitchen it's so gorgeous."

"This kitchen is like a dream come true." Trevor had understated the amenities the kitchen boasted, all commercial-grade, stainless-steel appliances Gia wished her café kitchen had room for. She pulled a high-backed stool out from the long center island with a rack of copper pots hanging above it. "Here, sit."

Savannah did as instructed.

Thor plopped down at the foot of her stool.

"What do you feel like eating?"

"If there's any soup, I wouldn't mind a bowl."

Gia opened the pantry door. Rows of packed shelves lined the small room. "I think it's safe to say he has any kind of soup you want."

Savannah hopped off the stood and joined her in the doorway. "You know what?"

"Hmm?"

"I feel kind of bad for Trevor."

Gia just lifted a brow and waited.

"All of this…" She gestured around the room, indicated everything beyond that one room. "And he has no one to share it with."

"He's got Brandy, and I've noticed him and Zoe spending a lot of time together lately. Just last weekend, he took her kayaking." When things got back to normal, Gia needed to find a day to go kayaking with Trevor again. She hadn't expected to enjoy kayaking, had been terrified the first time he'd taken her, but she'd come to enjoy it immensely. She'd never known the same peace she felt while drifting through the wilderness with only the sounds of nature surrounding her. "I think they'd make a great couple."

"Me too. Zoe's a sweetheart, and she's great with dogs, which would be important to Trevor. Plus, I don't think any of this would matter to her."

"No, probably not." Gia scanned the shelves of canned goods. "Do you want chicken noodle, or maybe chicken rice?"

"Sure, chicken rice sounds good." Savannah grabbed a box of Saltine crackers and returned to her seat. "What are you going to have?"

"I'll have the same." She rummaged through the refrigerator. "And I'll make a grilled cheese and tomato sandwich. Do you want one?" She'd already fed Thor before they left the apartment, so she offered him a treat from a jar in the pantry.

"No, thanks. Just the soup and crackers." She opened the package and nibbled on a cracker.

Thor ate his treat with less enthusiasm than usual. Maybe he needed some rest too. A morning without having to get up and rush out might be good for him. It might be good for all of them.

Gia poured a couple of cans of soup in a pot, set it on the stove, and then searched for a recycling can. She opened a door and flicked on the light. A powder room. She started to retreat, but something skittered across the floor, and Gia screeched and jumped back.

Thor shot to his feet and barked once but stayed where he was.

She'd never seen anything like the thing currently staring back at her, but it looked enough like a spider to bring a wave of pure terror. It stopped in the corner, its pointed tail curved over its lumpy back. She danced back away from it, keeping her gaze riveted on the creature. If it disappeared to somewhere else in the house, she'd never be able to close her eyes. "What on earth is that thing?"

Used to Gia's aversion to spiders, among other things, Savannah took her time getting up to see what it was. She crowded beside her and peered in.

Thor nudged his way between them, caught sight of the foul creature, and lunged, barking furiously.

Gia grabbed his collar and held him back. "No, Thor."

No way was she taking a chance of that barbed tail stinging him. Sweat poured down her face, burning her eyes. She didn't dare impede her vision by wiping them away, even with Savannah standing there. And even though Thor had begun to settle, she wasn't letting go of him. "Should I call one of the guards from out front?"

Savannah's laughter scraped along Gia's raw nerves.

"What's so funny?"

"You don't need to call the guards, Gia." She reached into the bathroom and grabbed a plastic container of baby wipes from the counter. After stacking the wipes onto the counter, she lifted a folded hand towel from the rack.

"That thing cannot possibly be—"

"It's just a scorpion, hon. It won't kill you."

"Hard to tell." Gia wrestled Thor away from the door to give Savannah room. "And what are all those lumps all over its back?"

"Its babies."

"It's ba…uh…" Her knees went weak, and she reached out to grip the wall. Visions of millions of little scorpion babies escaping their mother's back and scattering all over the house assailed her.

Savannah bent and used the folded towel to usher the creature into the container and closed the lid. "Will you walk with me to take her outside?"

Gia took a couple of deep breaths. Savannah had been kind enough to contain the beast when she knew Gia was afraid of it. Now Gia needed to pull herself together so Savannah wouldn't have to go outside and face her fears alone.

"Sure," Gia whispered. "But don't release him by the potty pavilion, or poor Thor will never get to use it again."

"You know what, Gia?" Savannah laughed. "Thank you. I just…I needed this tonight. One moment of normalcy, well, normal for you anyway, to put things in perspective."

"Well, then, I'm glad my terror worked out so well for you." She followed Savannah out the front door and across the courtyard, leaving Thor in the house since she'd left his leash in her room. She tried to ignore the sound of skittering feet inside the closed container.

Savannah stopped at the far end of the courtyard, where a line of bushes ran along the edge. "Is this far enough?"

That thing could never get far enough away—a chill raced up Gia's back, and she shivered—but she wasn't going to make Savannah leave the circle of light to ease her own admittedly irrational fears. "It's fine."

Savannah opened the container and freed its occupant.

"What are you two doing?"

Gia whirled toward the man's voice, instantly realizing she'd turned her back on the critter.

Chapter Sixteen

Hunt stood staring at them with his hands on his hips. Since his expression held more curiosity than anger, Gia whirled around to face the direction Savannah had released the scorpion and danced back a bit from the edge of the bushes.

Savannah patted her arm. "Gia found a scorpion in the house, and I had to get rid of it."

Hunt smirked and ran a hand over his mouth to cover it.

"Haha. I'm glad the two of you are finding so much humor in my distress. That thing had millions of little..." Gia wiggled her fingers around, trying to portray the image of what was probably less than millions of little critters swarming the creature's back. Why couldn't they see this was a problem? "Things on its back."

"Now, now, dear." Savannah put an arm around her back. "You come with me, and I'll fix you some nice warm soup to make you feel better."

Hunt gave up any semblance of discretion and laughed out loud.

Fine. If teasing Gia about her phobia of all things spider-like made Savannah feel better, so be it. At least she was smiling. "Fine. But I want grilled cheese too."

Hunt put his arm around her shoulders from the other side and kissed her temple. "Grilled cheese sounds good."

As they started to enter the house, Gia scanned the courtyard one last time to be sure the scorpion and her progeny didn't follow them back into the house. She didn't see anything. But a thought stopped her cold as she crossed the threshold. "You don't think any of those things escaped their mama do you?"

"No, Gia. It's fine." Savannah propelled her through the rest of the way with a hard shove to her back. "But you'd better get the door shut before it gets back in."

Hunt closed the door behind them and shook his head.

Thor bounded into the foyer, tail wagging hard enough to knock over anything he came in contact with.

"Hey, there, buddy." Hunt scratched the spot just behind his ears that sent Thor's eyes rolling back into his head. "How are you feeling, boy? Huh? Are you taking care of these ladies?"

Thor barked when Hunt stopped petting him and trotted beside him to the kitchen.

"Is Leo with you?" Savannah asked.

"No, he's following up on something, and I can't stay long, but I was in the area, so I wanted to stop and check on you two." He frowned at both of them. "And do I find you safely holed up behind locked doors? No, I find you outside in the courtyard, in the dark, alone. But for a scorpion."

Savannah lifted a finger. "And its babies."

"Ah, well, then, that's much better." Hunt pulled out a stool for Savannah, then sat beside her at the island.

Ignoring them both, Gia started slicing tomatoes and putting the grilled cheese sandwiches together. "Are you sure you don't want one, Savannah?"

"Um…yeah, why don't you go ahead and make me one. All that monster chasing seems to have brought back my appetite." She grinned.

That smile was well worth any amount of discomfort Gia had suffered. "What's going on, Hunt? Trevor said you got a phone call and had to leave earlier. Did something happen?"

"We got an ID on the woman in the lake."

Gia paused, the knife halting in the air mid-stroke. "Who was she?"

"Her name's LuAnne Swanson. She's a real estate attorney."

Gia's gaze shot to Savannah. "Do you know her?"

She frowned and shook her head. "The name's not familiar."

Hunt pulled up a picture on his phone and handed it to Savannah. "According to witnesses we've interviewed so far, the last time she was seen was Sunday night. She was having dinner at Correlli's with Buster Clarke."

"A social dinner?" Gia stacked American cheese and thinly sliced tomatoes on white bread, then buttered both sides of the bread and placed the sandwiches onto a skillet. She turned on the burner, added another can of soup, and turned on the gas beneath that pot too.

Thor ran to her at the scent of cheese.

"Sit, boy."

He plopped down, and Gia gave him a slice of cheese.

"No one knows if it was business or pleasure. They ate alone, and we haven't yet found anyone who overheard anything they talked about. Security cameras show him holding the door for her to enter the restaurant. His hand on her lower back as she walked through could have just been a friendly gesture, but it's not clear either way."

"It's hard to tell from this photo because it's just a close-up from the grainy surveillance video, but I don't think I've ever seen her before. It seems like she was pretty, though, and she looks to be around the same age as Buster." Savannah shook her head and handed Hunt's phone back to him. "So, now what happens?"

"I notified LuAnne's family while Leo went to interview the waiter who served them. We'll see what happens." Hunt washed his hands, dried them on a dishtowel, and returned to the counter next to Savannah. "How are you holding up?"

"I'm fine, thank you, but I don't appreciate being treated like a baby."

"What are you talking about?"

She sat up straighter. "I'm a big girl, Hunt. And, while I appreciate you guys trying to protect me, it doesn't help to hide things from me."

"I guess Michael couldn't keep his mouth shut, huh?" Hunt's jaw clenched.

"I'm no fool, Hunt."

"I never thought—"

She stared him down, but her expression softened. "I know you didn't, but you have to stop trying to hide things from me. How am I supposed to make decisions about my welfare if I don't have all the information I need?"

He shrugged and glanced at her from beneath his long, thick lashes. "I suppose just doing what you're told isn't on the table?"

"Ha!" She punched his arm. "How has that worked out for you in the past, buddy?"

"Touché." He sighed. "From now on, I'll be sure to keep you informed."

"Thank you, that's all I ask. It's not like I didn't realize on my own that Frankie Esposito might come after me, but you should have been upfront about it."

"You're right. I should have."

"And what kind of deals are you and Leo trying to make?"

He leaned over and kissed her head. "Whatever kind it takes to keep you safe."

Savannah stared him down for another moment, but she seemed to realize he wasn't going to elaborate, and she released his gaze.

Gia slid the grilled cheese sandwiches onto plates and set them on the counter, then filled everyone a bowl of soup, set them in front of each of their places as well, and went to sit. Savannah had already put out a pitcher of ice water, and Gia helped herself to a glass. "Did you find out anything about who broke into my house or the register at the shop? Do you think they're connected?"

Thor settled down beside her and propped his head on his front paws.

Hunt slumped against the stool-back. "No fingerprints. No footprints. No one caught on any surveillance camera we could find in the neighborhood, and we went door to door asking. But no matter how many times I go around and around, I always end up back at the same place. Thor."

Thor picked his head up at the mention of his name.

"What do you mean?"

His brow furrowed as he took a bite of his sandwich, chewed, swallowed, and wiped his mouth. "I just can't believe Thor let someone in the house, especially considering Klondike was there and how protective Thor is of her. It just doesn't make sense. Unless…"

Savannah's spoon clattered onto the counter. "Unless he knew the person."

"Exactly."

"You think someone I know broke into my house? And stole the money from the café?" Who would do that? And why? Anyone who knew Gia would know she'd spent her life's savings opening the café and purchasing the house in a rural development on the outskirts of the Ocala National Forest. Plus, she'd brought very little with her from her previous life. Mostly paperwork that had been thrown out or shredded when she found time to do it. She just didn't have anything worth breaking in for.

"Yeah, I do. It almost had to be someone Thor knows." He finished off his sandwich and set his empty plate aside. "Think about it. You take Thor all over with you. He spends his days at the daycare center with Zoe, who also takes care of a ton of other pets. It doesn't necessarily have to be a close friend or someone you know well. It could have been anyone he'd met that you were friendly to. It would have only taken seconds to sedate him, and if one person petted him and talked to him while another injected him, it's not so far-fetched."

So, what was she supposed to do? Walk around, not trusting anyone? Stop socializing Thor? Did she have to worry all day long in the café that one of the people she was talking to, gossiping with, serving, had betrayed her trust and broken into her home and harmed the one thing that meant more to her than anything else? Was it her fault? Had she failed Thor in teaching him to treat people kindly? When she first came across Trevor's guard dogs, she hadn't understood the need for them because he also had Brandy, a large German Shepherd. Now, she understood.

"Don't beat yourself up over it, Gia. You didn't do anything to invite evil into your life, just like I didn't." Savannah pushed most of her sandwich aside. "Thor is kind, sweet, and wonderful, as is his owner. Don't let someone else make you change that."

"Besides," Hunt added. "We don't know for sure yet. It's just an assumption. And, if you had been home at the time, and someone had tried to harm you, he'd have defended you, for sure."

They were both right, but it didn't do much to ease her growing fear. "It does make the most sense."

Savannah stood and cleared her place. "Anyway. I'm exhausted, and I need to go to bed."

"Will you be okay for a little while until I get cleaned up here?"

"I'm fine, Gia. You guys go ahead and enjoy a few minutes together while you can. Do you mind if I take Thor with me, though?"

"Not at all. You be a good boy, Thor, and get some rest." Gia hugged Thor and petted his head, then started clearing the counter. "I'll be up in a few minutes, Savannah."

"Thanks." She kissed Hunt and Gia. "Good night."

Hunt helped Gia clear the rest of the dishes, waiting until Savannah had sufficient time to reach the bedroom before speaking. "When I get my hands on Michael, he's going to wish he'd never said anything to her."

"Don't be too hard on him." Since there weren't many dishes, Gia didn't bother with the dishwasher. She began washing them by hand and putting them on a drying rack next to the sink.

Hunt opened and closed drawers until he found a dishtowel.

"I don't think he'd have said anything if he hadn't gotten so nervous."

Hunt frowned. "Nervous about what?"

She handed Hunt the frying pan to dry. "He seemed to get really spooked when Frankie Esposito came into the café."

With the frying pan in hand, Hunt paused. "What did Frankie want?"

"I'm not sure, actually." She set the next bowl on the rack. "He said he owns the Oakley Manor House and wanted to let Savannah know he was sorry for what happened to her."

Hunt set the pan and towel aside, folded his arms across his chest, and turned to lean against the counter. "And that's all he said?"

"No, he asked Savannah how Buster came to be looking at the house."

"What did she tell him?" Hunt's questioning had quickly taken on the fast pace she associated with his interrogation style.

Gia relayed the conversation as best she could remember, ending with his parting comment about Paige Clarke possibly killing him herself. "Why don't you seem surprised by that?"

"Let's just say rumor has it there was growing dissention among the Clarke siblings. No one's seen the old man for a while."

"The old man?"

"Carmine Clarke. Buster's father." Now that he was done grilling her, Hunt returned to drying. "Supposedly, he's not well, and his kids have taken over the business. Unfortunately, they're a bunch of spoiled brats who've lived too long on Daddy's generosity, and they do not see eye to eye on how things should be run."

"Paige and Robert seemed to get along well enough. Not that he said anything, but he kept a wary eye on her most of the time they were in the café, except when Paige and I went into my office alone."

"She's the little sister, and he's very devoted to her."

When she finished washing, Gia turned off the water and started putting away the dry dishes Hunt had stacked on the side. She enjoyed working in the kitchen with him. Too bad his hours kept it from becoming a more regular habit. "So, Buster was the odd man out?"

"Seems so."

"Does anyone know why he was looking at the Oakley Manor House when it belonged to his enemy?" It seemed if they could figure that out, it might help with the rest.

"I've asked that question of everyone we've spoken to, and the general consensus seems to be he wanted it to prove he could get it."

"Hmm...Nice guy, huh?"

"Like I said, spoiled."

"Do you think he sought Savannah out purposely because she worked in Angelina's office? I mean, there are plenty of other agents in plenty of other realty offices throughout the area. So, why Savannah?"

"Isn't that the million-dollar question," he muttered. Apparently, his talkative streak had ended.

"By the way, that's not the only thing Michael said."

"Oh?"

Gia paused so she could gauge his reaction. Savannah had already spilled the beans about Michael telling her what was going on, so Gia figured it was safe enough to mention the rest of the conversation. "He said you and Leo were running around trying to make a deal. Do you want to elaborate?"

"Not really." Hunt grinned. "But I will say, I'd do anything to keep my cousin safe, and if that means trying to work out a deal between the families, then that's exactly what I'll do. Fair enough?"

"I suppose." Gia finished putting everything away and wiped down the counters. "Do you want a cup of coffee?"

"No, thanks. I have to go. I really shouldn't have even stayed this long." He wrapped his arms around her from behind and rested his chin on her shoulder.

She studied his reflection in the window above the sink.

He nuzzled her neck. "Do me a favor?"

She wrapped her arms around herself, clutching his arms. "Of course."

"Don't let Savannah out of your sight, at least, as much as possible."

"Actually, that shouldn't be too hard, since she's going to be working in the café."

"Is she?" He turned her to face him and brushed a feather-light kiss against her lips.

"Mmm…hmm." She closed her eyes, enjoying the only moment she'd get alone with him for a while, possibly until he'd solved this case.

"Good. That's good. And don't let her get into any trouble." He set her back and pinned her with a pointed gaze.

"Of course, I won't let her get into trouble." Unless you considered going to the office to possibly confront Ward Bennett about his presumed connection to the Oakley Manor House trouble. In that case, all bets were off.

Chapter Seventeen

Early morning light finally filtered through the window around the curtains. Gia welcomed the sight. After another night spent tossing and turning, unable to shut her mind off, unable to get comfortable, despite the soft king-sized sleigh bed, and constantly getting up and down to check on Thor and peek in at Savannah, Gia gave up. She shoved the patchwork quilt back and got out of bed. "So much for sleeping in."

Thor lifted his head and looked at her, then laid it back down.

"I guess that means you're not getting up yet." She petted him for a minute, not wanting to bother him, but needing to reassure herself he was okay.

She navigated her way to the bathroom and didn't turn on a light until she closed the door. She eyed the deep jacuzzi tub, imagining how good the warm jets would feel against her stiff back, then turned on the shower instead. "One of these nights, before I leave here, I am going to soak in that tub."

But not today.

She showered quickly, slipped on a pair of black leggings and an oversized pink T-shirt, and dried her hair. Since she wore a minimal amount of makeup, especially since moving to Florida, where her complexion had become healthier thanks to year-round sunshine, it only took a minute or two to swipe some mascara on her lashes and add a bit of eyeliner. There was nothing to be done about the dark circles ringing her eyes, so she gave up and returned to the bedroom.

Thor curled on the floor next to the bed, wrapped around Klondike, and snoring softly.

She tiptoed toward the door, careful not to disturb them. Maybe she'd do a little exploring, find a nice room for hosting Savannah's reception. It would have to be big enough for lots of tables and a dance floor. Plus, there would have to be room for a buffet table, if they decided to go that route, and the DJ. And flowers, lots of flowers. Maybe one of the rooms with a fireplace, with Christmas decorations adorning the mantel.

A scream shattered the silence.

Gia slapped the light switch beside the living room door and squinted against the blinding light as she ran toward Savannah's room.

Pepper shot through the doorway from Savannah's room, between Gia's feet, and under the couch.

Thor ran from Gia's room, barking anxiously.

"Savannah?" She'd left the bathroom light on with the door open, so Savannah would have light if she woke during the night. "Are you all right?"

She tossed and turned wildly, tangled in the sheet. She screamed again, then muttered something as she tried to yank the sheets away from her.

Gia leaned closer, helping her pull the sheet away from her feet and legs.

"The clown, the clown, clown..." Savannah mumbled over and over.

Thor paced back and forth along the foot of the king-sized bed.

"Savannah!" Gia shook her shoulder. "Hey, wake up."

Savannah bolted upright and slammed her head into Gia's nose.

Tears sprang into her eyes, and she stumbled back.

"Gia?" Rubbing her head, Savannah squinted at Gia, her breathing ragged.

"Hey." She shook off the pain and approached the bed a little more carefully. "Are you all right?"

"What happened?" Savannah rubbed a hand up and down her throat.

Handing her a glass of water from the nightstand, Gia sat beside her on the bed. "You were having a nightmare."

"I remember." She frowned. "A little, anyway."

"You were talking about the clown again. Do you remember that?"

Savannah scooted back onto the bed, rested her back against the cushioned headboard, and pulled the thick quilt up to her chin. "I think so."

Gia petted Thor's head, then crawled into the bed and sat next to Savannah. "You were saying the same thing when I first found you outside the café. Do you think it has something to do with the kidnapping?"

She nodded slowly. "I...I can't...think... Something, though."

Gia stayed quiet, waiting while Savannah tried to sort through the nightmare and whatever might be actual memories.

"It's familiar. Something about where they held me, but I can't remember." She swallowed the full glass of water and set the glass down harder than necessary.

"They? Do you actually remember more than one person, or do you just think there were more?"

She weaved her fingers through her hair and squeezed. "I don't know."

"Don't get frustrated." Gia pushed Savannah forward and propped a pillow behind her back, then crossed her legs and got comfortable. Whether or not Savannah was able to go back to sleep, Gia wasn't going anywhere. "If bits and pieces are coming to you while you're sleeping, it means it's there, in your subconscious. You just need to wait for it to surface."

Savannah looked hopeful. "Ya think?"

"I do. I think once you relax, it'll come back to you. It's probably been coming back a bit at a time." She took Savannah's hand in hers. "But I also think you still need time to heal. I think maybe you're not quite ready to remember yet, and that's why you're having the nightmares."

Savannah tilted her head back against the headboard. "How do I get them to stop? I'm exhausted, and I'm afraid to close my eyes."

"If you want to go back to sleep, I'll sit right here until you wake. At the first sign you're having a nightmare, I'll wake you up." She'd also snatch Savannah's cell phone from the nightstand and Google circuses and carnivals in the area. The clown Savannah kept talking about had to mean something. Maybe she'd been held at an old fairground or something. Or maybe she passed a sign for a circus, or there was one visible from where she was held. Either way, it meant something, and Gia had every intention of figuring it out. "Or, if it would make you feel better to talk it out, I'll sit here and listen."

"You'll stay with me?"

"Absolutely."

Savannah fluffed her pillows and snuggled down under the blankets. "I'm sorry I woke you on the rare day you could have slept late."

"Don't worry about it. I was already up and showered by the time you woke up."

She yawned and closed her eyes.

Gia leaned across her, careful not to disturb her, and took her phone. She typed "carnival near me" into the search box. Nothing recent came up. Next, she tried "circus." A list of results popped up, but most were articles about protests involving the cruel treatment of circus animals. She tried "clowns" with no better luck.

"Anything?"

She looked down and found Savannah staring up at her. "I thought you were going to sleep."

"So did I, but it's not going to happen."

"Was I keeping you awake?"

"No." She scooted back to sit up. "I keep trying to remember, and bits and pieces of things come back, but I can't make sense of them."

"Do you want to talk about it?"

She took a deep breath and let it out slowly. "Not right now. If it's all right with you, since we both failed miserably at sleeping in, I'm going to jump in the shower and get dressed so we can go to the office. That note with OMH M 1 is bothering me, and I might sleep better if I know what it means. You still have it, right?"

"I do. I put it in my bag when I got undressed last night."

"Good. If I distract Ward, do you think you can drop it and pretend to pick it up or something, so it looks like we just found it there?"

Gia grinned. "I can do that."

They hurried through their morning routines. Savannah showered and got dressed, while Gia fed and took care of Thor, Klondike, and Pepper. After they were seen to, she climbed on a chair, removed the living room curtains from the rods, folded them, and placed them in the linen closet. "Now see if you two can keep out of trouble. Or I'm going to have to talk to Zoe and beg her to open a kitty room."

Klondike stretched and licked her paws.

"Don't ignore me."

She curled into a ball in a ray of sunlight and closed her eyes.

Thor nuzzled her hand, and she weaved her fingers into his thick fur. "You're a good boy, Thor. You always listen to Mama, don't you?"

"I seem to remember an incident involving a squirrel and a tree that didn't work out so well for you." Savannah stood in the doorway towel drying her hair.

Gia laughed. "That wasn't Thor's fault."

"Uh-huh." She gestured toward the window that overlooked a patch of tall pine trees. "Good call on the curtains. You ready?"

"Yup." Gia locked up and dropped Thor off at daycare, then drove to the real estate office. "You're sure you want to do this, right?"

"I have to know if that rat had anything to do with this."

"And if he did?"

Savannah shot her an evil grin and winked. "Then I'll sic Hunt and Leo on him."

"Seems fair." Gia took the note out of her bag, kept it hidden in her hand, and then followed Savannah into the office. A number of cars were parked in the lot already. "Do you know what Ward drives?"

Savannah pointed out a red Ferrari.

"Seriously?"

"He gets an unusually high number of big sales. I never really thought about it before—he's not married, has no kids, so I just figured he spent his money on toys—but he seems to make an awful lot of money." She studied the car as she walked past it.

"Could be he makes smart investments."

"Could be," Savannah conceded.

Tempest jumped to her feet and hurried toward them when they walked in. She shot Gia a nervous glance. "Hey, Savannah. How are you feeling? Are you sure you should be back to work already?"

"I'm not staying. I just stopped in to see Angelina. Is she in?"

"She's on the phone."

"Thanks. I'll wait." She said hello and introduced Gia to three other agents on the way across the room, then stopped at Ward's desk. "Hey, Ward."

"Savannah. How are you feeling?"

"Doing okay. Tired. I can't sleep at night because I keep remembering bits and pieces of what happened to me."

Gia wanted to slap a hand over her mouth. This was exactly the kind of thing Hunt meant by trouble. Spreading the word that she'd begun to remember any of her ordeal was not a good idea.

At least Ward didn't seem to react to the news.

Savannah glared at Gia, willing her to drop the note. "How's everything here?"

"Same ole, same ole. You know how it is."

Gia leaned against the desk, "accidentally" knocked a stack of papers onto the floor, and tossed the note into the middle of the pile as discreetly as possible.

Ward jumped to pick everything up.

Savannah rolled her eyes behind his head but still beat him to the note. She snatched it off the floor and held it close to her face to examine it. "What's this?"

"What's wha—" Ward caught sight of the note. "Uh..." He snatched it from her hand, crumpled it up, and tossed it into the trash. "Nothing. Just a reminder from a while ago."

"Really?" Savannah tilted her head and offered her sweetest smile. A sure sign there was gonna be trouble. "That's odd. OMH could stand for Oakley Manor House. And M one could easily be Monday at one. Funny that just happens to be the same time I was there showing that house. Don't you think? And what a coincidence; it also happens to be around the same time Buster was killed."

"Don't be ridiculous. It's an old note, and you can't prove otherwise, even if you are related to half the people investigating the case." He puffed out his chest. "People who really should be removed from that investigation, if they haven't already, since there's clearly a conflict of interest. Especially with you strutting around making accusations."

"Accusations?" She raised a brow. "What accusations are you talking about?"

He stacked the remainder of the papers together and slapped them down on his desk. "I'm not afraid of your cousin or your fiancé. I told you the note had nothing to do with Oakley Manor House or Buster getting killed. Now, don't you have something better to do than standing here harassing me?"

"Yes, actually, I do. I was just on my way to see Paige Clarke, offer my condolences on the loss of her brother." She fluttered her lashes and laughed softly. "Hmm…I wonder what she and her brother would think of a coincidence like that?"

Every drop of color drained from his face, and his mouth fell open.

She turned her back on him and started out, pausing to wink at Tempest. "Do me a favor? Ask Angelina to give me a call when she has time, please."

"Of course." Tempest's expression hovered somewhere between stark horror and appreciation.

"Thanks."

Gia cast a discreet look back at Ward as they walked out.

He pressed the phone against his ear and loosened his tie. Then the door fell shut behind her, blocking her view. "Do you really think that was a good idea?"

"That, my dear, was poking the bush. And of course it wasn't a good idea."

"So, now what?"

She shrugged and climbed into the car. "Now, we wait and see what Ward the weasel does."

Chapter Eighteen

Gia moved to the parking lot across the street and parked beneath the shade of an oak tree to wait. "What makes you think he'll do anything?"

"Because he was scared to death, and people make mistakes when they're scared."

Within five minutes of their conversation, Ward jumped into his Ferrari and peeled out of the parking lot.

"That didn't take long." Gia took her time pulling out behind him on the straight road. The last thing they needed was him spotting the tail.

Savannah snapped her seatbelt closed. "Don't lose him."

"I won't." She accelerated as he pulled farther away. "Where do you think he's going?"

"I don't know. His actions appear sinister right now, a reaction to being confronted with a suspicious-looking note. Truthfully, he could have called a client to confirm a meeting, which he is prone to do, and may be heading out to show a house."

Gia glanced at her speedometer. "At sixty miles an hour in mostly thirty-five mile per hour zones? I'm not going to be able to keep up with him if he goes through the school zone at that speed. Even if the schools are out for summer vacation, they still run summer camps."

Savannah tapped a nail against her phone. "Think I should call in a reckless driver and have him pulled over?"

Ward turned a corner, and the commercial downtown area gave way to the more rural wooded stretch of road leading out toward the fairgrounds. Towering pines stretched endlessly in every direction.

Gia checked the speedometer and pressed a little harder on the gas pedal. Thankfully, the roads were mostly empty. "Let's give it a minute."

"I sure would love to know where he's getting all his money." Savannah narrowed her eyes, her gaze riveted on the car in the distance ahead of them. "I've been racking my brain trying to remember which houses he's sold over the past few years, and I can't justify the toys he's able to afford."

"Is there any way to find out? A list of his sales, maybe?"

"Not without being able to get into his computer." She wrapped one arm across her body, resting her other elbow on her wrist, and tapped a nail against her lips.

"Can you?" Gia asked.

"Can I what?"

"Can you access his computer without him knowing?"

Savannah leaned forward in her seat, trying to keep Ward's car in sight as he inched farther away from them. "Theoretically, I guess I could, but I don't have his password."

"So, you'd need a computer hacker?"

"Yes, which I'm not." She swiped her phone and punched in the password.

"Neither am I." Gia was lucky she could do the basics on a computer.

"I'm calling his license plate in. We can't keep up with him, he's driving too fast."

Gia was focused on the problem of getting into Ward's computer. "Hmm…"

"What?" Savannah asked, distracted.

"I happen to know an information analyst who's a genius when it comes to computers."

"Alfie!" Savannah hooted, forgetting her call for the moment. "You think he'd do it?"

"I don't know, but it can't hurt to ask."

"As soon as—"

A bullet whizzed through the windshield between them and thudded into the back seat.

Gia slammed on the brake, and the back end fishtailed onto the sandy shoulder. She regained control and pulled back onto the road as another projectile hit the driver's side quarter panel. "Get down."

Savannah unlocked her seatbelt and slid to the floor.

Was that safer or not? If she hit something, Savannah could be crushed. But with someone shooting at them, she had no choice. "Call nine-one-one."

Savannah already had the phone out and was punching in the numbers.

Gia slid lower in the seat, trying to make herself as small a target as possible. Go on or turn around? She had no clue where the shooter was.

The back tire blew out.

Savannah screamed.

Gia fought the steering wheel, fleetingly grateful Thor wasn't with them. What if he'd been sitting in his usual spot in the middle of the back seat? The first bullet would have hit him.

"Gia!"

She yanked her attention back to the road ahead as she struggled to wrestle the car under control enough to keep it moving forward. If there was only one shooter, she just had to get past the point he could reach them. Or put some kind of barricade between him and them.

She spotted a narrow dirt road, slammed on the brake pedal, and skidded around the corner too fast. The back end swung around, and the passenger side slammed into a tree, crumpling Savannah's door inward. Gia unhooked her seatbelt as she swung her door open. "Are you okay?"

"Yeah." Savannah struggled to unwedge herself from the footwell.

Gia grabbed her arm and pulled.

As soon as Savannah rolled onto her back on the front seat, Gia pulled her out the driver's side door, half dropping her onto the ground. With a tight grip on her arm, Gia yanked her up and propelled her forward toward the shelter of the woods. "Go, go, go."

"Wait." Savannah tried to pull away. "My phone."

"Forget it." Gia shoved her forward, then plunged into the woods behind her.

Thick foliage swallowed them up, but they kept running. They had to put some distance between themselves and the shooter.

Gia tripped over a protruding root, stumbled, and recovered without going down. When her lungs screamed for air, and she couldn't draw another breath, Gia stopped and leaned her back against a tree. She slid down to squat, sucking air in desperate gulps.

Savannah crouched beside her, breathing just as heavily, and put a hand on Gia's shoulder. A trickle of blood ran down her hairline.

"You're hurt." She had to get Savannah out of there, assess how badly she was injured.

Savannah put her finger to her lips, then whispered, "I'm fine."

Gia nodded. It wasn't a huge amount of blood. She'd be okay until help found them. Although, Gia wasn't sure if Savannah had managed to convey their location before she'd lost the phone. She'd heard her talking, presumably to the nine-one-one operator, but she'd been too focused on trying to elude their attacker to register what was being said. She still couldn't talk enough to ask, but they couldn't wait there like sitting ducks.

They had to move, had to get deeper into the forest, away from the car, just in case the sniper came after them.

As soon as Gia started to stand, Savannah took hold of her hand and helped her up. Apparently, she'd just been giving Gia the time she needed to catch her breath.

In unspoken agreement, they moved farther into the woods, away from where they'd abandoned the car. When they came to a narrow stretch of swampy water, Gia stopped and leaned close to Savannah's ear. "Do you think this is far enough?"

Savannah looked around. "There's no kind of cover around here."

"What about the trees?" Certainly not ideal. Depending on the angle their attacker approached from, he could very well see them.

The wail of sirens saved them from having to decide. Gia started back toward the road.

Savannah grabbed her. "Just give it a few minutes. Wait until you hear car doors and Hunt and Leo screaming for us. Give them the time they need to make sure it's safe."

"And maybe catch whoever shot at us?" With any luck at all.

Savannah spared Gia the same look she gave her when Gia suggested maybe all of the venomous snakes would just magically go away. "He'll be long gone from his hiding place before they can find him."

"You're probably right." Gia found a boulder beside the stream, checked it for bugs, searched the stream's bank for alligators, looked up to be sure no snakes, venomous or otherwise, were hanging from branches above her and sat.

Savannah plopped down beside her, hugging her knees against her chest.

Gia yanked her feet up off the ground too. "Do you really think someone was shooting at us?"

"I guess it could have been kids throwing rocks or something, but it doesn't seem likely."

"No." She had to agree. "It doesn't."

"It also doesn't seem likely the shooter just happened to know where to wait for us, especially since we wouldn't have been traveling that way if not for following Ward." She slid her arms up her legs and folded them on her knees, then rested her chin and sulked. "I guess, sometimes when you stir a hornets' nest you get stung."

"I guess so." Gia leaned back on her hands and turned her face up to the sun, letting the hot rays ease some of the tension from her muscles. She was going to feel this tomorrow.

Savannah suddenly shifted and sat up straighter.

Gia jerked upright. "What?"

"You know what's equally unlikely?" She didn't wait for a response. "That Ward called someone to sit in wait and then lured us in this direction. How could he have known we would follow?"

"He couldn't have known for sure, even if he'd seen us in the parking lot across the street."

Savannah tilted her face up toward the sun's warm rays, quietly contemplating something. The cut on her temple didn't appear deep, but it was still bleeding slowly.

Gia strained to listen for sounds of pursuit, be it from the sniper or something more native to their surroundings.

"There is another explanation, you know," Savannah said softly.

"Oh?" Gia had a feeling there were hundreds of explanations they hadn't yet come up with. "What's that?"

"We weren't the targets." She lowered her gaze to meet Gia's. "What if Ward was the target, and the shooter spotted us behind him and took the opportunity to remove us from the equation?"

"Hmm...I hadn't thought of that." But she had to admit it was a possibility. A good one. She sat up straighter and folded her legs. "But who would want to kill Ward? And why?"

"I don't know, but Angelina is usually around in the mornings, and she wasn't today. I know she was supposedly on the phone, but we didn't see her, and there is a back exit from the office, one she could easily reach without being seen."

"So, you think Angelina could have gone ahead, positioned herself as a sniper, most likely up in a tree, and waited to take Ward out?" Somehow, Gia couldn't see the professional woman she'd met climbing up into a tree with a rifle slung across her back. "And if that was the case, we were behind Ward. Why would she have let him go by?"

"Who knows? Maybe she saw us coming and thought we were the more important to get rid of." Savannah lowered her gaze. "Or, at least, I was."

"Savannah! Gia!"

Gia sucked in a breath to answer the call, but Savannah slapped a hand over her mouth and shook her head. "We'll go to them. No need to draw attention to ourselves before we have help."

Gia nodded, and Savannah removed her hand. It didn't take long for them to meet up with a frantic Hunt and Leo.

Gia slid her arms around Hunt's waist and rested her head against his chest. Comforted by the solid, steady beat of his heart beneath her ear, she let her eyes drift closed.

He cradled her against him, kissed the top of her head. "You okay?"

She nodded, not yet ready to give up the safety and warmth of his embrace.

"Savannah, you okay?" Hunt called.

"I'm good," she answered from Leo's arms.

With one more kiss, Hunt set Gia back. Holding onto her arms, he looked her in the eye. "In case you weren't aware, this…episode, is what I would consider trouble. You know…as in, 'stay out of trouble.'"

"Ohh…is this what you were talking about?" She tried to smile but only half managed. "Next time, be more specific."

He pulled her in for another quick hug then tucked her beneath his arm. "I don't know what I'm gonna do with the two of you."

"You could start by feeding us." Savannah shrugged. "I'm starved."

He shook his head and raked a hand through his shaggy, dark hair. "All right. Come on. I guess we can question you just as easily over breakfast."

Because Gia's car was wrecked, they piled into Hunt's Jeep for the trip to the café. He checked in with the crime scene techs before joining them. Leo sat in the back with Savannah cradled beneath his arm.

Hunt swung a U-turn in the middle of the street and slowed as he passed Gia's car, then sped up. "Okay, let's have it. What were you two doing out here?"

Savannah pouted. "Maybe we were taking an early morning sightseeing ride."

Hunt shot her a warning glare in the rearview mirror. "Savannah…"

"What?" She offered her best innocent look back at Hunt in the mirror, which was almost enough to convince even Gia they hadn't been doing anything wrong. "Okay, fine. I'll tell you everything, but not until after we eat. I'm not getting yelled at on an empty stomach."

Hunt sighed. "Fine. No yelling."

"Promise?"

Hunt made an x across his chest, then lifted his hand in the air. "Cross my heart."

Savannah smiled. "You do know I'd have told you anyway, right?"

"Yeah, I know. I figure you're just being a brat to buy yourself a few minutes to collect your thoughts and to catch your breath after almost being killed."

She scooted forward on the seat and laid her head on his shoulder. "Thanks, Hunt."

He frowned. "For what?"

"For always understanding me."

He pressed his cheek against the top of her head. "You know it, kiddo."

Gia took the extra time Savannah had bought them to try to organize her thoughts. While there was a good possibility Ward Bennett had something to do with their attack, Savannah seemed to think there was an equal possibility Ward had been the target. Which meant, he could still be in danger. "You might want to have someone check in on Ward Bennett."

"What does he have to do with this?" Hunt asked.

"I'll explain it all in detail once we get to the café, but we were following him, and I thought a phone call he made prompted the attack on us, but Savannah suggested he may have been the original target, and we may just have presented an opportunity to get rid of us."

"And by us, she means me," Savannah said softly. "She just would have been collateral damage."

Chapter Nineteen

Hunt and Leo pulled chairs up to the desk in Gia's office so they'd have privacy to talk while they ate.

Willow set a tray in the center of the desk Gia had already cleared. "Can I get you guys anything else?"

"No, we're good. Thank you, Willow."

"You bet." She shut the door behind her as she left.

Gia set a cup of coffee in front of each of them.

"All right, tell me what you two got yourselves into." Hunt dropped onto a chair and snatched a piece of rye toast from a plate still on the tray.

Gia handed Savannah her slice of meat lover's breakfast pie.

She dug in, the first real interest she'd shown in eating since she'd returned. Nice way to avoid answering.

Gia saved her the trouble. "We stopped into the real estate office, and Savannah might have taken a poke at Ward."

"Details, please." Hunt gestured for her to proceed while he started on his western omelet. At least, with his mouth full, he'd have no choice but to honor his promise to Savannah. No yelling.

After a brief debate with herself over what information to omit from the story, Gia gave it to him straight. With Savannah's safety on the line, she couldn't take any chances. "Please, don't say anything to Michael about Tempest being the one to give us the note. She did what she thought was right, and we wouldn't know anything if not for her trusting me. I don't want to betray that trust. At the same time, there's nothing I wouldn't do to protect Savannah."

Hunt looked to Savannah. "How do you feel about not saying anything to Michael?"

She sat back and pushed her food around her plate. "Normally, I wouldn't dream of keeping anything from my brothers."

Hunt choked and covered his mouth with his fist.

Savannah grinned. "Well, anything like that, anyway. But Michael's been acting weird lately. Please, don't take this wrong, and don't go running off all gung-ho to interrogate him, but I get the feeling he knows more than he's saying. Every time I turn around, he's standing there. He's been in and out of the café all day long. And once, when I stepped out front for a minute's break, I saw him sitting on a bench across the street."

"Maybe he's just keeping an eye on you, concerned for your safety," Hunt said.

"Maybe, but it's still unusual behavior for him. Joey, no. But Michael, yes."

Hunt studied her for a moment as she kept her gaze on her mostly untouched breakfast. Seemed once she was off the hook about answering questions, her interest in food had waned. "All right."

Savannah's gaze shot to his. "You won't say anything?"

"No. At least, not right now. I agree with you; Michael hasn't been himself lately. I've been putting it off on his concern for you, but we'll just keep this between us for now."

Tears shimmered in her eyes. "Thanks, Hunt."

"It wouldn't be the first time I've kept a secret for you, little cous." The warmth and affection in his tone gave Gia a moment of regret she hadn't grown up with a family like Savannah's. What would it have been like to have siblings and cousins that always had your back, even when you messed up?

"Hey, now, I kept your share of secrets too." Savannah waggled her eyebrows.

Hunt's phone rang, and he stepped into the hall to answer.

Gia nudged Savannah's plate closer to her. "Why don't you try to eat, Savannah?"

She sighed and took a bite.

Gia took a couple of bites of her vegetable omelet, but it sat like a rock in her stomach.

Hunt shoved the door open. "Leo, let's go."

He jumped to his feet, kissed Savannah's cheek, and headed for the door. "What's up?"

"They found a print on the pad."

"A fingerprint?" Gia shot to her feet. "From the pad by my register, where the note I found with Thor came from?"

"Yeah."

"Whose print was it?"

She held her breath. If he didn't answer, maybe Savannah would give her cousin, Regina, a call and find out. Because whoever had hurt Thor was not going to get away with it.

"It belonged to Robert Clarke, Buster's brother."

Robert? That didn't make sense. Thor didn't know him, so why would he have let him in?

Hunt pointed back and forth between Gia and Savannah and leveled them with a glare. "You two are to stay out of trouble this time. You leave this investigation to us. I mean it."

Savannah stared after them, her bottom lip caught between her teeth, nails tapping away against the desktop.

Gia turned to her the instant the door shut. "So, are we going to stay out of trouble?"

"Probably not."

Gia held back a groan. There was nothing she could do about Robert right now, and Savannah would know that. They'd never get near him before Hunt and Leo picked him up, if he hadn't been apprehended already. So, there was something else churning in her mind. "I had a feeling you were going to say that. What do you have in mind?"

"Would you take a ride with me?"

"Seriously? After the last ride I took with you turned out so well?"

She grinned, but it was forced. "This ride will be different. I need to check something out before I say anything. If I'm right, no one should be there."

With a sigh, Gia stood. They both knew she was going to agree. "You'll have to drive."

"Thankfully, my car's still out back, since I rode with you out to Trevor's yesterday."

Gia collected the remains of their breakfast and carried the tray to the kitchen. "Hey, Cole, will you be okay for a while if I take a ride with Savannah?"

"You bet." Distracted, Cole ran a finger in the air in front of several tickets posted above the grill. "But I have strict instructions to remind you to stay out of trouble."

"Got it." Guilt niggled at her. She didn't like leaving him and Willow with such a large crowd.

"Go, Gia." He dropped eight slices of bread into the toasters. "Earl's on his way to help out, and Skyla's already out front with Willow."

"Thanks, Cole. If it wasn't for Savannah—"

"I know. And just like you're pitching in to help a friend, so are we."
He checked the tickets again. "Now go on, get out of here."

Ignoring the tug of guilt, she started out.

"And stay out of trouble," he called after her.

She'd certainly do her best.

"So...." Gia slid her sunglasses on. Since Savannah had left the
convertible top up, Gia figured she wanted to talk. "Where are we headed?"

"This might be a total waste of time..."

Gia really hoped that was the case.

"But you know how I keep waking up thinking about a clown?"

Uh oh. "Yeah?"

"Well, I got to thinking." She hit the turn signal and headed out of town.
"At first, I didn't remember anything at all. Then, I started dreaming about
being carried. I even woke up a little motion sick a couple of times."

"You didn't tell me that."

She shook her head. "I didn't really put it together at first. I thought
the nausea was just remnants of the sedative they used. Then, when it
happened at Trevor's this morning, I chalked it up to stress."

"But now you think it was motion sickness?"

"I do." Savannah made another turn onto a narrow residential street
lined with garages.

"Where are we?" It was a beautiful neighborhood, but Gia had never
been there before. Though the houses were large, the property they sat on
was not. It seemed there was no more than five or six feet between houses.
A row of garages faced the street. Yards separated the garages and the
houses they belonged to.

"There's a park up the road."

"It's interesting the way they have the community set up." Many of
the yards boasted screened pools, which took up most of the small yards.
Where did their dogs run? Even though the houses were beautiful, Gia
was happier with her small house surrounded by an acre of property
and large patches of prehistoric-looking woods scattered throughout the
neighborhood. "Why don't the houses face the street?"

"They face a walking trail." Savannah gestured toward a narrow gap
between houses. "It's a beautiful exercise trail that runs for over two-
hundred miles."

"Seriously?"

Savannah nodded and slowed to allow a group of young teens to cross
the street.

"Why haven't you ever brought me here before?"

"Gee, I don't know." Savannah raised an eyebrow. "With all the free time you have, and as much as you love exercising, I can't believe I didn't think of it sooner."

"All right, all right, no one likes a smart aleck."

"I wouldn't be too sure about that." She slowed even more as the lane narrowed. "I love a good wiseguy. As long as the sarcasm's not directed at me, of course."

"Of course." Gia leaned forward to see past Savannah to the trail, spotting what she could through the gaps between houses.

A woman with earphones jogged beside a golden retriever, its leash tied to a belt around her waist holding two water bottles. A young boy pedaled his two-wheeler with a man Gia assumed was his father running at his side with a big grin. A group of women strolled together, all pushing baby strollers and chatting amiably. Two teenage girls on skateboards weaved between them all, waiting for spaces to open up, careful not to come too close.

Picket fences, rows of hedges, and beautiful flower gardens surrounded houses facing each other from both sides of the trail.

"Dogs are allowed, as long as they're leashed, so we should take Thor one of these days and walk," Savannah said.

"I'd like that." Gia had never enjoyed walking. Then again, walking in New York City was a very different experience. Tons of people crowded the streets, packing together at each corner, then surging through the intersections the instant the lights changed to the tune of honking horns and the scent of corner street carts serving hot dogs and pretzels. "It seems so peaceful."

"It is. And there are tons of small parking lots at different sections of the trail where you can park, so you don't always have to walk the same section of trail."

The idea grew more and more appealing, and yet… "Why do I get the impression we're not here to enjoy the scenery?"

Savannah parked in a small dirt lot beside a park with exercise equipment and a playground. Children ran and laughed. Adults looked on from benches beside a lake with a fountain in its center. She climbed out, waited for Gia, and locked the car, then pocketed the key.

Though Gia was glad she'd finally come to her senses about locking the car up, Savannah's loss of trusting innocence saddened her.

"Come on."

Gia fell into step at her side as they crossed the park to the trail. "Where are we going?"

"In my dream, I was being carried by a man. All I could see of him was his shoulder. Everything else was just a blur. But when I looked past his shoulder, there was a clown. And the clown was laughing. Laughing, and laughing, and laughing. And then the screaming started in the background." She shivered. "It was terrifying."

"I bet." She took one of Savannah's ice-cold hands in hers and held it as they walked.

"But there was also something familiar about it, and when I was awake, in the daylight when it wasn't quite as scary, I was able to pull up an image in my mind."

They walked over an old wooden bridge overlooking a river. Gia scanned the shore for alligators. Seeing one from up there might be more fun than terror-inducing.

A gust of wind lifted her hair, and clouds built in front of the sun.

Savannah pointed to old, rusted, railroad tracks that ran along another bridge next to them. "At certain points, this trail follows the path of an abandoned railroad line that used to cross the state from one side to the other. Along the tracks are old warehouses. Many of them have large roll-up doors where the trains could pull up to them and load up their cars."

Savannah fell silent, walking hand in hand with Gia.

Gia figured she'd get to what she wanted eventually. In the meantime, she'd just enjoy the walk. They passed a yard where three peacocks roamed, and Gia stopped to take a picture. "Look how pretty they are."

"It is beautiful here. I used to walk here all the time with my pa when I was little."

"That's an awesome memory to have." She tucked the phone back into the waistband of her leggings and resumed walking.

"Yes, it is. There's another memory I have from walking this trail as well."

They came to a stone wall, ivy crawling up its sides, signaling the end of the neighborhood they'd been walking through. After crossing a wide street, the trail resumed, only now it was bordered on one side by woods and a lake, and on the other by a stretch of what appeared to be warehouses.

Thunder rumbled as dark storm clouds gathered overhead. A streak of lightning, not nearly far enough in the distance, shot from a cloud to the ground. "I think maybe we should go, Savannah."

"It won't be long now."

Boats dotted the gravel yard surrounding one of the warehouses, tractor-trailers in various stages of disrepair scattered around another. Savannah kept walking, her gaze focused straight ahead, her grip on Gia's hand tightening.

Thunder shook the ground. Gia looked up into angry, roiling clouds that were destined to open up at any moment. She'd never get used to the speed with which the storms developed in Florida.

Savannah stopped in front of one of the warehouses and pointed to it. On one of its doors, someone had painted a clown face, its eyes squinted, its mouth open wide in laughter.

"I knew it," Savannah whispered.

"Savannah?" Their peaceful stroll suddenly took on a more ominous tone.

"The motion sickness, the man's shoulder, even the sound of peacocks screaming in the distance." Savannah's breath hitched, her gaze glued to the image. "And the clown's face. Laughing. Always laughing. It's expression never changing. Its eyes flat. Dead. I always used to clutch Pa's hand a little tighter when we walked past this place."

A couple of fat raindrops plopped on Gia's head. One slid down her cheek.

"Come on." Savannah tugged her hand and started across the seemingly abandoned sand yard.

"What?" Gia pulled back. "Come on where?"

Savannah stopped and turned to face her. "I doubt anyone's here. It's been abandoned for years, so there's no reason for anyone to have stayed, now that I'm gone."

A few more raindrops pelted her. "What are you talking about?"

"I remember someone carrying me inside. I saw the clown's face over his shoulder." Savannah looked up at the warehouse. "This is where they kept me."

"I figured out that much, Savannah. The part I can't figure out is why you're moving toward it."

"I have to see inside."

"See what?" No way was Gia going in there. And neither was Savannah.

"I have to find some evidence that I'm right before I say anything to Hunt or Leo."

"No. Absolutely not. We are not going in there." This was definitely the kind of scenario Hunt had been talking about when he said, 'stay out of trouble,' and she had every intention of following that directive.

"Have I not gone along with more than one of your cockamamie schemes?"

Touché. Gia groaned.

Thunder rumbled, even as a bolt of lightning sizzled and cracked nearby. The sound of rain pounding against the uppermost tree branches reached her an instant before the deluge soaked them.

Gia grabbed Savannah's hand and ran toward the warehouse door.

Chapter Twenty

Gia eased the warehouse door open, wishing it was any door other than the one with the clown face on it. But that's where Savannah remembered being carried, so that's where they entered. Savannah was right; the clown was terrifying. At least the door wasn't locked, which saved them from having to stand out there, in front of the clown face, trying to decide what to do. She'd take her chances inside.

She crept forward, over the threshold, barely breathing. Blackness greeted her; the windowless interior made darker by the storm. She felt along the wall beside the door, found a switch, and flipped it up. Overhead lights flickered on, illuminating the entirety of the big open space. At least, it was easy enough to tell the building stood empty. "Now, what do you want to do?"

Savannah looked around. She took a deep breath and coughed. "I remember that smell, kind of like rotting vegetables. And something else too. Flowers. I remember smelling flowers."

Gia tried not to gag on the stench or the knowledge that Savannah had been held prisoner there. "You said that at the hospital too."

"Leo?"

Gia turned to find Savannah holding the phone pressed against her ear.

"I need you and Hunt to meet me somewhere right away." She squeezed her eyes closed and waited while he spoke.

Why was he talking for so long? She'd have expected him and Hunt to run out right away, no questions asked.

"Trust me, Leo, there probably isn't anything more important than this right now."

Gia held her breath.

"Thank you." She rattled off the address without giving him any more information, then hung up.

Okay, she could breathe again. "What was that all about?"

"They're on their way."

"I didn't expect you'd have to convince them to come." Gia's voice echoed through the steel structure. Rain pounded against the roof, leaking through to form puddles in several places.

Savannah kept the phone clutched against her chest, clinging to it like a lifeline. "Robert's interrogation is still going on, and they wanted to stay and watch."

"Watch? What do you mean watch?" Gia didn't trust anyone else to interrogate him. She'd seen Hunt interrogate witnesses before, and it was downright scary. If anyone could get to the bottom of why he'd broken into her house and harmed Thor, Hunt could. "Aren't they questioning him?"

"No." She took a step farther into the room. "Apparently, they've been removed from the case."

"What? Why?" They couldn't do that. Not when they might have the person who'd hurt Thor in custody.

"I'm not sure. Leo was pretty vague about what happened, only to say the interrogation was already underway when they arrived, and the chief had removed them from the case. Hunt was trying to convince the powers that be to allow them to witness the interrogation, but he didn't seem to be having much luck. Leo was completely frustrated."

Gia could definitely feel his pain.

Savannah started to move, slowly making her way along the front wall of the building.

Gia stuck to her side like glue. "Does anything look familiar?"

"You mean other than that horrifying clown that will haunt my nightmares forever?"

Bile burned up Gia's throat. "Yeah, other than that?"

"No." Savannah turned in a slow circle. "But I'll take my chances with a venomous snake over that clown any day."

"Please, don't tempt fate," Gia whispered and scanned the concrete floor. "Maybe we should wait outside."

"All right." Savannah kept moving forward in the opposite direction of the door they'd entered. "Just let me walk the perimeter once, and then we'll go out."

Gia nodded and walked beside her.

The concrete floor held years' worth of stains, though Gia couldn't make out what any of them might once have been. "Do you know what this warehouse was used for?"

"Not originally, but Pa told me they used to store carnival equipment that wasn't in use here." She led Gia up a stairway to a platform where a big, roll-up style garage door stood. A small doorway stood next to it, with a grate covered window in its center. Savannah pointed outside. "See the tracks down there?"

"Yeah." Gia looked past the tracks, searching for anyone showing the slightest bit of interest in the warehouse, but the area was deserted. She longed for the sunshine to return and bring the walkers back out in force. *Come on, Hunt, where are you?*

"The trains were able to pull off the main line into these areas, pull right up to the cargo doors, and pick up what they needed."

"Mmm-hmm. That would be convenient." She followed Savannah back down the stairs. "Do you know why the railroad doesn't run anymore?"

"Um." She tilted her head and frowned, as if listening for something. "Actually, I don't."

They skirted the perimeter of the building but didn't find anything. When they returned to the door, Gia stopped and waited, vibrating with nervous energy. "What do you want to do?"

Please, say you want to leave.

The rain seemed to have lightened up, pounding less violently against the roof than it had been when they'd entered.

Savannah sucked in a deep breath, then blew it out slowly. "We can wait outside now."

Oh, thank you! Gia resisted the urge to turn tail and run. "You're sure?"

She nodded. "I think I just needed to prove to myself that it's just a building. Hopefully, conquering my fear of it will allow me to finally get some sleep."

Gia reached for her hand. "I hope so."

"Thank you for coming with me. I know it couldn't have been easy for you, especially knowing all kinds of critters could have been holed up in here."

It wasn't the possibility of critters that tormented Gia, but the fact that someone had held Savannah there against her will. She squeezed Savannah's hand and kept that thought to herself. "Of course. I'll always be with you. Come on."

She led Savannah out the door they'd entered. By mutual, unspoken agreement, they stood on the trail with the rain pouring down on them rather than by the door.

Hunt's Jeep pulled up a few minutes later, its lights flashing.

"I didn't realize cars were allowed on the trail."

Savannah grinned. "They're not."

"Ahh..."

Leo hopped out of the passenger's side. "What's going on? What are you two doing out here?"

"Don't tell me; let me guess." Hunt rounded the front of the Jeep and looked up at the building. "You had a sudden attack of health consciousness after your near-death experience and thought it would be a good idea to begin your new exercise regime out here in the rain. At least, that had better be your explanation."

"To tell you the truth, I was gonna go with that, but then y'all went and ruined it by figuring it out." Savannah hooked a thumb over her shoulder without turning around. "Since I don't want to have to admit you were right, I figured I'd just go with this is the building whoever kidnapped me held me in. I remembered the clown on the door from when Pa and I used to walk here, but it didn't come back to me right away."

Hunt shook his head and lowered his gaze.

Leo clenched his teeth together so hard Gia thought they might shatter.

But, to their credit, neither of them gave Savannah a hard time. Neither of them said anything at all. Gia feared their silence might even be more dangerous as they started across the rain-soaked sand.

"Oh, and Hunt, for the record," Savannah called after him. "Apparently, no one likes a smart aleck."

She winked at Gia and climbed into the back seat of the Jeep to wait.

Gia slid in the other side, then reached between the seats to turn off the air conditioning. "It's freezing in here."

"Probably not if you weren't soaking wet." Savannah turned around and knelt on the seat, then rummaged through the back.

"True." Gia slumped back against the seat, her arms wrapped around her for warmth.

"Lucky for us, Hunt practically lives out of this thing." Savannah pulled two sweatshirts from the back. She sniffed them both, then handed one to Gia.

"Thanks." She pulled the black hoodie over her head and kept her hands inside the too-long sleeves to warm them. "So. Now what?"

Savannah shrugged into a dark green zip-up sweatshirt and rolled the sleeves three times. "I figured I'd better go into the office and let Angelina know I'm giving my notice. If you want, you can help me clean out my desk too. I just want to get it done and over with, so I don't have to go back there."

"Okay, then. We could do that." Though she'd prefer to avoid another run-in with Ward the weasel. "What about Ward?"

Savannah shrugged, the too-big sweatshirt making her seem even more delicate. "What about him?"

Gia kept her head against the back of the seat, her eyes beginning to grow heavy as Hunt's scent cocooned her, bringing a sense of comfort and safety. Oddly, she felt safer sitting there in the back of Hunt's Jeep with Savannah right next to her than she had since Savannah first went missing. "Do you still want to try to get into his computer?"

Savannah picked at one of the rhinestones on the tip of her nail, and it popped off the bottom point of the heart. "If he had anything to do with this, I want to know. So, yes, if we could find a way, I'd like to get into his computer and find out where all his money's coming from."

"And what about the sniper who came after us the last time we were at the office?"

Savannah tapped her nail against her phone for a minute; a habit Gia was beginning to think of as her thinking tap. She snapped her fingers. "I've got it."

"Got what?"

She held up a finger and scrolled for a number, then hit send and switched the call to speaker.

"Hello?" A woman's voice answered.

"Angelina? Hi, it's Savannah."

"Oh, Savannah, how are you? I'm so sorry I haven't had a chance to call you back. Tempest did give me the message, but I've been a bit swamped trying to sort through what clients you're currently working with."

The comment sounded suspiciously like a reprimand, and Gia bristled. What did the woman expect? Savannah had just been released from the hospital. Surely, she was entitled to a few days off.

"Actually," Savannah said, "that's what I wanted to talk to you about. I'm going to be taking a leave of absence for a while."

Angelina remained quiet.

"I'd like to stop by the office later tonight, if that's okay. I still have my key, and I don't really feel up to running into everyone and having to answer questions." She looked at Gia.

Gia nodded her encouragement. As far as she was concerned, Savannah needed to get out of that office and cut ties as quickly as possible. And going in after-hours would alleviate the potential of running into Ward.

"I'd like to clean out my personal items from my desk, and I could leave you a list of all of my clients and what stage of the process each of them is in."

"That would be very helpful, thank you." Finally, Angelina's voice softened. Gia couldn't fault her too much; she was probably just overwhelmed. "That would make it much easier for me to reassign everything. I am sorry to lose you, though. You're a great agent, and I do hope you'll return to us as soon as you're able."

"Thank you, Angelina, I'd like that. I just…I need to work through a few things first before I'll feel comfortable showing houses again." She ran one nail tip around the edge of the phone between the screen and the case.

"Of course, I completely understand. I have to admit, I showed a house to a new client this afternoon, and I was more than a bit nervous walking into an empty house with him."

"I'm sorry. That certainly does make doing the job difficult."

"At best," Angelina said. "Anyway, you feel free to come in and get your belongings whenever you're comfortable. And you can leave the list on my desk. If it's okay, I'll stop in to your friend Gia's café one day over the weekend and pick up the key."

"That would be perfect, thank you again, Angelina. It's been a pleasure working for you, and I appreciate your understanding." After saying good-bye, she hung up. "Now we have permission to go in after hours and permission to access Ward's files."

Gia stared at her wide-eyed. "That's how you interpreted that conversation?"

"Okay, fine, I have permission to access my files on the computer, but if I happen to see what's in Ward's, oh well. At least, it won't be considered breaking and entering. Probably."

Chapter Twenty-One

Gia dialed Alfie's number. Their plan hinged on him saying yes, since neither Gia nor Savannah had any computer hacking skills, or any real computer skills at all. She held her breath until he answered.

Alfie answered with, "Hi, Gia, how are you?"

"I'm doing okay. How about you?" It was good to hear his voice. Alfie had lost his best friend several months before, and he still had a hard time, sometimes not coming around for a couple of weeks at a time.

"Things are pretty good," he said.

"How's Babe?" Alfie had adopted the third kitten from the litter Thor had saved.

"Don't tell her I said so, but she's a terror." The affection in his voice belied the complaint, and he laughed, something she'd like to hear more often. "She starts running around the house randomly like someone flipped a switch, crawls onto my keyboard and stretches out for a nap while I'm trying to work, and steals my comfiest chair every time I get up for something."

"Sounds just like Klondike."

"It's amazing, isn't it?" His grin came through the line as if he was standing in front of her.

Gia needed to make more time to spend with him. She missed him. "It certainly is."

"I wanted to stop in to see Savannah, but I had a wicked tight deadline to meet, and I barely made it. How is she?"

"She's doing okay, as well as could be expected, anyway. She's going to come to work for me in the café."

"Oh, that's great. I'm so happy she's okay,"

"Me too."

"And I will definitely stop in this week."

"That would be nice, Alfie. It would be great to see you." While she enjoyed chatting with Alfie, she didn't have the time to spare at the moment. Hunt and Leo should be out any time now, and she didn't want them to overhear her conversation. If she told them their plan, she and Savannah would have to defy them when they said no.

"Listen, Gia, I'm sorry."

"Sorry?" Had she missed something? She might have zoned out for a moment. "Sorry for what?"

"I wanted to come in, to be there for you when Savannah was missing, like you were for me when I needed you. I know you must have needed all the comfort and encouragement you could get, and I figure I'm an awful friend, but I...I just couldn't." He sniffed and blew his nose. "It brought back too many painful memories."

"Oh, Alfie, you have nothing to be sorry for. I completely understand."

"You're sure?"

"Of course, I am." Her heart still ached for his loss.

"Thank you for understanding. I don't know how I would have gotten through these past months without all of you." He sniffled again. "Anyway, with everything that's going on, I don't imagine you called just to chat, so what's up?"

Now that she had him on the phone, she felt kind of bad asking him to go with them. She didn't want to get him in trouble, but they really needed the information. "Do you know anything about computer hacking?"

"Of course, I do." He laughed. "There's not much I don't know about computers. What do you need hacked?"

An idea came to her, a way to get into Ward's computer without having to involve Alfie directly. "Savannah needs to check something on a coworker's computer, but it's got a password, and she can't get in. Is there any way you could talk us through hacking it?"

Alfie laughed so hard she thought he was going to rupture something. When he got himself under control, he sighed. "Ahh, Gia. I love you dearly—and thank you for that; I haven't laughed that hard in months—but I've seen you on a computer. It's painful to watch. Why don't you just tell me where to meet you? I'll get you in, and then I'll take off. No questions asked."

"I don't want to get you in any trouble."

"I'm assuming this has something to do with Savannah's disappearance?"

"Yes, it does. At least, we think it does. We're trying to find out." She was careful to be completely honest with him. They were asking him to risk not only Hunt's wrath, but possible legal recriminations.

"Then I'm in. And don't worry about it; it's not the first thing I've ever hacked. And since I enjoy the challenge so much, it certainly won't be the last."

Hmm...maybe he wasn't as fragile as she thought. "Thank you, Alfie. I can't tell you how much I appreciate it. And when you do come into the cafe, breakfast is on me."

She gave him the address, told him to meet them in about an hour and wait in the car for her to come get him, then said good-bye.

Savannah sat staring out the window. "He's such a sweetheart."

"Yes, he is."

She shifted in her seat. "What do you think is taking Hunt and Leo so long?"

"I don't know, but I was thinking of going in to look for them. I mean, the place was empty. What could they possibly be doing in there?"

Savannah's phone rang, and she frowned at the display. She started to put the phone against her ear, then pushed back her still wet hair, hit the speaker button, and laid it on the center console instead. "Hey, Joey, what's up?"

"Pa asked me to call you and ask if you borrowed any of the rainy-day money," Joey blurted without so much as a hello.

Savannah frowned. "Of course not. Why would I do that without asking him?"

"He doesn't mind if you did. He didn't even want me to call at first so you wouldn't feel bad if you had taken it, and he said you could have all of it if you needed it."

"Joey," Savannah snapped, "I said I didn't take it. Now, what's going on?"

He sighed. "Pa didn't feel like making dinner, and you know how he feels about my cooking, so he told me to take some money from the jar and go pick up pizza from that new place down the road from Gia's café."

"Okay, and?" Savannah massaged her temples.

"And it's gone."

She froze. "The money or the jar?"

"Just the money; the jar's still in the cupboard."

That ruled out her father having misplaced it, although he could have spent it and forgotten.

Gia looked out the window at the abandoned warehouse, avoiding looking at the clown face that would certainly give her her own share of nightmares. What was taking Hunt and Leo so long?

"How much is missing?"

"All of it. About four hundred dollars, give or take. He thinks."

"All right. Okay." Savannah leaned forward and looked out the windshield toward the warehouse. "Is Pa okay?"

"He's fine, just concerned about you." He hesitated for a minute. "Are you okay?"

"I am, Joey. I'm fine. Good, actually. Do you have money to go get Pa's pizza?"

"Yeah, no problem. I'll take care of it."

The rain had slowed to a drizzle, and Gia again considered getting out and going in search of Hunt and Leo.

"All right, I'll be by later on. I have to go to the office and clean out my desk. I'm going to be working for Gia at the café for a while."

"Oh, wow. That's awesome."

"Thanks. You take care of Pa, and I'll be there when I can. I'm just waiting for Hunt and Leo to come out, and I'll let them know what happened."

"Okay, thanks, Savannah."

"You bet. Give Pa a kiss for me."

"How about I just relay the message?" He disconnected, cutting off his laughter.

Savannah just stared at the phone as if it held some kind of answers. "What do you think is going on?"

"I have no idea, but that makes cash missing from the café, my house, and your house." Gia didn't want to voice her opinion, that someone they knew had to have taken it. She didn't want to upset Savannah further, but what other option was there?

Savannah looked up at Gia. "We have five dogs, Gia. Five. Big dogs. That money did not walk out on its own, and no stranger walked into that house."

Seemed Savannah had come to the same conclusion on her own.

Hunt and Leo ran toward the Jeep and hopped in.

Hunt scrubbed a hand back and forth over his wet hair, shaking water everywhere.

"Hey," Gia yelled. She'd just begun to dry out and warm up. "You're worse than Thor."

Hunt looked in the rearview mirror and opened his mouth, but stopped mid-retort. "What's wrong?"

"Someone stole Pa's rainy-day money," Savannah said.

"What?"

"Joey called, and he said Pa's rainy-day money is gone." Savannah gripped both front seats and slid forward. "You do realize that's too much of a coincidence, right?"

"Yeah, I do." He shifted into gear. "Where did you park?"

Savannah told him.

"Are you coming with us?" He glanced in the side mirror.

"Actually, I have a couple of things to do, and then I'll be there."

"Fine." He made a U-turn in the middle of the empty trail. "I'll drop you off and go out there now. If you two can stay out of trouble long enough, that is."

"I'm going to the office to clean out my desk, and I have to leave a list of my clients and where they're at in the buying process for Angelina to reassign them."

Hunt narrowed his eyes at her in the rearview mirror. "And that's it?"

"Pretty much." Savannah deftly switched gears. "What took you guys so long in there?"

Hunt pulled into the parking lot next to Savannah's Mustang and shifted into park but left the Jeep running. "I wanted to make sure we did a thorough search before we lost access."

A ripple of shock ran through Gia. How could the chief have removed them from the case? And why? Also, how could she have forgotten? "What did you find?"

Hunt pulled a plastic bag from his pocket and held it up. It contained a gold Rolex with a broken leather band. "I found this on the ground right outside the back door."

Gia turned the bag so she could see the face of the watch better. Even through the wet mud caked on the watch and smeared inside the bag, she recognized it. "I've seen that watch before."

"Where?" Hunt asked.

"Frankie Esposito was wearing it when he came into the café."

Leo looked something up on his phone, then held it out to Hunt. "I guess that's no surprise, considering Francis Esposito owns the warehouse where it was found."

"Yeah, but..." Gia shook her head. Something didn't add up. "I saw the watch on Frankie's wrist after Savannah was found, when he came in to apologize."

Hunt stuffed the bag back into his pocket, handed Leo's phone back, and opened his door. "I'll check into it."

Gia started to get out, but stopped when Hunt's phone rang.

"Hang on a sec; I have to answer this."

She flopped back against the seat but left the door open, enjoying the sunshine peeking from behind the clouds. A rainbow crossed the entire sky. She'd never seen rainbows like she did in Florida before. Their beauty could brighten even the darkest days.

Hunt hit the button for the Bluetooth. "Hey, Regina, what's going on?"

"Listen to me," she whispered urgently. "Everyone is supposed to keep their mouths shut, and I'll get fired if Chief Shaw finds out I called you, but there's been another arrest warrant issued in Savannah's case."

"Who's it for?"

"Hunt, I want you to promise me you'll let the detectives take care of it."

"I'm sorry I can't do that, Regina." He clenched both fists tightly around the steering wheel. "But I can promise to keep your name out of it."

"Hang on." She moved away from the phone. "Yeah, tell him I'll be right there. Hunt, you still there?"

"Yeah."

"I have to go, so I guess that'll have to be good enough. Robert Clarke is looking to make a deal, and he's probably going to get it. The lawyers are hashing it out now. He admitted to writing Paige's number on the pad, but he says he just ripped off the top page or two and handed it to someone because they asked for it. He claims he didn't write the note found with Thor."

"Who'd he give it to?"

"He also admits to passing the sedative given to Thor, or at least a sedative, but he swears he didn't know what it was going to be used for."

"Regina." Hunt's tone held a note of warning. "Who did he pass the number and sedative on to?"

"Hey, Leo, are you there with Hunt?"

"I'm here, Regina," Leo answered, but he didn't appear to be any calmer than Hunt.

"Good, make sure he doesn't run off and do anything stupid."

Leo looked over at Hunt. "I'll do my best."

They all knew chances were whatever stupidity Hunt ran off into, Leo would be running beside him.

"Give me the name, Regina," Hunt bit out between clenched teeth.

She sighed. "Michael Mills."

Chapter Twenty-Two

"There has to be some mistake," Savannah said, as she had at least a hundred times since Hunt and Leo had dropped them off in the parking lot and gone to look for Michael.

Again, Gia agreed. Michael had been acting strangely, but she found it hard to believe he'd have had anything to do with Savannah's kidnapping or the attack on Thor. Though she couldn't deny it, him having stolen the money did make sense. Her blood boiled just thinking that he might have betrayed her and Thor's trust, gone into her home, and hurt Thor. But she'd already told Hunt she wouldn't press charges if that turned out to be the case. Whatever was going on, if Michael did have any involvement, he was family, and he'd need help.

Savannah also refused to press charges if it turned out he was involved in her kidnapping, though her face had been purple with rage when she'd said it.

Hunt had promised he'd do his best for him, though it had taken a lot of convincing, and he stopped short of promising not to punch him in the mouth, but it wasn't up to them if the D.A. chose to bring charges. Especially if it turned out he had been involved in Buster and LuAnne's murders. Hopefully, he and Leo would get to Michael before the detectives did.

Gia pulled into the parking lot across the street from the real estate office and pulled up beside Alfie's blue MINI Cooper. "Do you want to park here or go into the lot?"

Savannah studied both lots for a moment. "Let's park close to the front door, so I can put my stuff right in the car. It would be too much to carry across the street."

"Sure thing." Gia gestured for Alfie to come get in her car.

He nodded and unfolded himself from the driver's seat, then leaned back in and grabbed a bag. He got into the back seat and patted the black duffel bag. "Got everything I need right here."

"I...uh..." Gia studied the bag. "Didn't realize hacking was so involved."

"No worries. I'm sure I have a lot of stuff I won't need, but better safe than sorry, right?" He grinned like a kid on Christmas morning. They may have unwittingly unleashed a monster.

Savannah shot her a sidelong glance, obviously sharing her concern.

Hoping not to draw attention by leaving the car parked haphazardly, Gia parked in the closest parking space to the real estate office's front door.

Alfie rummaged through his bag.

Gia looked at Savannah. "Are you sure you want to do this now?"

"Yup. Positive." She appeared perfectly calm and more determined than Gia had seen her since her ordeal.

That alone was worth the risk. "Come on, then, let's go."

"Will I be needing this?" Alfie held up a black knit ski mask.

"Uh..." *Oh, boy.* "I think you'll be okay without it."

Savannah just grinned. "Who knows? Maybe he's on to something."

When they entered the office, Savannah called out. Silence greeted them, but they ran through the office anyway, peeking in Angelina's office, the meeting rooms, cubicles, and bathrooms—even a small storage closet.

"I think it's safe to say we're alone." Savannah pointed out Ward's computer to Alfie, then leaned over his shoulder to watch him work.

Gia stood behind his other shoulder with one eye on the computer and the other on the front door. They'd locked it behind them, but she felt trapped with all of the blinds closed. It not only blocked anyone's view inside, but also blocked her view of the parking lot. She'd never see anyone coming in time to get out from behind Ward's desk and look innocent.

Alfie opened his bag and pulled out a pair of thin black rubber gloves.

Actually, that wasn't a bad idea. "Do you have any more of those in there?"

"Absolutely. I believe in always being prepared." He handed her and Savannah each a pair. He cracked his knuckles, wiggled his fingers, and went to work. Two minutes later, they were searching through Ward's files.

"Alfie, that was downright impressive." Gia shook her head, amazed by skills she could never hope to possess.

"Thanks, but that was pretty easy. I was kind of hoping for more of a challenge." He typed a couple of commands. "What do you want to know?"

"We can probably take it from here, if you want to go." Savannah straightened and stepped back so he could stand.

He whirled on her. "Go? Why would I want to go? I can get whatever you're looking for a whole lot faster than you can."

"You're sure?" Gia asked.

"Are you kidding me? This is the most fun I've had in years." He turned and bent back over the keyboard.

She really was going to have to make more time to hang out with him. Maybe he'd enjoy kayaking with her and Trevor. She'd already made Savannah a fan; maybe she could do the same for Alfie.

"Now, shoo." Alfie waved over his shoulder. "You two go do whatever else you have to do, so we can get out of here. If I find anything suspicious, I'll call you."

Gia wasn't sure leaving him was a good idea. "How will you know what you're looking for?"

He rolled his eyes. "I'm an information analyst. I'll know exactly what belongs here and what doesn't."

Gia looked to Savannah. It was her call.

"Mostly, I want to know how many houses Ward's sold and how much he's made in commissions, if you can find that out." She shrugged and moved away. "Thanks, Alfie."

He nodded, but his full attention was already on the computer as his fingers flew over the keys so fast Gia expected to see smoke.

Savannah unlocked the file cabinet in her cubicle and started sorting through files. "Could you put these on the desk, please? I'll get everything together for Angelina first, then we can clean out the desk and get out of here."

"Sure thing." Gia piled the files in the center of the desk. She lifted a picture of her and Savannah from the desk, their heads bent together, both of them smiling conspiratorially. Hunt had taken it at a family barbeque. It was one of Gia's favorite pictures of them.

"Gia?"

She lowered the picture back into its spot. "Yeah, sorry. I got a little sidetracked."

Savannah handed her another stack of files, then took one of her own from atop the cabinet. She sat behind the desk and started sorting through folders, opening them, and jotting notes on a legal pad.

With nothing to do, Gia wandered. She walked past Tempest's desk, noted the garbage pail full of used tissues. Had Tempest known what was going on with Michael? Is that why she'd passed the note? To shift any focus to Ward and away from Michael? Had she really even found the note on Ward's desk? Maybe it was Michael's, and she'd lied about where she found it and given it to them to divert attention from him.

Savannah laid a hand on Gia's shoulder from behind. "Everything you're thinking right now—forget it. He didn't do this. I know my brother, and he doesn't always make the best choices, but he's a hard worker, and he loves his family. And you and Thor are family. He'd never do anything to hurt someone he cares about. Especially me."

"I want to believe that. I really do." Guilt wedged itself in her heart.

"Then believe it. I don't know what's happening with Michael. I admit he's been acting weird, and I thought he might know more than he's saying, but he didn't kill Buster. My brother might be a lot of things, but he's no killer. Of that, I'm absolutely certain. The rest, well, I guess we'll see what happens."

Gia nodded and wiped tears from her cheeks. When she'd needed support, when other people, supposed friends, had abandoned her amid a host of allegations related to her ex's financial corruption, Savannah had stood by her side with the same conviction she now used to defend Michael. Gia would give him that same faith as well. It was the least she could do for Savannah.

"Besides, if Tempest did lie about where she found the note, why would Ward have acted so weird about it? And why would someone have taken a shot at us?"

Gia shook off any further misgivings. "You're right."

Savannah's answering smile was a little uncertain. "There was no reason for Ward to act like he did if he wasn't concerned about something."

"Come on." Gia stared at the closed blinds again. They were taking too long. "Let's get this done and get out of here. Are you done with the files?"

"I am. I just need some help collecting them and carrying them into Angelina's office."

"That's going to have to wait a minute." Keeping his attention fixed on Ward's computer screen, Alfie waved them over. "I've got something."

Gia and Savannah each leaned over one of his shoulders and looked at what had him so excited. Maybe it was because she wasn't a computer whiz, but Gia had no clue what she was looking at. "What is it?"

Alfie ran a gloved finger along a couple of lines, careful not to make contact with the screen. "If I had to guess, I'd say it's a list of people and companies your friend Ward is syphoning money from."

"Syphon—" Savannah's breath whooshed out. "I don't know what I expected to find, but it wasn't this."

Gia searched the list for any familiar names. "I can't believe he'd leave something so incriminating on his work computer."

Alfie winced.

"Alfie?"

"Well… I didn't find anything in his work files, and it seemed like you guys really needed something, so I sort of hacked his personal records remotely."

She didn't know whether to yell at him or hug him. "We won't be able to pass any of this on to the police, since we don't have a warrant."

"No," he agreed. "But I can tell you what he's doing if you want to know. Then maybe we can find a way to catch him legitimately."

"Oh, we definitely want to know." Savannah's eyes glistened with anger.

"Okay." Alfie pointed out names and numbers as he spoke. "All of the people he's stolen from have been past clients. It seems he gets most of the well to do clients who work with the agency. I believe he's probably getting their account information from the loan documents, but that's mostly just a guess."

"It does make sense." Going forward, Gia would think twice before giving out any financial information.

"Then, he routinely syphons small amounts of money from all of them."

"And no one has noticed?"

Alfie shrugged. "Even if they did, it's not likely they'd be able to figure out who was doing it with the way he has it all set up. I'd say some figured out what was happening, though, because occasionally an account drops off. I would assume the owner figured out they were being robbed, transferred their assets, and closed out the accounts."

"Question is, how is he always the one to land the big deals?" Savannah muttered half to herself.

"I'd say it has something to do with the thirty-five percent of his profits that are being wired into an offshore account that belongs to Angelina Lombardo."

Savannah gasped. "That rat."

Knowing Angelina was involved made Gia fear for Savannah's safety even more. Ward was one thing; the Esposito family was something else entirely. "Will anyone be able to tell you hacked in?"

"Not likely."

"If you were able to figure it out that quickly, why wouldn't anyone else?"

"Because I already knew I was looking for something on this specific person, and I hacked into a computer he's used to access personal information before. If I was just looking for an unknown entity, I might not have been able to find him. And definitely not as quickly. He's good, Gia. Or someone working with him is."

That's what she was afraid of. "I don't know what to say, Alfie, thank you."

"You're welcome." His fingers flew over the keyboard again, and everything disappeared.

"Wait. We didn't write down any of the information." There had to be a way to at least warn the people he was robbing, even if just by anonymous notes.

"I took a screenshot of all of it and sent it to a random email account I set up. I can give you copies when you need them."

"Alfie, you're a genius."

His eyes widened. "You're just figuring that out?"

She laughed.

"Now, I'm going to get out of here so you guys can finish what you're doing. I'll wait in the parking lot across the street and call you if anyone pulls into the lot."

"Are you sure, Alfie?"

"Positive." He stood, pulled out a granola bar from his bag, then hefted the bag over his shoulder and grinned. "Hacking makes me hungry."

Gia let him out with a promise to call and keep him updated and locked the door behind him. She turned and leaned back against the door. "Now what?"

"Now, we pile all of this on Angelina's desk, collect my belongings, and go see Pa." She lifted a pile of folders. "Then I'm going to bite the bullet and tell Hunt and Leo what we found and let them sort it out."

Gia grabbed another pile of folders. "Are you okay?"

"I'm fine. But right now, Pa's upset someone stole from him, Joey's nervous and upset because Pa's upset, Michael is..." She lowered her gaze. "I don't know what Michael's gotten himself into, but from what we've found here, and knowing Angelina's involved, I'd say it's a safe bet whatever Michael had going on with the Clarkes had nothing to do with what happened to me if any of the Espositos were involved."

Gia couldn't argue that. The chances of the Clarkes and the Espositos being involved in the same thing were probably slim to none.

Savannah set the files on Angelina's desk, then ticked off points on her fingers. "First, Tempest finds a suspicious note on Ward's desk with the day and time I'd be at the Oakley Manor House. Then we find out the warehouse I was held against my will in belongs to Frankie Esposito, who coincidentally lost his watch there after wearing it into the café to see if I remembered anything about who took me. On top of that, Angelina, who is one of Frankie Esposito's cousins, is somehow involved with whatever's going on with Ward."

That was a mountain of circumstantial evidence that was hard to ignore.

"And, don't forget, we were leaving this office after mentioning the note to Ward when a sniper took not only one, but several shots at us."

"That's all true."

Savannah tilted her head. "And yet you're not convinced?"

Was she? Kind of. But there was one gaping hole in Savannah's theory. While Ward and Angelina had both been in the café the day the money went missing from the register, the Espositos did not break into her house and hurt Thor. How could they? He didn't know them, and everyone agreed he probably wouldn't have let them in. But, even if he did, Savannah's five dogs most definitely did not let one of the Espositos, a stranger, walk into that house. Not to mention, since his wife's death, Savannah's dad rarely left home…Except for the day Savannah went missing. He'd been at the café that day. "How often does your dad use the rainy-day money?"

"Almost never. Why?"

"So, it's conceivable someone took that money the same day they took the money from my house and the café, but he didn't notice it missing until today?"

"Sure." Savannah placed the last of the piles on Angelina's desk, put the notes she'd written on top, and leaned a hip against the corner of the desk. "Why do you ask?"

"I'm not sure. Let me think about it for a few minutes." She definitely didn't want to hurl unfounded accusations without thinking them through completely.

Savannah stood. "I'm gonna go find a box to put my stuff in so we can get out of here."

Gia's phone rang, and they both jumped.

Savannah pointed a finger at her, her other hand pressed against her chest. "Haven't you learned your lesson about leaving that ringer turned on when we're up to no good by now?"

She looked at the screen. Marie Winston's name popped up.

Savannah looked over her shoulder. "Is it Alfie?"

"No. It's something I should have remembered to do before now. "Why don't you give Alfie a call and let him know it's safe to leave now. Even if someone does come in at this point, we're not doing anything that's not legitimate."

"Sure thing." She took out the phone and made the call as she left Angelina's office.

Gia answered Marie's call. "Hi, Marie, I'm sorry I haven't gotten back to you by now."

"Oh, no problem at all. I'm sorry to call so late, but you said you were going to make a decision by the weekend, so I just wanted to thank you for considering me for the position and let you know I found something else."

"Oh, okay." Relief rushed through her. She'd liked Marie and probably would have ended up hiring her if she hadn't canceled her other interviews and given the position to Savannah. "Thank you for letting me know. I wish you the best, and if things don't work out, you can always give me a call."

"Thank you, I'll do that."

Gia hung up, turned the ringer to silent, now that they wouldn't need a warning call from Alfie, and wandered around the room. The office was large, the desk in its center imposing. She could imagine the authoritative woman sitting behind it, wielding her power. Everything on the desk was lined up in perfect order, including a row of Post-it notes along the top of her blotter. On the notes were abbreviations just like those on the note Tempest had given her; 125 EHR TH 2, MD W 10, and so on. The handwriting appeared to be the same. Maybe the note didn't belong to Ward, after all. But then how had it ended up on his desk? Or had Tempest taken it from Angelina and lied?

Bookshelves lined the lower half of one wall. Framed certificates and awards hung on the wall above it; Angelina's real estate license, a community achievement award, a letter from a first-grade baseball team thanking her for their new uniforms.

Framed photographs displayed on the top shelf were more personal, portraying a softer version of Angelina; a picture of her by the shore, smiling as she reached toward a dolphin swimming close by, another of her sitting by a campfire, bundled in a blanket, toasting a marshmallow. Gia had a hard time convincing herself the woman in these pictures and the Angelina she'd met were one and the same.

Another picture caught her attention. She picked it up to look closer, mentally thanking Alfie for remembering to bring gloves. The photo showed Angelina on what appeared to be a platform in the top of a tree, a rope tied to her waist, her arms held high in the air. Other people dotted platforms and bridges in the background, seemingly looking toward her and cheering.

Gia called out to Savannah in the other room.

Savannah poked her head into the office. "What's up?"

"Do you know where this was taken?" Gia turned the picture so she could see it.

"Yeah, it's one of those tree-top obstacle course places. I don't know which one; there's a number of them around here. Why?"

She handed the picture to Savannah. "Look closer."

Savannah held it close, studying it carefully. "Do you think this means Angelina is the sniper who shot at us, supposedly from a tree?"

"Possibly, but look closer at the people in the background."

She did as instructed but shook her head a minute later and handed the picture back to Gia. "Am I supposed to recognize someone?"

"Maybe not, I don't think you were in the café when she came in, but this woman right here..." She pointed to a woman standing on the next platform over from Angelina, looking on with a big grin. "Is Paige Clarke."

Chapter Twenty-Three

Gia walked up to Savannah's front porch with more questions than answers. At least, Savannah was out of the office and wouldn't have to go back any time soon. She hefted the box of stuff from the office onto her hip to hold the door open for Savannah.

"Hey, a little help here," Savannah called to her brother, Joey, in greeting.

"Just a sec," Joey called from where he sat in an armchair, his feet propped on an ottoman, frantically pounding at a video game controller with his gaze riveted on the TV screen where some kind of spacecraft swirled around his avatar in a dizzying array.

Mr. Mills hurried into the small foyer. "Here, give me that."

Savannah swung the box out of his way and kissed his cheek. "Don't worry about it. The box is light; I'm just giving Joey a hard time."

He smiled and hugged Savannah and then Gia. "Put that stuff down and come on into the kitchen. There's plenty of pizza left if you want me to heat it up. I had Joey get extra when he said you were stopping by."

"Thanks, Pa. Let me just put this stuff in my room, and I'll be right there."

"Of course, of course. Take your time."

Gia followed Savannah halfway down the hallway to her room, though she used it more for storage than anything else, now that she spent most of her time at Gia's.

Savannah dropped her box in the corner and gestured for Gia to do the same. She took two small plants out of the box. "The rest can wait. I'll put these in the kitchen until we move back into your house."

A pile of clean laundry had been dumped on the bed; the dryer sheets still clung to a sweatshirt. Gia picked one up to fold it. "You do know you can bring your stuff to our house, right?"

"Our house?" She grinned. "I do, thank you, but I don't have the heart to tell Pa I'm moving out. I know he knows on some level, but as long as I don't clear out my room, it's not the same."

Gia got that. Mr. Mills spent most of his time in his room, sitting by the window, overlooking a towering oak tree he fondly remembered as his wife's favorite. No matter how much his kids tried to get him to go out and do things, keep busy, he almost always refused. He said he spent enough time away from his wife while continuing to raise his children alone; now, he chose to spend his time with his Sara, immersed in memories of their shared life together.

"Come on." Savannah snatched a pair of leggings from Gia's hands mid-fold and tossed them onto the bed. "We can do that later. I want to visit with Pa for a while. Plus, I think Alfie might be right; hacking does make you hungry."

Savannah took the plants to the kitchen, watered them, and set them on the windowsill above the sink. "Sit, Gia. Relax."

She took a seat at the table.

"Oh, that's nice." Mr. Mills set two cans of Diet Pepsi on the table for Savannah and Gia. "Your mama, she loved plants, you know."

"I do; I remember, Pa." Savannah pulled out a chair and sat. "She used to take me out to the garden with her, but I spent more time making mud pies than learning anything about gardening."

Somehow, that didn't surprise Gia.

"You used to come in covered from head to toe in mud." He laughed at the memory.

Savannah laughed with him.

"There's pizza in the oven. I put in four slices, so I hope you're hungry." He set out two plates. "I'll be in my room if you ladies need me."

"Aww, Pa, why don't you sit with us for a bit?" Savannah took his hand and pointed to the chair next to her.

Though Gia and Savannah had both grown up without their mothers, Savannah had the good fortune to have a father who adored her, a good family man who'd raised a close family who truly cared about each other.

Gia checked the pizza. Warm enough. If Savannah was going to eat something, she wanted to get it in front of her before she changed her mind. She used a potholder to pull the tray out and set it on a trivet in the center of the table. "Would you like a slice, Mr. Mills or something to drink?"

Mr. Mills clasped her hand in both of his. "Gia, dear, when are you going to stop calling me Mr. Mills and start calling me Pa?"

"I…" A well of emotions flooded her.

"You're family, dear, not company."

"Thank you, Pa." she managed to whisper past the lump in her throat.

"Sure thing." He patted their still joined hands. "Now, be a dear, and fetch me a plate. Seems I'm hungrier than I realized."

"You got it." Grateful for the moment alone to gather her wits, she turned her back and went to the cabinet for a plate. While Gia's brothers had welcomed her, and Joey was indeed a brother to Gia, Mr. Mills had always remained a bit distant. Now, he'd shown her more kindness than her own father ever had. She took a deep breath and grabbed a dish from the cabinet.

"Is that pizza I smell?" Joey dropped onto a chair. "Grab me a plate too, will ya, Gia?"

"Joey!" Savannah punched his arm.

"What?" He pointed at Gia. "She's already standing at the cabinet."

"It's fine, Savannah. I don't mind." Truthfully, she'd do anything for her adopted family. And, at the moment, she was feeling particularly generous. She handed him a plate and shoved a few more slices in the oven to heat. She'd seen Joey devour a whole pie by himself on more than one occasion.

"Hello? Anyone home?" Footsteps pounded down the hallway, and Michael strode into the kitchen. "What's going on? I smell pizza; is there any left?"

Gia recovered first. "Sure, you can have one of the slices on the table, and I just put more in the oven."

"You might want to add a few more from the other box." Hunt stood in the doorway, shoulder leaning against the doorframe, arms folded across his chest.

Leo stood at his side, cutting off Michael's only escape route.

Michael looked back and forth between them, then at Joey. When his gaze finally landed on Savannah, he flopped back in the chair and lowered his face into his hands.

"Hey, Pa, how are you?" Hunt reached across the table to shake hands with him while Leo grabbed a couple of folding chairs and placed them around the table.

"Doing okay." He shook Hunt's hand then returned his grip to Savannah's. "Now that my little girl's back."

"Joey." Hunt patted Joey's shoulder on the way past, then took a seat across from Michael.

Savannah kissed Pa's temple and got up to help Gia. Together, they doled out pizza, served drinks, and cleared everything once everyone finished. By unspoken agreement, and despite numerous glares across the table, no one said a word to Michael until Pa had finished eating and bid them all good-night.

"He had a good time tonight, don't you think?" Joey asked Savannah, as Pa shuffled through the doorway toward his room.

"He did. He seemed happier than he has in a long time. Who knows? Maybe he's ready to come out and join the world a little more," Savannah answered with her gaze narrowed on Michael.

The instant he heard Pa's bedroom door close, Michael bounded to his feet. "Well, this sure has been fun and all, but—"

"Sit down, Michael." Hunt stood and faced him, his expression rock hard.

Michael stood his ground, folded his arms across his chest, and tucked his trembling hands beneath them. "What's your problem, man?"

Hunt's fists clenched. "Do not make me put you back in that chair, Michael."

"I'd like to see you try, cous." Michael's grin only provoked Hunt further.

He grabbed the edge of the table, and Gia had a vision of him tossing it across the room.

She jumped up and out of the way.

Savannah followed, retreating to the doorway with Gia.

"Do you need to go get some air?" Leo jumped to his feet and shoved Hunt back. "I can do this myself if you can't handle it."

Hunt's breathing came in harsh gasps; his jaw clenched tight. He shook his head. "Nah, man, I've got it."

Leo patted Hunt's chest and turned on Michael. "I really suggest you just sit down, shut up, and let us get to the bottom of this. It would go a lot easier for you that way."

"Is that a threat?" Michael demanded.

"Hey, what's going on?" To his credit, Joey didn't take sides, even though he clearly didn't have a clue what was going on or why Hunt and Leo appeared to be ganging up on Michael. He looked to Savannah for answers. "What's happening here, Savannah?"

Savannah's face turned red. Her hand shook violently as she pointed at Michael. "Why don't you ask him?"

"Savannah, please." Michael held his hands out to the sides. "I don't know what you all think, but whatever it is, you guys have it all wrong."

"Well, then…" Savannah returned to her seat, crossed one leg over the other, and folded her hands in her lap. "Enlighten us."

Gia took a seat next to Savannah, inching her chair even closer to Savannah's.

Michael looked longingly at the doorway, blocked by Hunt and Leo, and flopped back onto his chair. "Look, Savannah, I never meant for anyone to get hurt. Especially you. You have to believe that."

Leo sat on Savannah's other side.

Hunt paced back and forth like a caged tiger.

Joey stood beside his chair, looking confused.

"You are my brother, Michael, and I would do anything to help you." Tears shimmered in Savannah's eyes, but she didn't let them fall. "But I have to know what you've gotten yourself involved in."

He stared at her but didn't say anything.

She took a deep, shaky breath and blew it out slowly. "Did you kill Buster Clarke?"

Michael gasped and jerked back as if she'd slapped him. "Are you crazy? Is that what this is about? How could you even think that?"

Joey fell into his chair, his mouth agape.

"Honestly, Michael, I don't know what to think anymore. Did you steal Pa's rainy-day money, the money from the drawer at the café, the cash from Gia's house?" She stood, spread her hands, and leaned on the table. "Are you the one who sedated Thor?"

Michael ran a hand over his mouth, tears spilling over and running down his cheeks. "I'm sorry, Savannah."

"It's not me you need to be apologizing to."

"Gia…" He turned to her, held her gaze. "I am so sorry. I never meant to hurt Thor. I…"

He sobbed and cradled his face in his hands.

"Okay. Enough of this." Hunt stopped pacing. "Sit up, Michael. Now."

He lifted his head and dropped his hands into his lap.

"Are you ready to talk now?" Hunt demanded.

He sniffed and nodded.

Hunt turned a chair around, straddled it, and rested his hands on the seatback. "Robert Clarke was arrested this afternoon. He confessed to giving you Paige's number, though he swears he doesn't know why you wanted it."

Michael snorted and ran a hand over his hair. "He's a liar."

"So, he didn't give you the phone number?"

"Oh, no, he gave me the number, but he knew exactly why I needed it. He was the one who approached me." He slammed a fist on the table.

"Did he also give you the sedative you used on Thor?"

His gaze shot to Gia, then quickly away. He nodded.

"And the one used on Savannah?"

Joey burst from his chair and over the table before anyone could react. His fist connected with Michael's jaw, and both of them tumbled to the floor. Joey yanked him up by the front of his shirt and punched him again.

Blood spurted from Michael's nose, but Joey didn't let up.

Hunt and Leo finally got hold of him—probably not as quickly as they could have—and wrestled him away from Michael.

"Did you hurt my sister?" Joey screamed, as Hunt and Leo hauled him off the floor.

"Enough, Joey." Hunt left Leo to deal with Michael and shoved Joey against the far wall, then held him there with a hand splayed against his chest, while Joey seethed and stared daggers at Michael.

Michael managed to get to his feet, but he didn't sit. "I'm sorry. I…"

Leo righted Michael's chair and pushed him into it.

"I was in trouble, and I didn't know what to do." Michael sniffed and wiped the blood from his face with a napkin. "I've been gambling in the Esposito casinos, and I got in over my head. I owed too much, but I worked out a plan with them to pay it off, then Frankie Esposito called the loan in before I could come up with the money. When Savannah got snatched, I did everything I could to get the money, but I still came up short."

"Except ask for help," Hunt yelled. "Help you know full well everyone in this family would have given."

He nodded and wiped his bloody nose again.

"Hunt," Leo said softly, "Let him tell it, okay?"

Hunt squeezed his eyes closed, dropped his head back, and shoved his hands into his hair. He stayed like that for a few seconds, then nodded and sat.

Michael eyed him warily as he continued. "I didn't have trouble borrowing Pa's money, because the dogs know me well, but Thor was a problem. The first time I went out there, he wouldn't let me in. Then, when Robert Clarke approached me, we got to talking. He already knew Savannah was missing, and I told him what was going on. I said I needed something to knock out a dog that wouldn't harm him, and he met me outside the café with it. He also handed me a sheet of paper, well two sheets actually. I guess he ripped off two by accident. But he handed me Paige's number and said she offered to help me out if I needed it. She'd give me a loan to pay off Frankie so I could get Savannah back. So I agreed. What else could I do?"

"How do you know Robert Clarke?" Leo asked.

"I went to school with him."

By the time he'd finished, Hunt was breathing heavy. "You're saying you had nothing to do with Savannah's kidnapping?"

"Not directly, but indirectly, it was all my fault." He started to cry, deep, racking sobs. "I'm so sorry, Savannah. Can you ever forgive me? I never meant for you to get hurt."

Savannah stood and went to him. She put an arm around him and pulled him close. "It's all right, Michael. We'll figure it out. I'm mad as all get out, but we'll figure it out. That's what family does."

"How sure are you that Frankie Esposito was the one who kidnapped Savannah?" Hunt asked.

Michael's sobs tapered off. "I can't be a hundred percent sure. Paige had Robert deliver the money to Frankie, and then Savannah turned up, so I figured it was him. Honestly, I didn't care, as long as she was back and safe. I assume Frankie had his thugs grab her. Men like him don't get their hands dirty."

They were interrupted by pounding against the front door. "Police, open up."

Michael jumped to his feet, looking back and forth between the doorway and the kitchen window like a caged animal.

"Michael..." Hunt looked over his shoulder, then back at Michael, while Leo went to answer the door. "Listen to me. I have never been this angry with anyone before, but Savannah's right, we're family, and you need to trust me now."

He nodded.

"Stay put. I'll go in to the station with you, and we'll straighten it out."

"Okay."

Several officers swarmed the room with Leo.

A tall man in a suit swaggered in behind them.

Hunt turned to him and clasped his hands together behind himself. "Chief Shaw."

"Captain Quinn." He gestured toward Michael. "Mind telling me what's going on here?"

Hunt shrugged. "Family dinner."

The chief pointed a finger at Hunt. "What did I tell you? Did I or did I not remove you from the Clarke investigation for tampering with evidence?"

"You did, sir."

"So, what are you doing sitting here with a man we have an arrest warrant for?" He lowered his finger, propped his hands low on his hips, and pinned Hunt with a hard gaze.

Hunt rocked back on his heels. "Eating. Sir."

"And I'm supposed to believe you are not questioning a suspect in my investigation?"

"With all due respect, sir, how would I know he's a suspect in your investigation? Or have you forgotten I was removed from said investigation?"

"Oh, no, I haven't forgotten." He took a step closer to Hunt and puffed out his chest. "I haven't forgotten I removed you from the investigation for that stunt you pulled with the pad. Tampering with evidence is a crime, Captain, in case you weren't aware."

Hunt stood quietly at attention.

"We were lucky to get a print from that page at all after you scribbled on it to retrieve the information from the page above it. Of course, it will probably be ruled as inadmissible."

Wait? What was he talking about? The pad that came from the café? Gia wasn't about to let Hunt get in trouble for that. She shot to her feet. "Hunt didn't scribble on that pad."

"Excuse me?" Chief Shaw turned on her.

So did Hunt and Leo.

She ignored them.

"I did." At least, she was standing right there and had handed Hunt the pencil and hadn't objected. "I scribbled on the top page, hoping to figure out what someone had written last on it after whoever attacked Thor left a note written on that same paper." Sweat trickled down her back. She hated lying, never did if she could avoid it, but she couldn't let Hunt get in trouble, not when everything he'd done had been to protect Savannah. "I wasn't aware the pad would be evidence in a police investigation at the time, and since it was my property, I believe I was within my rights to do so."

"So do I." Savannah slid her hand into Gia's and stood at her side.

Chief Shaw looked back and forth between Gia and Hunt.

Gia stood perfectly still, careful not to fidget, not to shift her gaze from his.

Giving up on his rant, the chief pointed at Michael. "Arrest him."

Joey stood and shoved his chair in. "I have to go try to explain this mess to Pa."

Two officers took Michael into custody, handcuffed him, and read him his rights.

With one last dirty look for Hunt, Shaw turned and followed them out.

"I don't know what to say, Gia. Thank you." Hunt kissed Gia's cheek. "Did I ever tell you you're the best?"

She smiled and fluttered her lashes. "Why thank you, Captain."

When he and Leo were gone, and Gia and Savannah were left alone, Savannah grabbed Gia's arms and looked up into her eyes. "I don't know how to thank you, Gia."

"You don't have to thank me for sticking up for Hunt, Savannah." She'd done it because she felt it was the right thing to do.

"Not for that. Well, for that too, but mostly for what you're about to do next." She sort of smiled, but her face scrunched up into the 'you're-not-going-to-like-this' look she usually reserved for Hunt.

"Oh?" *Uh oh.* "What's that?"

"You said Paige Clarke left you her business card?" She released her and stepped back, then waited for Gia to nod before continuing. "I need you to call her and ask her to meet with me."

Gia did not like where this conversation was heading. "What do you want to see Paige for?"

"To thank her," she said sweetly, and with so much venom, Gia cringed.

It was unusual Gia couldn't follow Savannah's thoughts, but at the moment, she was a closed book, a fact that sent a surge of anxiety rushing through Gia. "Thank her?"

"Sure." Savannah shrugged. "If not for her, who knows what might have happened to me. She may have even saved my life."

"May have?"

"Mmm-hmm."

Suspicion snuck in. "Why 'may have?' I'd say she definitely did, if she paid what basically amounted to ransom to see you returned safely."

"Perhaps, but something in Michael's story just doesn't add up." Savannah paced back and forth across the tile floor. "The Espositos and the Clarkes are mortal enemies, so why would Paige offer to pay Frankie? It's not like she knows Michael, or me, for that matter, so why help us?"

Gia hadn't thought about that, but Savannah was right, as much as she hated to admit it. "I don't know, Savannah. It's not that I don't agree with you, but I'm not sure it's a good idea for us to meet with Paige."

"You don't have to come with me—"

"You can stop right there. You are not going alone." No way would she let Savannah confront that woman by herself. "We could ask Hunt and Leo to—"

"No. We can't ask them for help right now."

"Why not? Maybe one of us could wear a wire in case she says anything incriminating; then, they could get it on tape. Plus, they'd be able to come to our rescue if things go wrong." Things going wrong was a definite possibility for them.

Savannah pursed her lips. "That's not a bad idea, but what do you think the chances are of them agreeing to that? Besides, Hunt was already in trouble for tampering with evidence and interrogating a witness after he was removed from a case. He'll be lucky to be reinstated, even with you going to bat for him."

She had a point there. "But—"

"And if Hunt and Leo say no, then we have to go against their wishes. Haven't you learned by now? If you don't want no for an answer, don't ask the question." Savannah scowled as she paced. Then she stopped and snapped her fingers. "I've got it. What about Alfie?"

Again, Gia didn't follow her train of thought. "What about him?"

"If he was as excited as he was about hacking a computer, can you imagine how excited he'd be to go on a stakeout?"

Chapter Twenty-Four

"Can you hear me, Alfie?" Gia whispered from Paige's study. The microphone and earpiece she was outfitted with weighed heavily. If Paige caught them…She took a deep breath to steady her nerves.

"Loud and clear." Alfie's voice in her ear brought at least some reassurance, though she'd have felt better if Hunt and Leo were sitting out there.

Alfie had been beyond excited when Gia had called and asked him about surveillance equipment and had shown up with a briefcase full of electronic toys. His MINI Cooper was now parked a block away, and he had explicit instructions to call Hunt if anything went wrong.

The door opened, and Paige walked in and extended a hand. "Gia, it's good to see you again."

Savannah gasped softly.

Gia didn't dare look at her to see what was wrong. The last thing she wanted to do was alert Paige to any kind of problem. Instead, she stood, wiped her sweaty hand, hopefully discreetly, on her jeans, and shook Paige's hand. "It's good to see you, too, Paige. This is my friend, Savannah."

Savannah gripped her hand, a smile covering whatever had caused her earlier reaction. "It's a pleasure to meet you, Ms. Clarke."

"Paige, please."

"Paige. I wanted to come personally to thank you. I've spoken to my brother, Michael, and it seems you most likely saved my life. And his. I am so grateful to you for that, thank you." Savannah's gratitude seemed so sincere; Gia knew she meant every word of it. No matter what happened from that moment moving forward, Savannah would be forever grateful to Paige Clarke.

As would Gia.

Paige waved for them to return to their seats in the small seating arrangement, then sat in an armchair across from them and crossed one leg over the other. "I wouldn't be too grateful for Michael's sake yet. He still has to pay back the loan."

"I've come to take care of that for him."

What!

Blindsided again. Savannah hadn't mentioned anything about that to her, and Gia hadn't seen it coming. She didn't know how much Michael owed, but it had to be a lot. Savannah just didn't have that kind of money.

"It's a substantial sum, Ms. Mills."

"Savannah, please." She sat up straighter. "I've been saving money for my wedding for some time now, and I would like to use it to pay what my brother owes you. If it's more than what I have in savings, I will get the rest from my brothers and my cousins. He can pay us back when he has it."

Paige studied her. "You are a very special person, it seems. A good sister. No wonder he was so frantic to save you."

Savannah gasped. "Oh, no, I can't believe I forgot to offer my condolences on the loss of your brother. Please, forgive me. With everything else that's gone on, my mind is a bit scattered. I'm so very sorry for your loss."

"Ah, thank you. Yes, my brother, Buster." She uncrossed her legs and slid forward to perch on the edge of the chair, hands resting on her knees. "He and I weren't as close as you and your brother, I'm afraid."

Savannah reached out and patted her hand. "I'm very sorry to hear that."

"Yes, me too." Paige's eyes filled with regret.

Savannah frowned as she sat back. "Do you mind if I ask why he was so determined to buy the Oakley Manor House?"

Paige stood. "Can I offer you something to drink?"

"No, thank you."

"Gia?"

"I'm good, thanks."

She went to a small bar in the corner, dropped a couple of ice cubes into a glass, and poured ginger ale over it. She took her time, her back to them. When she finally turned, glass in hand, she leaned a hip against the mahogany bar. "Buster was obsessed with that house since we were kids. He always swore one day he'd own it. My father would slap him upside the head and tell him that house was off-limits. It belonged to the Espositos, and any attempt he made to deceive them would result in an all-out war and deaths for our family."

"And yet..." Savannah tilted her head. "He tried to buy it anyway."

She nodded and swirled her drink, watching the ice move round and round the cup. "Yes. It seems so. To be honest, I think the biggest reason he wanted it so badly was because he couldn't have it."

Why would anyone risk their lives for such a reason? Risk the lives of family members just to prove a point? For what gain? Wealth? Power? Revenge for some past slight? Gia didn't understand, would probably never understand, since there was nothing she wouldn't do to keep her new family safe.

Savannah stood. "Well, I just wanted to say thank you and offer to pay my brother's debt to you."

"You're welcome. I respect you for coming to your brother's aid." She set her drink on a coaster on her desk, jotted something on a piece of paper, and then handed it to Savannah. "That is the amount needed to satisfy your brother's debt. You can contact me at the number below it, and I will send Robert to pick up the money when you're ready to pay it."

Gia jumped up, desperate to be out of there. "Thank you for seeing us, Paige."

She smiled warmly. "Any time."

Savannah started toward the door, and Gia breathed a sigh of relief.

Then Savannah paused. "You know, there is something else I don't understand?"

Paige sipped her ginger ale. "What's that?"

Savannah turned on her. "Why you did it?"

"Excuse me?" Paige's smile faltered.

Gia wanted to grab Savannah by the arm, slap a hand over her mouth, and haul her out of there. Instead, she stood quietly next to her, willing her to stop talking. It didn't work.

"As angry as I am with my brother right now," Savannah said. "My first instinct is to help him, to protect him."

Paige set her drink aside and leaned back against her desk, hands resting on either side of her. Relaxed. Not at all perturbed by Savannah's veiled accusations.

Savannah took a step closer to Paige. "Buster didn't intervene when Robert jumped me in that bedroom."

Gia's knees went weak. What was Savannah doing?

"Nor did he try to help when you injected me with the sedative. So, I have to wonder, why kill him?"

"What do I do?" Alfie whispered frantically in Gia's ear. "Should I call Hunt now?"

Paige was staring straight at them. There was no way Gia could answer him. Hopefully, he'd figure it out, because they were most definitely going to need help.

Paige smiled and looked down. "How'd you figure it out?"

"Your perfume. A floral scent. The instant I smelled it, as soon as you walked in, everything came crashing back. I remember smelling it just before I blacked out, subtle, but memorable under the circumstances."

"I would imagine so." She nodded. "I'm sorry you figured it out."

Savannah lifted her chin in defiance. "I'm not."

"You do know I can't let you leave now, right?" To her credit, Paige did appear disappointed about that. Or maybe not. Her neutral expression made it hard to tell.

Savannah shrugged. "As long as that's the case, would it hurt to tell me why? I really want to understand. Does it have something to do with your friendship with Angelina Lombardo?"

Paige's eyes went wide in surprise, the first real emotion she'd shown since they'd arrived. "How...?"

"There's a picture in her office. The two of you aren't standing together, but you're looking at her and cheering her on. Enemies don't do that for one another. Friends do."

"Angelina." A tear tipped over Paige's lower lashes and rolled down her cheek. "Angelina and I have been friends for a long time. We went to school together, away from here, and things there were good. We were the best of friends, probably not unlike you and Gia here, who stood by you knowing you would probably die tonight."

Gia shuddered. She'd stand by Savannah no matter what, but she had no intention of dying, or letting Savannah die, tonight. However, she had no clue yet how to stop that from happening.

"But neither of our families would allow Angelina and I to be friends," Paige continued as if she hadn't just threatened their lives. "So, when we returned home, we had to keep our friendship secret. But now, with my father ill, dying, we could have been friends again, could have lived in peace. Robert would have been okay with it. To be honest, most of us don't even know what originally started the feud between our families, anyway. Money, power, greed?"

Gia could almost feel bad for her, if not for the fact she was going to kill them when she was done talking.

Alfie remained eerily silent, and she hoped he'd figured out to send back-up. Then again, if Hunt got there before Paige killed them, he'd probably murder them himself.

Paige scoffed and shook her head. "But Buster wouldn't let go of that stupid house. He insisted as soon as Father was gone, he was going to get it. He was determined to escalate the war between our families, a move that could only have caused pain and death on both sides. His hunger for power had become dangerous."

"So, you and Angelina helped him get what he wanted?" Savannah frowned "I don't understand why?"

"I told him to go see you. I knew about the debt your brother owed Frankie from Angelina. When you walked into that room at the Oakley Manor House with him, and I took you down, Buster was confused. I told him you were going to tell Frankie you showed him the house, then I told him to go into the bathroom and get rope. When he did…"

"When he did, Angelina killed him." Savannah nodded as if she could envision the whole encounter.

The tears Paige had so easily shed for her friend, dried up at the thought of her brother. "Yes, she caught him off guard and was able to take him out. By the time he grabbed the nail gun and tried to fight back, he was as good as gone."

"What about the woman who was killed? LuAnne Swanson?"

"She found out Frankie owned the house, went to see Angelina at the office, and spoke to her about it. We had to get rid of her before she could tell him Buster had gone out there. Don't you see? Frankie would have been furious. He'd have considered it a slap in the face, and he would have retaliated. That would have reignited the feud all over again when most of us were willing to let it go. Can't you understand? I watched enough family members die for no reason. So did Angelina. With Buster and Frankie both out of the picture, the people we love would have been safe."

Compassion gripped Gia, but only for a moment.

Paige scoffed. "LuAnne was dead before we brought her to the house and dumped her in the lake. We should have gotten away with it, will get away with it once you two are out of the picture."

"Except Robert got careless and left a print on the pad at Gia's," Savannah goaded.

"Oh, please. Robert is never careless. He does exactly what he's told. Now, if Buster had been more like him, well…" She sighed. "Anyway, we needed Michael to get picked up so he'd tell the police Frankie took Savannah to hold for ransom until his debt was paid off."

Brilliant. If not for the fact that so many people's lives had been carelessly disregarded, ruined, taken, Gia might have been impressed with the planning of it all. "Did Frankie actually call in that loan?"

"No," Paige admitted. "Angelina did."

There couldn't be too much more to the story, and Savannah seemed to have run out of questions. Gia had to stall, give Hunt and Leo a chance to get there. "So, this entire thing was an elaborate plot to kill Buster and let Frankie go to jail for his murder."

"We had no choice. Don't you understand how many more people would have died if those two weren't taken out of the picture?"

Gia ignored the comment, mostly because she could actually understand that in her own twisted way, Paige seemed to think she'd been doing the right thing.

"I suppose it was you who put his watch out at the warehouse?" Savannah asked.

"Of course. We woke you up just enough for you to see the clown face on the door while Robert was carrying you in. It's pretty specific and unique, so it shouldn't have been hard to find once you remembered."

Savannah tilted her head. "And if I didn't remember?"

She lifted a brow. "The police would have gotten an anonymous tip."

"I still don't understand how you could do that to your own brother." The fact that the man she killed had been her brother seemed to be the one thing Savannah couldn't get past.

"When Angelina first came to me with her plan, I said no. I talked to Buster instead, begged him to let sleeping dogs lie, to keep from escalating any tension between our families. But he just wouldn't let the Oakley Manor House go. Don't you understand? If he'd have bought that house, Frankie would have sought revenge the instant he found out. Someone would have died. Probably Buster. My way, at least, it ensured only the two who were engaging in the war suffered. Buster probably would have died anyway, and Frankie would have gone to prison if he was caught. If we hadn't done what we did, there would have been collateral damage."

"You mean more collateral damage than just Savannah and her brother?" Anger surged through Gia. She could have had sympathy for Paige, if not for the fact she'd freely used innocent people with no consideration for their safety. "More than LuAnne?"

"I'm truly sorry for that." She went to her desk and pressed a button on what looked like a phone. "Robert, I need you in the study."

"What are you going to do with us?" If she didn't plan on killing them in the study, Hunt might have a chance of saving them when they emerged from the house.

Paige frowned and pressed the button again. "Robert."

The study door swung open.

Paige looked up. "What took you so—"

Gia whirled toward the door and braced herself for Robert's attack.

"Freeze, Paige." Hunt stood in the doorway, his weapon aimed at Paige in a steady hand.

Paige hooked an arm around Gia's neck from behind and pulled her tight against her body. She held a letter opener from the desk against her throat. "Back up and let me out of here, or Gia dies."

Gia flung her hands up, keeping them where Paige could see them and hopefully have no reason to kill her.

"There's nowhere to go, Paige. Robert is already in custody." Hunt's voice remained perfectly calm.

Gia's insides turned to mush. She had to think. Had to stay calm.

Paige pressed the letter opener harder against her neck.

Something trickled down Gia's throat right where the blade stung. She sure hoped it was sweat. She squeezed her eyes closed. They shot open an instant later, lest she miss a cue from Hunt.

Hunt released his finger from the trigger and held both hands up, the gun still held in one, pointed toward the ceiling. "All right, calm down, Paige. We can talk about this, but you have to let Gia go."

"I'm not talking about anything, and I'll let Gia go as soon as I'm out of here." She inched forward, keeping a firm grip around Gia's neck. She whispered in Gia's ear, "Stay calm and move with me, and you might just live through this night, Gia. No real reason to kill you now that the cat's out of the bag. As long as you help me escape, I'll let you go."

Gia nodded as best she could without impaling herself on the blade. She moved slowly with Paige, keeping pace with her, her body the only barrier between Paige and Hunt. Her confidence built the closer they got to Hunt. Surely, he'd never let Paige out of there with a weapon against Gia's throat.

"Move away from the door, and call your men off." Paige moved the letter opener away from her throat, barely an inch, but it was all the opening Gia needed.

She shoved her hand between the blade's point and her throat as she spun toward Paige, forcing the other woman to loosen her hold from around Gia's neck.

Savannah pounced, slamming a desk lamp against the top of Paige's head.

It shattered, and Paige staggered but stayed on her feet.

Hunt yanked Gia out of the way away even as he grabbed hold of Paige's wrist.

Savannah half-dragged Gia away from the scuffle as Hunt forced the letter opener from Paige's hand.

"Are you all right?" Savannah shifted the hair away from Gia's neck, then jumped up. "Stay there."

Gia was too dazed to do anything other than follow her order.

Savannah returned an instant later and dropped to her knees beside Gia with a box of tissues from the desk. She pulled out a couple and pressed them against Gia's neck.

"How bad is it?" She was afraid to look. She could feel the sting as if the blade was still pressed against her throat.

Savannah held up the tissue, where only a few spots of blood had soaked in and grinned. "I think you'll live."

Relief rushed through her, and she sagged back against Savannah and laughed. Probably not an appropriate response given the circumstances, but she was too relieved it was over, and Savannah would be safe, to care. Tears streamed down her cheeks as Savannah hugged her.

Hunt hauled Paige to her feet. "You are under arrest for the murder of Buster Clarke and the kidnapping of Savannah Mills."

Leo appeared over Hunt's shoulder and took over. He cuffed Paige and led her past Savannah on their way out of the office.

Savannah patted Gia's shoulder and surged to her feet. She held up a hand to stop him on his way past. She leaned close to Paige. "At least, you and Angelina will be able to continue your friendship unimpeded in prison."

Chapter Twenty-Five

Gia packed the few clothes she'd brought when they'd arrived at Trevor's back into her bag. "Are you sure you don't want to stay another night? Trevor said it would be okay."

Savannah snuggled Pepper, then put her into the carrier. "Nah. After everything that went on last night, all I want to do is go home."

Thor barked.

Gia petted his head. "Well, I guess I'm outnumbered, but we are definitely coming back to explore the mansion before the wedding."

"Oh, absolutely." Savannah grinned. "And since Trevor agreed to a Christmas wedding, we are going to decorate every last inch of this place."

Hunt grabbed the two remaining bags. "Is this everything?"

"Yup, unfortunately, we weren't really here long enough to unpack much." A fact Gia regretted, but Savannah was right. It was time to go home.

Leo walked in and grabbed the two cat carriers. "Sorry, I'm late, I was on the phone with Chief Shaw."

Gia froze. "What'd he want?"

"Everything's worked out. Hunt's fine, and there will be no disciplinary action since you're the one who doctored the note." He winked at her and pointed at Hunt. "Oh, also, Ward Bennett was picked up but then released."

"Released?" Savannah asked. "Why?"

"That wasn't unexpected. We had no admissible evidence he did anything wrong. The information Alfie got was obtained illegally, so we can't use that." Hunt shrugged. "We had to let him go."

Outrage prodded Gia. "What about the note Tempest found on his desk?"

"Not admissible. Besides, he says he found it on Angelina's desk and took it because he wanted to go to the police and tell them the truth, but he feared for his life."

Since Gia had seen all of the other notes just like it on Angelina's desk, Ward's story seemed plausible, though she didn't buy a word of it.

Savannah propped her hands on her hips. "Do you believe him?"

"Who knows?" Hunt shifted the bags to a more comfortable grip. "He probably did take the note off Angelina's desk, but I think it's more likely he wanted to use it as leverage to get out of having to pay a share of his profits to her."

"I wouldn't worry about it too much, though." Leo winked. "It seems an anonymous email went out to all of the people Ward was stealing from. It didn't name him, but it let them know their accounts were compromised, and all of the accounts were closed. Mr. Bennett may start over, but his current cash flow is gone."

"Did anyone find Angelina?" Savannah asked.

Angelina had disappeared right after Paige's arrest.

"She was picked up early this morning, on her way out of town."

Gia still feared retaliation from one of the families, but with Angelina out of the picture, it was less likely. The Clarke family had lost all three of the siblings, one to death and two to prison. Frankie Esposito had sent a bouquet to the shop, addressed to Gia and Savannah, with a note that simply said, "Thank you." Maybe they'd be okay, after all. "Was Angelina the one who shot at us on the road that day?"

"No, actually, that was Paige." Hunt's phone rang, and he put the bags down to check the screen. He sent the call to voicemail and stuck the phone back into his pocket. "When you went into the real estate office that day and found the note, Angelina overheard the conversation and realized Ward had taken it from her desk, so she sent Paige to sit in wait for him, called Ward and sent him down that deserted road for Paige to pick him off. But then she spotted you two tailing him, and called Paige back and told her to get rid of you two. She had a feeling you were getting too close."

"Will Paige be able to argue that you and Leo were not part of the case when you arrested her?" Paige going free was Gia's biggest fear.

"Nah. We were still on the force, so it's fine. Anyway…" Hunt picked the bags back up. "That was Chief Shaw calling. I need to get done and return his call."

While Hunt and Leo loaded up the car, and Hunt returned his phone call, Gia took Thor to the potty pavilion one last time.

Savannah walked with her. "I spoke to Pa earlier."

"How's he holding up?"

"About as well as could be expected. Michael is facing charges, so he's going to have to deal with that. Hunt and Leo think he'll make out okay, though, especially since none of us are willing to testify against him. He's going to have to testify, but they expect the D.A. to go easy on him in return."

"That's good. I'm glad." Michael wasn't a bad guy, and he was torn to pieces over his part in putting Savannah in danger, but he'd do the right thing. And the support he would get from his family would make all the difference.

"Me too." Savannah said. "And now that he doesn't have to worry about his debt, since Paige already paid Frankie and Paige and Robert are both going to prison for a long time, he's going to straighten himself out. He's done gambling. It was a hard lesson, but those are the ones that stick best."

"Yes, they are," Gia agreed.

"Anyway." Savannah led Gia to the bench they'd first sat together on when arriving at Trevor's, and they sat together again. "We have strict instructions from Cole and Willow to take two days off. How do you want to spend them?"

It didn't matter to Gia, as long as they spent them together. "Did you have something special in mind?"

"I was thinking we could go home and curl up on the couch with a bowl of popcorn and watch an old movie or two. Then, after a good night sleep…" She crossed her fingers and held them up. "We could go shopping for gowns. And then—I've already okayed it with Trevor—we are totally coming back here to check this place out."

Gia hugged Savannah close, then whistled for Thor. "Sounds like the perfect weekend."

Keep reading for a special excerpt of
A WAFFLE LOT OF MURDER
An All-Day Breakfast Café Mystery
by Lena Gregory

For diner owner Gia Morelli, her seasonal fall menu calls for two main ingredients—maple syrup and murder . . .

While the first hints of autumn grace Boggy Creek, Florida, Gia misses the colorful harvest traditions she left behind in New York. On a scramble to make new fall memories—and promote her irresistible pumpkin spice waffles—things take a dark turn when she gets roped into the Haunted Town Festival, a spooky celebration held on deserted farmlands. The desolate area conjures plenty of eerie vibes at night, but Gia and her best friend, Savannah, are nearly frightened to death upon the discovery of the event organizer's body buried in the nearby woods. More alarming, the local rumor mill says the woman's shady dealings may have egged someone into sending her to an early grave. Now, there's no shortage of creepy clues to feast on as Gia and her pals try to stop a killer with a very scary appetite . . .

Look for A WAFFLE LOT OF MURDER, *on sale now!*

Chapter One

"That letter is not gonna open itself, ya know." Savannah snatched the envelope Gia had been turning over and over for the better part of five minutes, slid the tip of one rhinestone-studded maroon nail beneath the flap, and slit it open.

"Yeah, well..." Gia climbed back onto her step ladder and returned to the cornucopia she was arranging on a shelf behind the All-Day Breakfast Café's counter in honor of fall's impending arrival. At least, everyone assured her fall was coming. Hard to tell without the leaves changing color and the crisp clean air that would have heralded the change of season in New York. Whatever devastating news awaited her inside the envelope could wait until she was done decorating. "Remember what happened last time I received a letter from the town council?"

"That's a little dramatic, don't ya think?" Savannah waved her off and started reading. "How long has this been sitting here? It's dated over a week ago."

Gia spread some hay around the shelf beneath the arrangement. "I don't know. A few days, I guess. I picked up the mail on Friday but didn't get to go through it all until this morning."

"Mmm-hmm..." Savannah shot her a knowing look and lifted a brow. "AKA, you saw the town council return address, tossed the letter aside, and ignored it for the weekend."

And there's the down side of having a best friend who knew you too well. "It's possible it went something like that."

Earl and Cole, who were both sitting at the counter drinking coffee, and good enough friends to get away with it, laughed.

Earl, the elderly gentleman who'd been her first customer when she'd opened the café, pointed to her work in progress. "You have an empty space there."

Gia straightened, then leaned back, careful not to tumble off the step ladder. Sure enough, he was right. She shifted a couple of gourds to fill in the hole "Better?"

He wiped his mouth with a napkin and set it aside, then pushed his empty plate away, sat back and studied her creation. "Yup."

"Makes me realize fall's comin'." Cole, who worked the grill a few days a week to help her out and to alleviate his own post-retirement boredom, stood and took his and Earl's empty breakfast plates, then rounded the counter to put them in the bin Gia kept there. "I gotta get started prepping to open."

"Sit a few more minutes. Have another cup of coffee if you want. I already cut up all the vegetables last night." Though they'd had a huge Sunday morning breakfast crowd, the evening had slowed enough for her to get started preparing what they'd need for Monday morning.

Savannah held the letter out to Gia. When she didn't take it right away, Savannah shook it. "Look."

Gia made no move to take the letter. Her last experience with the town council had left a bitter taste in her mouth, but if Savannah's enthusiasm was any indication, this letter might not threaten such dire consequences. "I guess they're not trying to shut me down again."

"Nope. On the contrary, this is awesome. Who knows? Maybe they want to make nice after your last encounter." She grinned and thrust the letter toward Gia again. "Now take this, and see for yourself."

Gia set the small pumpkin and gourd she was holding aside, climbed down from the step ladder, and took the letter from Savannah.

"See?" she squeaked.

"Savannah, I haven't even started reading it yet."

"Well, I'll save you the trouble. You've been invited to participate in the annual Haunted Town Festival." She squealed and clasped her hands together.

After quickly scanning the letter, Gia tossed it onto the counter. "It says I've been cordially invited and I can have a table and a house. What does that mean, exactly?"

Savannah grabbed a can of Diet Pepsi from the small refrigerator beneath the counter, despite the perfectly good soda fountain sitting right above it, and popped the top—how she managed it with those long nails, Gia had no clue. "The Haunted Town Festival is huge, probably the biggest event of the year around here."

"All the proceeds go to the animal shelter, so people come from all over to support it." Cole refilled his and Earl's coffee cups.

"Thanks," Earl said and took a sip. "He's right. All of my kids come with their kids, been doing it every year since they were little, and none of them have ever missed a festival."

Cole lifted the coffee pot toward Gia.

"No, thanks." She'd already had three cups—any more and she'd be too jittery to work. "What do they mean by a table and a house?"

"Okay." Excitement brightened Savannah's already brilliant blue eyes. "So, the Festival is held on the old farmlands just outside of town. There are a large number of abandoned outbuildings out there, and most of them are used for themed houses. Like haunted houses and the like. You get to set up your house with whatever theme you want, and then, on the night of the Festival, you have a bunch of people work your house and scare the people coming through."

"Those houses are hard to get. The same groups get them every year." Earl frowned. "I wonder whose house opened up?"

"I heard Tim and Cathy retired and moved up to Pennsylvania to be by their youngest who just had her third baby in less than five years," Cole said.

"Certainly sounds like she could use the help," Earl agreed. "But what did they do with their plumbing business?"

"Their oldest son took it over, but he must have decided not to do the house this year. Who knows?" Cole shrugged. "Maybe it was too much, with taking over the business and all, or maybe he just didn't want to do it without the rest of the family."

"Either way, I guess you lucked out that a house is available." Savannah tapped a nail against the letter. "There's a number right there. You'd better call right away. That house will go fast, if it hasn't already. I sure hope they held it for you, being they sent an invitation and all."

"I don't know." It sounded involved, and if it was too much for someone who'd been doing it for years, how was she supposed to pull it off? Of course she didn't know why the last person had backed out. "What about the table? What's that?"

"The table is great advertising, the chance to get word out and offer a variety of samples from your menu. We can put out a few different dishes, easy to eat things you can pick up and eat on the go; homemade muffins, scones…" Cole snapped his fingers. "Oh, you know what would be perfect? Some of those pumpkin spice waffles you were playing around with last week."

"And don't forget the cold brew coffee." Savannah grabbed an order pad and pen and started jotting notes. "Maybe we could even do a smaller version of your breakfast pies, like make them in little mini pie tins people could carry with them or sit at one of the picnic tables and eat."

The table sounded like a great idea, get word out about her business, let people taste some of her menu items. "Maybe I could just do the table and not the house."

"Nah," Cole said. "The table is work and great advertising, but the house is the fun part."

"Then it's settled." Savannah scooped the letter off the counter and held it out to Gia.

Gia held up her hands. "Wait, guys—"

"And don't forget home fries. They'll be sure to bring in customers." Earl winked at Gia.

"Thank you, Earl, but I—"

"You know what?" Savannah fished her cell phone out of her oversized mustard-yellow bag, checked the number on the letter, and dialed. "I'll just call them myself."

"Wait. I didn't even—"

She held up a finger and turned away. "Hello? Yes, hi. I'm calling for Gia Morelli at the All-Day Breakfast Café…Yes…Sure, I can hold…"

"Savannah, wait—"

She turned back toward Gia and covered the mouthpiece. "You're the one who's always talking about missing fall in New York, missing the old traditions you had, driving out on Long Island… Yes, I'm still here."

Earl picked up where she left off. "Hitting up the farm stands, pumpkin picking…"

"Roasted sweet corn, apple cider," Cole added.

She shot them a dirty look. "You two aren't helping matters."

They just laughed at her. Traitors.

Savannah sighed. "I'm on hold again."

"All right, so maybe I have been missing New York, and perhaps I've mentioned it once or twice."

Savannah pinned her with a you've-got-to-be-kidding-me glare. "Ya think?"

Gia scowled, though she couldn't really argue. As much as she loved Boggy Creek, straying from the familiar was proving difficult at times, especially with the arrival of her favorite season.

"Well, you'll never stop missing your old traditions if you don't start making new ones," Savannah said.

"I guess you're right."

"Of course I am." She smirked. "I wouldn't have said it if I wasn't."

"I think the table is a great idea, but maybe we could skip—"

Savannah held up a finger and returned to her call. "Yes. Yes, we haven't decided on one yet, but I'll get back to you later on and let you know…"

"Looks like you're doing the Festival." Earl laughed out loud with no regard whatsoever for the look of horror that had to be plastered on her face if the sinking feeling in her gut was any indication.

"But I—"

"Ah, let her have her fun." Cole grinned at Earl. "Now for the good part."

"Oh, what's the good part?" At the moment, nothing sounded good, or fun. It all seemed like an overwhelming amount of work and less time she could spend with Thor, her Bernese Mountain Dog. Hard to believe he had just turned a year old and she'd had him for almost that long. At the same time, it seemed he had been a part of her life forever and she couldn't imagine being without him.

Earl nodded toward her, his eyes filled with understanding. "First off, I know that look. It's the same one my daughter-in-law gets every time she's invited to something that doesn't include her little girl. So let me ease your mind. Thor can be with you while you set up and work on the house, and he can be there before and after the haunting hours. Guests are allowed to bring their pets, but Zoe gets a bunch of high school students together and sets up an old stable as a doggie day care center for the workers."

Zoe had been watching Thor since Gia brought him home, and she was amazing. "I guess that would be all right."

"It's for his own safety. During the peak hours, you are 'haunting' your house, so it's dark and creepy, and you can't really keep an eye on him."

"Speaking of pets, have you ever considered some kind of pet breakfast food?" Cole turned the pad Savannah had been using around and jotted something down. "We could make something up and offer it at the Festival to get an idea if people and their pets like them."

Hmm…that was a good idea. A homemade breakfast treat for dogs. She could set up a stand by the door of the café for them. "I like that idea. Maybe something with peanut butter. Thor loves peanut butter."

"And bacon," Earl added with a grin. "Who doesn't love bacon?"

Gia was beginning to warm to the whole event. At least, the table part of it. The house she wasn't so sure about. She'd never even visited a haunted house, never mind trying to set one up and work it.

"Woo hoo!" Savannah pumped her fist in the air. "We got it!"

"The house?"

"Yup. Now we just have to come up with a theme."

"A theme?" Gia's stomach turned over. What had Savannah gotten her into?

"Yeah, you know, like vampires or werewolves or something."

"Nah." Cole shook his head. "How about something different? Something unusual."

"Clowns." Earl tapped the pad Cole was jotting ideas on. "Write that one down. Every single one of my kids is terrified of clowns. We could do a circus themed house."

"We?" Hmm…maybe, if they all pitched in and worked on it with her the whole thing wouldn't be so bad. She had to admit, it would be nice to spend time with her friends somewhere other than work.

"Of course. What? Did you really think we'd throw you to the wolves without backup?" Earl grinned. "Besides, you don't really think I'd miss this, do you? I bet some of my kids would love to participate too. And my grandson is old enough. It sure would be nice to spend some time doing something fun with him."

"Don't forget Willow and Skyla," Cole tossed out. "And maybe Trevor and some of the kids who work in his shop want to join us too."

"And my brothers." Savannah frowned. "Wait…Didn't the Ramseys do clowns last year?"

"Oh yeah, you might be right." Cole scratched clowns off the list. "How about zombies?"

Savannah waved off the idea. "Zombies are overrated. Besides, every haunted attraction has zombies."

"True." Cole tapped the pen against the pad, his brow furrowed in concentration.

Apparently, the Haunted Town Festival was a serious event in Boggy Creek. At least, it was to her friends.

Gia warmed to the idea. An event that involved the entire community sounded great. It would be good for business, and she was always looking for ways to immerse herself in the community. She'd grown to love Boggy Creek over the past year. She wanted to be a part of everything that made it so special. Still…she had no clue what she was doing. And Gia had never been very adventurous. She preferred the familiarity and safety of her comfort zone. In spite of that, the one impulsive decision she was forced into making—her move to Boggy Creek, Florida—turned out to be the best thing she'd ever done.

Savannah waved a hand in front of her, trying to recapture her attention. "Ghosts? Aliens? Horror movie monsters?"

They tossed around ideas for the next few minutes, until Cole glanced toward the clock hanging above the cut out between the kitchen and dining room and jumped off his stool. "Yikes! We got so carried away we forgot we had to open."

Gia headed for the front of the shop, where a couple already waited on the sidewalk for her to unlock the door.

Savannah fished her keys out, then slung her bag over her shoulder. "And I have to get to work. I have paperwork to do, and I have to get in touch with a seller to find out what time I can get my potential buyer into a house."

Gia unlocked the door and held it open for her two customers. "Good morning. Have a seat wherever you'd like, and I'll be right with you."

Savannah scooted behind the couple before Gia let the door go. "I'll pick you up about seven, and we can go see our house and decide where to set up the table. Barbara Woodhull, one of the event coordinators, is meeting us out there at seven thirty."

"Sure thing." There was no point in arguing. Apparently, her friends had decided she'd be participating, so Gia gave up. Besides, she might even enjoy it. She'd been missing fall, which had always been her favorite season. She had been a bit homesick and down lately, despite her love for Boggy Creek and its residents. Maybe a new annual tradition would help ease some of the nostalgia that had been hounding her. But she still couldn't help wondering what she'd gotten herself into.

Chapter Two

Still not convinced she was doing the right thing, Gia climbed out of Savannah's new Mustang convertible and ran her fingers through her tangled curls. Riding with the top down in the little blue sports car was amazing but left her long, dark hair looking like a rat's nest.

Savannah ran a hand over already perfect long blonde hair. She'd been smart enough to pull it back into a bun before they'd left. She smoothed her long cream-colored skirt.

Oh well. Live and learn. Gia scanned for critters as they crossed the deserted hard-packed dirt field that barely passed for a parking lot. "Are you sure it's okay to be bumbling around out here when it's getting dark?"

Savannah lifted a brow. "Gia, the event takes place after dark."

"Oh." She swallowed hard and forced a laugh. "Right."

"Besides, Cole opened this morning, so we couldn't come out here until you closed."

"True." But it didn't make her any more comfortable on the deserted farm after dark. When half the town was lingering around, it would probably seem less frightening. Of course, that was the idea of the event, to scare people. It seemed they'd found the perfect setting.

Streetlights surrounding the lot lit up as she followed Savannah toward an old outbuilding that had seen better days. Rust spotted the corrugated metal where jagged holes had rotted through the walls. One spotlight shone above the large, partially open garage style door—at one time, they must have kept tractors or other farm equipment in the building. Another spotlight lit the small, closed door next to it.

Savannah pushed the roll-up door, and it screeched as it opened. She stepped into the lighted interior and yelled, "Barbara?"

Gia followed her in.

An enormous black animal crouched beside a pile of wood.

Gia screamed and lurched back.

Savannah caught her and laughed, then pointed to the stuffed black wolf the size of a small car, Gia's horror was reflected in its black eyes. Its lips curled back, revealing brown stained fangs and a row of jagged teeth.

"Scary, huh?" Savannah didn't seem fazed by the creature that appeared to be pouncing toward them. She patted its muzzle. "You should see it when they turn it on. Debby from the animal shelter does a huge section in the woods. She's been offered a house every time one opens up, but she prefers the section of woods between the last two houses. Because she runs the event, she likes to let donors have the houses. Anyway, they hook this monstrosity up to an air compressor and set it in the trees. Then, every time the pressure builds up, the whole thing shoots forward into the path. You can hear the screams from all the way in town. Scares the life out of me every year, even though I know it's coming."

Gia walked around the wood base the animal stood on. If this was any indication of the attention paid to detail for this event, it must be amazing. "Where did they get something like this?"

"A theater company used it for a prop one year, then donated it to Debby for the Festival."

"Donated?"

"Debby can be very persuasive, and she's quite passionate about the Festival. It brings in a good portion of the funding she needs to run the shelter and provide food, blankets, veterinary care. Some of the animals she takes in spend their whole lives there, and they need care."

Gia's heart ached to think of Thor having ending up in the shelter forever, not that the animals there weren't well cared for. Debby treated them all like her own—but nothing could be the same as going home to a family that loved you. Thor had brought so much to her life at a time when she'd desperately needed it.

Savannah shot her an I-told-you-so look. "You can go out to the shelter and pick out another one after the Festival."

"I never said—"

"You didn't have to; it's written all over your face."

"Yeah, well, Thor's been amazing. With just the two of us in the house, surrounded by all that property, there's no reason I can't bring home another one."

"Or two."

"Don't push it." But she couldn't deny she'd been thinking the same thing. Sometimes Savannah's intuition was scarier than the big black wolf staring her down. "And you stay out of my head. It's creepy."

Savannah laughed out loud, and a pang of love shot through Gia.

She'd never had another friend like Savannah, someone who knew her so well, accepted her for who she was, despite her faults, cared about her so much, and would do anything in the world for her without an instant of hesitation.

"Thanks, Savannah."

"For what?"

"Just for being you and for being such a good friend."

"Always." Savannah gave her a quick hug, then stepped back, looked around, and frowned. "I wonder where Barbara is. It's not like her to be late. From what I hear, she runs this event like a drill sergeant."

"Maybe she got held up at work." Gia started forward, strolling between piles of props, wood, paint cans.

"She doesn't work. As far as I know, anyway. Even though Debby is technically responsible for the event, Barbara Woodhull and Genevieve Hart put this whole thing together every year, coordinate everything down to the last detail. I can't imagine them doing that while holding down jobs."

"You don't know them well?"

"Not really. I've seen them around; Barbara seems a little stand-offish; she attends community events but stays to herself, if you know what I mean. You've probably seen her around town, early forties, always dressed to the nines. Come to think of it, I've never seen that woman have to stick on a ball cap or tie her hair up in a sloppy knot to make herself presentable." Savannah shrugged. "Anyway, Genny seems like a real sweetheart, very friendly. I've never participated in the Festival before, though I attend every year. Too bad you arrived too late to go last year. At least then you'd have an idea of what goes on."

Gia hadn't been in a position to enjoy a festival or anything else when she'd first arrived in Boggy Creek, but Savannah didn't need to be reminded of that. She'd stood by her side through it all.

Savannah picked up a rusted pickaxe, examined it, then tossed it aside and brushed the powdered rust off her hands. "Only local businesses sponsor and work the Festival, and the real estate office I work for doesn't participate."

Savannah called out again, then fell into step with Gia. "If you see anything that sparks an idea for a theme, let me know. People have dibs on some of this stuff, like the wolf that's only here because it's too big to store anywhere else. Mostly, this building houses things that have been donated throughout the year, so a lot of it is up for grabs."

"What's Debby's theme?"

"Werewolves. Everyone dresses like werewolves and stalks their victims...uh, I mean guests..." she grinned, "through the woods between houses. It keeps people from getting bored while they're waiting their turns."

"Some of this stuff is great." Gia held up a hardhat with an ax blade embedded in it, the handle sticking out. Then she pointed to a box filled with doll parts. "And some of it's just plain disturbing."

"No kidding." Savannah shivered. "And don't get any ideas; you're not using dolls, or pieces of dolls, or anything with creepy eyes that will be staring at me the whole time."

It was Gia's turn to laugh as she tossed the hardhat onto a small pile of wood scraps. "Hey, you're the one who was so gung-ho to do the scary stuff. I'd have been content hanging out at a table with food all night."

"Yeah, well…" They'd reached the closed back door of the building, and still no sign of Barbara Woodhull.

Gia turned back to the prop she'd just discarded, an idea taking hold. "Hey, do you think anyone's using the hardhat with the ax?"

"I don't know. Why?"

"Check it out." She picked up a shovel someone had propped next to the back door, one side of it covered in something red and sticky-looking that reminded her of congealed blood. "If we use the hard hat, this shovel, and the pickaxe you found when we came in, maybe we could do a haunted mine theme?"

"Hmmm…Maybe." Savannah tapped a nail against her lips. "We could make the house look like an abandoned mine. If we black out the windows, we can even create the illusion of being underground."

Claustrophobia threatened to suffocate Gia, and she tossed the shovel aside. "Maybe not."

Savannah frowned. "What? I thought that was a pretty good idea."

"We have to be able to work the house all night, and I don't want to feel like I'm trapped underground for hours on end."

"True." But Savannah's enthusiasm waned. "I can't imagine where Barbara could be. I'm sure this is where she said to meet her, and the door was partway open."

"Why don't you try calling her?"

"Good idea." She pulled her cell phone out and dialed.

Gia brushed splattered dirt off an old door someone had left propped against a pile of tires, the glass from its window missing, leaving a gaping hole they could cover with black fabric, then someone in a mask could poke their head through to startle unsuspecting guests. "What about some kind of a—"

"Wait." Savannah took the phone away from her ear and listened. "Do you hear that?"

Gia strained to hear. From outside, a muffled version of "Thriller" blared through the night. She couldn't help but smile. "Barbara's ringtone, I imagine."

"She must be out back. Come on." Savannah pulled the small door open and held it for Gia.

As soon as she sucked in the humid air, she choked.

Savannah paused. "You okay?"

She pressed a hand against her chest, willing away the tightness. "Yeah. I didn't realize how musty and moldy it smelled in there. Not to mention everything is covered in dirt and dust."

"For sure. Most of that stuff's probably been sitting around someone's storage shed or basement for years." Savannah started down the road, her sandals' three-inch heels sinking in sand that was much softer than that of the hard-packed dirt parking lot.

The ringtone stopped. The hum of insects filled the night, louder than Gia had ever heard. Or maybe that was just because she was trying to hear past it. "Try her again."

Savannah dialed but didn't press the phone to her ear. "Thriller" sounded again, and they followed the sound across the narrow dirt road that wound around past the back of the building and then between two fairly large, rotting wood sheds.

"This is the road the guests will follow. It winds between all the houses and through the woods. It ends by a big field down that way." Savannah pointed toward an open space.

With darkness mostly on them, Gia couldn't make out much more than a lack of trees or buildings in the distance. "How much land is out here?"

"I have no idea, but what's used for the Festival is only a small portion. If you head down that way," she gestured past the scattered row of buildings, "there's an abandoned orange grove and several abandoned farms that aren't part of the fairgrounds."

"Hey, look." Gia bent and peered under a bush a few feet into the wooded area bordering the road. Light flashed on and off to the sound of "Thriller."

Savannah turned on her phone's flashlight and handed it to Gia. "Here. Shine this into the bush so I don't stick my hand into a bunch of thorns or anything."

It was the *or anything* that worried Gia most. She shone the light beneath the bushes and held her breath while Savannah took a quick peek before reaching in and grabbing the cell phone, which had once again stopped ringing.

"Can I help you ladies?"

Savannah whirled toward the woman's voice, lost her balance, and fell over, sprawled half on the dirt road and half on the grass. Barbara's phone fell face up in the dirt.

"Oh goodness, I am so sorry." The woman wiped mud from her hands onto her already dirty jeans, careful to avoid the mud-covered knees, then reached out a hand to Savannah. "I certainly didn't mean to startle you."

"It's okay." Savannah took the woman's hand and climbed to her feet, then dusted herself off. The cream skirt was probably beyond saving, but at least she hadn't broken an ankle falling off her heels. "I'm Savannah Mills, and this is Gia Morelli. We had an appointment scheduled with Barbara Woodhull for seven thirty, but she didn't show up."

The woman looked at her watch and frowned, then used her wrist to wipe the sweat from her forehead. "Oh my. That's not like Barbara to be late."

"When I called her phone she didn't answer, but we followed the ringtone to the bush right there and were just picking up the phone." Savannah bent and retrieved the phone from the dirt and brushed off the blue, rhinestone-studded case.

"Hmm... That's weird." The woman squinted at the phone, through bloodshot, red-rimmed, swollen eyes. She sniffed and pulled a crumpled tissue out of her pocket.

"Are you okay?"

"Oh yes." The woman waved off the question and wiped her nose. "Allergies. I've been working on my house for the past couple of hours, and the dust and mold that's collected on everything all year is killing me."

A bulky man with a full head of long, thick gray hair and the lined face of someone who'd seen a lot of stress in his life shoved through the door Gia and Savannah had just exited. He wore a black T-shirt with Security emblazoned across the front. He took one look at the woman and frowned. "Genny? Is everything okay?"

"Yes, oh dear...maybe not. I don't know." She started to chew on her thumbnail, then scrunched up her face, looked at the dirt caked beneath her nails, and lowered her hand to her side. "I'm sorry to bother you, Jeb. These women had an appointment with Barbara, but she didn't show up, and they found her phone in the bush there."

"No bother at all, ma'am. That's what I'm here for." He nodded toward Genny, then turned his attention to Savannah. "What time were y'all supposed to meet up with Barbara?"

"Seven thirty."

"Huh..." He scratched his head. "Well, I haven't seen her around here tonight; have you, Genny?"

"Uh, no." Deep lines furrowed her brow. "Actually, I haven't seen her since last night, but she never lets that phone out of her sight. If she doesn't have pockets, she usually holds it in her hand."

The phone in Savannah's hand vibrated, then "Thriller" blared from the speaker.

All of their gazes shot to the phone. The initials KC popped up on the screen along with a background image of a man and a woman locked in a heated embrace, the woman facing the camera, her eyes closed, her long dark hair spilling over her shoulders.

Genny gasped.

Jeb took the phone from Savannah and studied the screen. "You said you found this out here?"

"Yes, right there beneath the bush." Savannah pointed. "We were trying to call her to see if she was running late, and we heard the phone ring, then saw it light up."

"All right." He handed the phone to Genny, and she stuffed it into the back pocket of her jeans.

So much for preserving evidence. Of course, they didn't even know if a crime had been committed, but still. You'd think he'd be a little careful just in case.

"I'll have a look around, but she probably lost her phone earlier, then went to retrace her steps hoping she could find it," Jeb said. "You ladies don't worry about a thing. I'm sure she'll turn up."

Despite Jeb's seeming lack of concern for Barbara's whereabouts, a sense of unease crept over Gia. His theory made perfect sense, and yet, despite Genny and Jeb being there, the acres and acres of property had the deserted feel of someplace long abandoned. And, if not for the floodlight positioned by the back door, it would now be fully dark.

Genny smoothed back strands of frizzy brown hair that had come loose from her pony tail with a shaky hand, leaving a smudge of dirt along her forehead. "Can I ask what you were meeting with Barbara about? Maybe I can help you."

Gia glanced at Savannah, not knowing if they should continue or not. Savannah shrugged.

Gia held out a hand to Genny. "I'm Gia Morelli. I own the All-Day Breakfast Café, and I was invited to participate in the Haunted Town Festival."

Genny's worried gaze transformed instantly, excitement brightening her dull brown eyes. "Oh that's wonderful. Welcome, welcome. I'm sorry Barbara wasn't able to greet you. I'm sure something came up. But I'd be happy to show you around."

"Are you sure it's not too late?" The thought of trampling through the old farmland in the dark, when who knew what critters waited out there searching for prey, didn't appeal. A shiver tore through her. "We could come back tomorrow if that would be better."

Savannah rolled her eyes.

Gia ignored her. She couldn't help it if her experiences with wildlife were limited to stray cats in the alley behind the deli where she'd worked in New York City, an occasional rat on the subway, and pigeons that gathered in the park.

"Oh no, no. Don't be silly, dear. No need to come back. I know these grounds as well as, if not better than, Barbara. The circuit breaker is right inside. Just let me turn on the lights, and we'll get started." She hurried away, all thoughts of Barbara apparently forgotten.

Gia leaned closer to Savannah, afraid her voice might carry across the open field where Jeb had been swallowed up by the darkness, or into the cavernous metal storage building Genny had rushed into. "Are you sure it's safe out here at night?"

"Of course it is, Gia."

"Then why do they have a security guard on duty?" Hah. Gotcha there.

"Because people have started setting up their houses and stuff already. The lighting has been run, supplies are being stored in houses with no locks, and they worry about vandalism. Nothing more sinister than kids being kids, Gia. Sneaking into an old abandoned farm that has the added bonus of creepy props? Are you kidding me? What kid wouldn't be all over that?"

Me for one. She kept the thought to herself. She had a feeling Savannah's childhood had been drastically more adventurous than her own, especially since she'd grown up with a houseful of brothers.

Rows of lights Gia hadn't noticed lining both sides of the dirt road flickered on.

The brush beside them rustled, and something skittered into the darkness. Savannah elbowed her in the ribs. "It was a lizard."

Gia laughed. "All right, all right. I'm trying here."

"Okay, ladies. Follow me." Genny started down the road. Her heavy-duty flashlight led the way, even with the lights lining the road. "Are you taking the empty house or just a table?"

"Both," Savannah blurted before Gia had a chance to change her mind.

"Wonderful." Shining the light into the center of the empty field, Genny gestured them forward. "The tables will be set up there, in the center of the 'town.'"

Thankfully, she continued down the dirt road without venturing out into the overgrown field. "That higher grass will be cut down before the event.

The tables will be set up ahead of time. I believe the one that's available is at the front, right by the entrance."

"That will be a great spot, Gia." Savannah gripped her arm. "People waiting in line will have to go right past you. They'll have time to eat while they wait to enter the haunted section."

"Oh yes, it's definitely a great spot," Genny gushed. "The exit is on the other side of that last house there, so they'll pass pretty close to you on the way out too. Plus, there's picnic tables set up just to the side of you. It really is a prime location."

"Which house opened up?" Savannah asked.

Genny gestured with the flashlight, then stopped in front of a wood building the size of a small ranch and opened the door. "This one right here."

"Wow." Savannah walked around the side of the storage building, then looked down the road, and retuned to them. "Right in the middle. That's great."

Gia stared at the pitch black interior. The scent of mold and something else, grease or oil, maybe, wafted out. Her eyes started to itch. She sneezed and rubbed her eyes. Boy, Genny wasn't kidding about allergies. If she was going to spend any kind of time in this building, it was going to have to be aired out. And doused with Lysol. Maybe bleach. And Febreeze. And maybe she'd burn a few candles.

Genny reached a hand in and flipped a switch by the door. Bright, fluorescent overhead lights lit the interior. "Naturally, you can't leave these overheads on the night of the event. You'll have to use some kind of dimmer, decorative lighting. But this is great for set up. Not all the buildings have so much light. I had to hang drop lights in mine just to see my hand in front of my face."

Savannah followed Genny into the long, narrow building. The shape of the empty building reminded Gia of every summer camp she'd ever seen in a horror movie. "What about a dormitory?"

"I love it." Savannah whipped a pad and pen out of her purse. "We could set up a bunch of beds and stuff, make it haunted? Or maybe have monsters, like nightmares or something? We could call it Nightmare House."

"What a fabulous idea and different from anything else we have." Genny oohed and aahed as Savannah relayed her vision for the event. "I'll tell you what; I'll approve it right now. I love it."

"Can you do that? Really?" Savannah pressed her pad against the wall and frantically wrote ideas. "We don't have to wait for Barbara or Debby?"

"Not at all. You just move right ahead."

"Awesome, thank you." When Savannah's pen stopped working, she shook it, but it had given up. She stuffed everything back into her purse. "Thank you so much, Genny. We're really excited to be included."

Gia waited out front with Savannah while Genny locked up. "Thank you very much for showing us around. I can't wait."

Somewhere along the line, Savannah's excitement had become contagious. Unfortunately, the cost did have to be considered.

"Well, if you ladies are okay to see yourselves out, I'd like to get finished up in my own house so I can head home. It was nice meeting you both, and I'm looking forward to working the event with you."

Gia and Savannah said their good-byes, and Genny hurried off back the way she'd come.

Savannah fell into step beside Gia as they headed back down the dirt road toward the storage shed. "Isn't this exciting?"

"It is…"

"But?"

"I'm just worried about the cost."

Savannah waved off her concern. "Don't even worry about it. It won't end up costing that much. At least, the house won't. We'll try to use a lot of the junk we find lying around here, and we can ask around town for donations."

"Where are we going to get beds, Savannah? Even if we find cheap ones…"

Savannah laughed. "Don't be silly. They don't have to be real beds. We'll just get some old blankets and build platforms or something underneath to make them look like beds."

"I guess that would work. Then afterward, we can donate the blankets to the animal shelter."

"See." Savannah punched her arm. "Now you're getting the hang of it."

They walked through the storage shed and out to the parking lot.

From down the road, blue and red lights raced toward them, accompanied by the peal of sirens.

Printed in the United States
by Baker & Taylor Publisher Services